Ali

Daddys
Good
Gi...

Swallow
Your
Pride

Sarah Blue

SARAH BLUE

SPOTIFY PLAYLIST

Earned It – The Weeknd
A Well Respected Man – The Kinks
Fetish – Selena Gomez, Gucci Mane
The Best I Ever Had – Limi
Freak – Doja Cat
Dirty Mind – Boy Epic
I Wanna Be Yours – Arctic Monkeys
Cola – Lana Del Ray
Please Me – Cardi B, Bruno Mars
Bulletproof – La Roux, GAMPER & DADONI
Bad Habit – Steve Lacy
Adore You – Harry Styles
You Get Me So High – The Neighbourhood
Applause – Lady Gaga
golden hour – JVKE

I Think I'm In Love – Kat Dahlia
Electric Love – Børns
Wildest Dreams – Taylor Swift
Someone To You – Banners
ily – Surf Mesa, Emilee

CONTENT MESSAGE

If you do not like the term daddy, now is your time to close the cover, and walk away. We can both act like this never happened.

If you're a daddy's girl, then this book is for you. For a full list of content or triggers of this book, please visit my website.

authorsarahblue.com/content-warnings/

For daddy... I mean Pedro Pascal.

Jessa

A Funeral, a Douchebag, and a Job Offer

I MET my dad on three occasions; the first was when I turned ten years old and my mother introduced us over moderately-priced food at our local Applebee's. She was basically like, 'hey, here's this man who never knew you existed, his name is Collin and oh yeah, he's your dad.' The second was when I graduated college, he congratulated me and handed me a check for fifteen-thousand dollars and told me he was proud of me. This last time is morose, as I look down into the coffin and see the shell of the man he once was.

To be completely honest, I don't know why I'm here.

My half-brother, Zach, invited me. Though I didn't know I had a half-brother, until I received the invitation for the funeral. And by invitation, I mean a curt text message from an unknown number. I thought about not coming, Collin Kemper never meant much to me while he was alive, but now that he's dead, it feels real. The concept of ever having a real connection or relationship with him isn't even an option anymore. As much as I hate to admit it, I was hoping that finally having my father in my life was an option. There's a reason I was already on my way down to Florida and it wasn't

just because I was running away from my life in Virginia—
mostly. I thought I was running toward something, and that
something is now in a casket.

The realization that I'm an orphan sinks in at this
moment—I know I'm twenty-five—can someone really be an
orphan when they aren't a child? But the fact is, half the time
I'm floundering, I don't know who decided I should have to
pay bills, have responsibilities, and carry around crippling
debt. Most of the time, I still feel like I'm eighteen and that I
have all the time in the world to figure out who I'm supposed
to be. Lately, it feels like I have no path or direction. I was
hoping that coming here would help me figure out what I'm
supposed to do, who I'm supposed to be.

It's this deep desire of wanting a connection that made
me come today. Knowing that I have a half-brother—that I'm
not alone. I suppose there was a need for closure too.
Though, this isn't what I had hoped for. I was hoping I'd
come to Florida and be able to forge some sort of relationship
from my estranged father, and now that I know he exists, a
relationship with my half-sibling as well.

I haven't been able to speak to Zach yet, but as I briefly
look into the coffin and walk to my seat, I seek him out. He's
speaking with an older woman who has a pinched expression.
She's blonde and pretty in her own way, but she looks tense.
When I tilt my head, I can't help but see certain comparisons
between Zach and myself. We both have dark brown hair,
brown eyes, and a similar olive tone to our skin, but so do
about twenty other people in the room. I look down at the
pamphlet for the service and read.

Collin Kemper, loving husband and father leaves behind his wife of thirty-eight years, Abigail Kemper and his son, Zach Kemper.

I swallow thickly, both at the fact that I'm not mentioned and the realization that I'm a child from an affair. I look around guiltily, like I have something to be ashamed of—logically I know the guilt is unfounded—before continuing to read.

Collin was a man of faith who was devout to his church, constantly donating his time and money. When he wasn't busy running his successful sports supply company 'Kemper's', you could find him at any type of athletic event. Collin was a passionate fan of the Buccaneers, the Lightning, and the Rays. He will be greatly missed in so many communities; we only wish he could see what an impact he had on so many lives.

I cough into my hand and refrain from an eye roll. He could give to so many others, but he couldn't seem to give me —his child—more than a second thought. I keep myself composed as I sit through the ceremony and watch as others mourn a man I barely knew.

It's only when the ceremony is over and nearly everyone has left that I approach Zach. My nerves are nearly shot, and I have no idea how to even start the conversation. He's nearly ten years older than me, and we know nothing about each other.

"Jessica?" he asks, tilting his head.

"Yes, but I go by Jessa."

"Okay. I'm glad you could make it. Follow me," he says, and I can't help but feel disappointed. He doesn't make small talk as he leads me down the hall and opens the door. I try to put my feelings on the backburner. Zach lost his father, the person who raised him. I lost someone who handed me fifteen-thousand dollars and his DNA. He steps in first and I follow, even though there's an impending feeling of doom making havoc in my stomach.

When we step into the room, there's a man sitting behind a desk, he's in his late sixties and he's rummaging through some paperwork. The same blonde woman is in the room. I've learned that she's my late father's widow. She doesn't even look at me as I stand there fidgeting with my fingers. I try to keep my head down and figure out exactly why I'm a part of whatever this is. But there's one more person in the room I can't help but glance at.

I hadn't noticed him before, which is saying something, because he's devastatingly handsome. He's likely in his late thirties with black hair, a shaven face, and dark green eyes. He glances at me from his chair, putting on his glasses and looking back at the man behind the desk. I feel like I'm invisible in this room, and all I want to do is run away, not that I have anything to run toward. If anything, I'm already running away from something. I'm so in my own head I don't hear the man behind the desk speak. I raise my head to look at him, and he gives me a small smile before repeating himself.

"Miss Peters, please take a seat," he tells me, and I agree. "We're here to read the last will and testament of Collin Kemper." I swallow and wonder why the fuck I would need to be a part of this. "The four of you are the only ones mentioned in the will, so I will proceed."

Abigail coughs into her fist and glares at me before looking back at the lawyer. "To my devoted wife, Abigail, you shall continue to have all of our shared properties, shared assets, and my 401k." Abigail nods, seeming pleased enough. I wonder why he has to put his wife in his will, wouldn't all his things automatically go to her?

"To my business partner, Aiden Carlson, I bestow all of my sports memorabilia, my season tickets, and my extensive whiskey collection." I turn to the man I now know as Aiden and watch as he smiles, covers his mouth, and shakes his head.

"To my son, Zachary, I gift you my Porsche, the vacation home in the Keys, and forty percent of Kemper's Sports Supply." I look over to Zach and his brow crinkles, his mother and Aiden look confused and they all turn to look at me. I would really like to crawl into a hole and disappear right now.

"To my daughter Jessica, I leave to you ten percent of Kemper's Sports Supply and the cottage in Clearwater." I blink rapidly a few times. All eyes are on me in the room, I can't help but tug on my black dress, pulling it over my knees.

"This is simply ridiculous," Abigail says, attempting to rip the papers out of the lawyer's hands. "He was on a lot of medications, surely he wasn't thinking properly."

"Mrs. Kemper, he wrote this will before he was even ill. Collin was in a clear state of mind before making these decisions.

"This means Aiden has the most shares in the company. There's no way that Collin would do this to his family."

I look over at Aiden, not at Zach or Abigail. Aiden seems completely calm, like he knew this was coming.

"It's okay, I don't need—" I start to say, when the lawyer cuts me off.

"You will have to go through the proper channels if you don't want to receive these gifts." I was just going to say the shares, because I need a place to live right now, so that gift is definitely staying with me. The lawyer hands me a thick, large manila envelope, and I take it.

"This is ridiculous, don't worry, Mom, we'll fight it," Zach says to his mother before glaring at me. Definitely not the sibling introduction I was hoping for, not by a long shot. The room is tense and I feel itchy and unwanted, so I step out. My heels click against the hardwood floor as I leave the building and stand outside, taking some deep and even breaths. The air is heavy with moisture, and I can feel myself beginning to sweat. I can't tell if it's this horrific Florida weather or the disaster that I just walked away from making me sweat profusely.

I will not break down. I can't afford to—literally.

"You all right?" a deep voice says, and when I look up, it's Aiden. He's a lot taller than I thought he was when he was sitting down. His all black suit fits him well, showing off his tall, muscular figure.

"Honestly?" He nods like he doesn't want some bullshit answer. "No, this is definitely not what I was expecting when I came here today."

"What were you expecting?" he asks, and I grimace.

"I was hoping I would have a brother, maybe find some closure."

He removes a flask from \the inside of his suit jacket, taking a heavy swig and holds it out in offering. I immediately clutch it in my hands and take a large sip. I wince when the whiskey burns my throat and then hand it to him. He takes the flask back with a smirk, and I'm happy at least one person here doesn't seem to despise me.

"What does having shares mean? Does it mean I have a job?" I ask, feeling like a complete idiot. My degree is in digital design, not business. Do I just have stakes, or am I part of the decision making? I'm truly not sure. All I know is that I need something, sleeping in my car or hotels here and there is not working out.

"Do you need a job?" he asks, and I bite my lip and nod my head. He pulls a card out of his pocket and hands it to me. His face doesn't hold much expression, but at least it's not hostility. *Aiden Carlson, CFO Kemper's Sports Supply. 3625 Henderson Avenue, suite B.* "I'll see you on Monday," he says and he begins to walk away.

"Wait," I say, following after him, my heel hitting the pavement the wrong way, causing me to start to fall. His long fingers wrap around my forearm as he pulls me upright. I can feel the heat in my cheeks, but he doesn't look at me like I'm a clumsy idiot, he just holds on longer than he should. As soon as I'm standing completely straight, he lets go. I clear my throat. "Do you know where this cottage is?" I ask softly. I only booked the hotel for one night. I'm not sure what my plan was next. If things didn't go well, I'd probably head back to Richmond, as much as I dread going back there and facing everything I left. I was hoping maybe I would be calling Florida home before I got that text from Zach. It seems like I might be getting my wish in a round-about way.

He taps the envelope in my hands, I nearly forgot I was holding it. "Everything should be in there." I tilt my head at

him and wonder just how close he was to my father. I nod
and give Aiden a tight smile.

"Thanks again."

"Watch your step to the car, yeah?" he says with a smirk.
I can only imagine how pink my cheeks are right now as I
turn, very carefully, to make sure I don't eat shit on my way to
my dated Chevy Malibu.

As soon as I get into the driver's side, I delicately open the
envelope. There are a few documents inside about my shares
for the sports supply company and the deed to the cottage,
whose address I plug in my phone. A set of keys come
jangling out, and lastly a handwritten letter. My hands shake
as I unfold the ripped-out piece of lined paper and read.

> Jessica,
> If you're reading this, that means that I failed
> you. I want to let you know that I did love you, and
> I'm sorry that it wasn't in a way that you deserved.
> At my core, I was a coward, afraid to face my wife
> and live up to my decisions. You were never a mistake.
> The only mistake I ever made was not being a proper
> father to you. I hope that you find the cottage as
> peaceful as I did. While I know that shares in
> Kemper's doesn't fix anything, I hope that it gives you
> some stability to follow your dreams. I wish I wasn't
> such a prideful man and that I could have done
> better by you. Know that you are loved and special.
>
> -Dad

A tear stains the letter as I delicately fold it up and place it back into the envelope for safe keeping. I lean my head against the headrest of the car and continue my breathing from earlier. His words were ones I always wanted to hear, but I wanted them from his lips, not off a page beyond the grave. I feel frustrated, sad, and overwhelmed as I back out of the parking spot and listen to the directions on the GPS to get to the cottage I just inherited from a man I barely know.

I'm not sure what I expected, but a small, light-blue house directly on the beach was not it. The house is well kept, with immaculate siding, white shutters, and flora that has clearly been maintained throughout the front yard. I take the folder, the house key, and my purse as I get out of my car and walk up the two steps to the bright pink door with a lighthouse welcome sign hanging on the front.

I swallow, turn the key in the lock, and open the door. The inside is modern, opening up into the living room that has a beige couch, TV, and nautical decor throughout. To the left is the simple eat-in kitchen and to the right are three doors. I open the first one and the room has mostly stuff piled in it, a lot of beach chairs, wooden lighthouses, and boogie boards. The second door is a full bathroom that's simple, yet efficient. The last is the owner's suite. There's a queen bed with—you guessed it—lighthouse themed sheets and decor. There is a private bath, fully decorated with a lighthouse soap dispenser, a wooden lighthouse on the wall, and even a toilet seat cover decorated with even more lighthouses.

I sigh, tossing my purse and the envelope on the nightstand before lying down on the bed. The bed is far softer than I imagined, and I watch as the fan spins rapidly. When I turn to the nightstand, there's a picture of my father, smiling widely as he holds up a fish that he caught.

I'm not sure if it's the photo or the heavy weight of the day finally hitting me, but it's then that I finally break. Tears streaming down my face as I grieve the man I never got to know, his pretty words, the disappointment of meeting my brother, and the overwhelming nature of my father's last wishes.

It's pretty fucked up when I think about it. The way I never had a dad but wanted one so badly. If I'm being honest, I just want someone to take care of me for once. I guess my father is doing that in his own way, in a way he couldn't handle while he was alive.

But even so, these are financial things. Is this job and the cottage happening at a time I absolutely needed them? Completely. But yet, I feel I'd give it all up to just have someone actually care about me in the slightest. I groan and reach into my purse, taking a Xanax before lying back on the soft sheets, hoping that sleep doesn't evade me and that I can shut my mind off for at least a few measly hours.

Jessa

Everyone Knows

I SPENT THE WEEKEND CRYING, eating, and watching the *Real Housewives of Atlanta*. I also spent a good majority of the time slowly spiraling and wondering what the fuck I'm doing. Can I really accept this cottage? The shares? The job?

It didn't take long for me to come to the conclusion that I could absolutely accept these gifts, but I still worry about the repercussions. The way Zach and his mother looked at me, like I was an abomination or some sort of mutant, it has me unsteady. I wonder if he plans to take legal action like he said.

The worst he could do is ask for a paternity test—which has already been done. As much as I might wish Collin was an actual father, he did pay my mother child support, not that I really ever saw any benefits of that money.

I try to not go down a rabbit hole of thoughts about my mother. She had her addictions, her problems, but she did love me, at least as much as she was capable.

I'm on my third pint of Chunky Monkey for the weekend when I look at the time. It's past midnight, and I have a job that starts tomorrow. Not that I have any clue as to what the job was, but desperate times and all. There are also four voicemails and ten text message notifications waiting for me on my phone. I don't want anything to do with my ex, but something has prevented me from blocking his number. I vanquish him from my mind as I focus more on what I need to do moving forward.

Not wanting to look like a complete idiot, I read through the documents about my shares and did some research as to how it works. Kemper's is a privately owned S corporation, meaning none of the shares are traded publicly. I have no idea what the shares are worth, but based on the contract it seems as though the board has to agree on whom shares are sold to. So it seems like Aiden or Zach would be my only options if I decide to go that route. Not that I'm sure I want to. It seems like there's potential to make money through profits for just being a shareholder itself.

Maybe I need a lawyer. I'm only able to understand half of the terms in the will and Google can only help so much. It's also nice having a stake in something my father created, he wanted me to be a part of the family business. He had to die for us to get here and for me to find out I had a sibling, but it has to be worth something.

Meeting Zach was difficult, and maybe it's blinded optimism or this lingering desire for a family, but I have hope that maybe he will come around. I don't even know if he holds a position at the company or just owns a huge chunk of it. But I'm willing to give him another chance, I just hope that he's open to it.

I turn out the light and toss and turn as I wait for what tomorrow is going to bring.

Kemper's Sporting Supply is not a store, apparently. I guess I had no idea what I was walking into. I spent all weekend researching what being a shareholder meant—with little fucking success—I didn't think to research the company beyond information about my shares. It's very clearly the headquarters. It's a small glass building with minimal decor. There's a low hum of voices answering phone calls and common office chatter as I walk to the receptionist's desk.

"Hello, can I help you?" she asks. She's pretty, her skin is sun-kissed and her blonde hair sparkles with highlights from the sun. Her dress is casual and her face is welcoming as I smile back.

"I'm Jessa Peters. I'm supposed to meet with Aiden."

Her eyes widen, and she nods her head. "Oh yes, Mr. Carlson is expecting you, follow me." She stands up from behind her tall desk, and I trail her as she continues talking as we walk throughout the cubicles and closed door offices on the left. "My name is Penny. I work the front desk, if you ever need anything."

"Thanks, Penny. I'm Jessa." I cringe at saying my name twice, but the tall blonde woman just gives me a smile instead.

"Oh yes, everyone knows who you are." I'm about to ask her what she means as she stretches out her arm. Aiden is sitting at his desk, dressed far more casually than he was at the funeral: a simple black polo shirt and lightweight pants. He talks in a bored tone over the phone as he waves me in, giving Penny a nod. She retreats out of the office, shutting the door behind her.

Aiden's office is sparse. There is a small imperial red plant in the corner, but besides that, no other personal touches. No photographs of him and his family, no memorabilia, nothing that indicates that this is a place that he comes and goes every day.

"No, you listen. Kemper's has supplied the equipment for UCF for over a decade. If you're going to fuck me, Gary, at least have the decency to do it when I'm present," Aiden says over the phone, and I look out the window, where a homeless man sits on the curb, panhandling for change. *Maybe I should just leave.*

There's an awkward silence while I wait to hear what Aiden says next. "Okay, tell them we'll match it." His tone isn't as curt as before, and I play with the hem of my dress as I wait for him to finish up his conversation.

There's no goodbye or great speaking to you, he just hangs up the phone and looks at me. I look back at him and blink a few times. Not one to handle awkward silences well, I raise my hand like an idiot and wave. "Hi."

"Jessa," he says, picking up a file and looking over it for a moment. "Did you find the cottage fine?"

"Yes, it's really nice."

He nods and clears his throat. "Have you gotten a lawyer?"

"What?"

"To explain your shares and to protect what Collin gifted you."

"I know the gist of it," I say, knowing damn well I can't afford a lawyer right now.

"I'd strongly advise you to do so."

"About the job," I cut in, not wanting to dwell on it any longer.

"What experience do you have?"

This, I came prepared for. I grab my portfolio and place it on his desk. He flips the front and his gaze travels over the pages. He doesn't give me any indication of what he thinks; he doesn't hum or speak. He just looks at the work I've done: the websites, the email marketing, even a few logos.

"Your background is in design?"

"Yes. I graduated from Virginia Commonwealth University with a degree in design and applied arts. Most of my work has been freelance since I finished school. I've had other side jobs to balance my income, but designing is my passion."

He looks over the last few pages and rubs his chin. "Most of our stuff is outsourced. I need to talk with Huck in human resources to see what we would be able to offer you. Would you be amenable to other office work?"

I perk up, sitting up straight in my chair and nodding my head. "Of course, I'm a hard worker. I won't let you down."

I swear a look passes his face, but it's too quick for me to register the emotion. "Is Zach working here going to be an issue for you?"

"No, sir," I say. It slips out casually, and Aiden stiffens only for a second before clearing his throat.

"Now that he's a shareholder, I imagine he will be here more often. His position was in sales previously, but I'm not sure how he plans to continue his role."

"And you're the CFO?" I ask curiously.

"And CEO until further decisions are made." I look at him and wonder how he got into such a high position. Aiden looks fit, and still relatively young to be a CEO of a company.

I have a million questions I'd like to ask him. Like how he became business partners with my father and what he was like as a person. But none of them slip off my tongue as he stands up and ushers me to follow.

There's a cubicle right outside of his office that he leads me to. "You can take this desk. We'll need to talk to Huck about your contract and pay. In the meantime, I'll have Penny set you up with what you need to get started."

"Okay," I reply, sitting on the stiff chair and glancing around the bland cubicle. As I shift my weight on the chair, I groan. This is going to need to get replaced. Aiden walks off when Penny approaches me. She has her own laptop as she runs through what I might need to do my job. There's already two monitored computers at the station, but we discuss what I have at home versus the office and the software I already pay for.

I shift in the seat, and she laughs.

"Yeah, I think everyone shoved that chair in here because it's the worst." I give her a small smile, not wanting to come off as a diva on my first day. Once we have a list of items I'll need, she heads back to her desk to order them. Their IT guy is supposedly coming in tonight, and he will set me up with an email and a login.

I nervously tap my foot against the concrete office floor. What if this is a mistake? Surely life doesn't give you this many lemons at once. It's like my negative thinking summons Zach to my cubicle.

"Jessica," he says dryly. I want to correct him and remind him that I go by Jessa, but I decide not to rock the boat any further.

"Hi, Zach."

"What are you doing here?" he asks.

I try to put my most confident foot forward, sitting up straight and looking him in the eye when I speak. "I work here now. I think maybe we got off on the wrong foot. The funeral was a hard time—"

He scoffs, tapping the top of the cubicle before walking away. I sigh and rub my face, even though I've told myself over and over to stop touching my face as much. It's a bit of a nervous habit, one that's been impossible to break.

While I don't expect everyone to like me, I've never felt such strong hatred from one person before. It makes my stomach hurt and my flight response tingle. It's an unwelcome feeling, having someone who doesn't want me around.

I rub my face again and groan. *This was such a bad fucking idea.*

Aiden has an irritated look on his face as Zach follows him to his office and the door is slammed louder than necessary.

Penny comes back over to my cubicle, looking back at the door before looking at me. "You've really caused quite the stir here at Kemper's."

"I didn't mean to," I say.

"Oh, honey. It's not your fault. Everyone here loved Collin. When he got sick, we were all devastated. When he was on his deathbed, we learned about his secret daughter. It was a shock to us all."

I look out into the hallway. "Everyone knows?"

She grimaces and nods her head. "Everyone knows. I'm guessing that's why Zach's been a bigger dick than usual." She covers her mouth after she says it and shakes her head. "Sorry, I shouldn't say things like that."

I smirk at her and shake my head. "If the shoe fits."

"He was always kind of a tool before, but ever since his dad got sick he's been on a real power trip. We all heard about the shares," she says softly. I get the feeling that Penny isn't inherently trying to gossip with me, but maybe looking to fill me in and help me understand the dynamic of the office.

I blink at her a few times and wonder why Zach would be giving out all this information. Penny shakes her head. "Zach really likes to talk about himself." She shrugs before looking at Aiden's door and then back at me. "Hey, want to get some lunch."

I smile at her and nod. "That would be great."

"Do you like Mexican food? There's an amazing food truck right around the corner."

"That sounds great." I grab my purse off the desk and follow Penny to reception. She unlocks the bottom drawer and takes out her purse, slipping it over her shoulder as we exit the office. The heat and humidity slaps us in the face as we walk a block over. Penny has sunglasses covering her eyes, and I make a note to put a pair in my car, purse, really anywhere, so I don't get blinded every time I go out.

"So, where are you from?"

"I've lived mostly in Virginia."

"Never been. Well, we sat in traffic in Virginia on our way to Maine that one year, but I've never spent time there." I nod as we wait in line at the food truck, not missing Virginia traffic, but the way my commute this morning went it seems I traded it in for some otherworldly hellscape that is a Florida commute. "So you knew Collin was your dad?"

"I'd only ever met him twice." Her brows furrow and she nods her head.

"He didn't seem the type to just abandon his kid."

I sigh and fidget with my purse strap. "Men have a way of disappointing you like that."

She nods back and sighs dramatically. "You're right about that. So the funeral was the first time you met Zach?"

"Yes, I didn't know my father had other children."

"Woof, this story keeps getting more messed up." Penny seems genuine. I don't feel like she's trying to pull information out of me for nefarious reasons. I get a sense that she knows I'm lonely and need someone to talk to; it's a serious contrast to how I feel around Zach.

"You don't have to tell me how messed up it is, I'm living it."

"Well, I'm here if you need me. I know it can be hard to make friends in a new town," Penny says, lightly touching my forearm. I give her a smile and I feel relieved that I have at least one person in this new town to count on. Possibly Aiden too. He's been hard to read, but he's been nothing but kind to me.

We order our food, and Penny suggests we take it back to the office with how hot it is today. I agree completely as we both sit at reception and eat. While we're eating, a red-faced Zach storms past, giving me a dirty look before leaving the office completely.

"Sounds like someone just got put in his place," Penny says with a smirk. I don't reply, wanting to be able to mend whatever possible relationship there could be with Zach. That won't happen if I'm already gossiping about him in the office.

Aiden walks up to reception. He doesn't look fazed in the

least as he rests his elbow on the table. "Jessa, when you're done, will you come to my office?"

I go to pack up my food so I can speak to him right away, and he shakes his head. "No, finish your food, take your time. I'll see you shortly," he says, waving me off.

Penny and I both watch him leave, and she sighs once he's safely in his office. "At least the person who matters the most in the office seems to like you."

"What?"

Penny shakes her head and takes a bite of her burrito bowl. I try to eat, but I'm so anxious about speaking to Aiden that I wind up wrapping it up and putting it in the fridge for later. I steel my spine and straighten my dress before walking into his office.

Aiden

Dead People Can Be Annoying

ZACH KEMPER CAN FUCK ALL the way off. I never truly understood how the little prick was Collin's son. I guess the fact that Collin had a secret child all these years changes how I feel about the man. But at the same time, I still consider Collin a mentor of sorts. I don't think Zach liked how close his father and I became over the years. He certainly doesn't like that he has a sister he didn't know about or the fact that I just gave her a job.

But I also know it's what Collin would have wanted, and truthfully, she is filling a position that we need. It's not a pity filled job offer. I was impressed when I looked at her portfolio. She's genuinely talented, unlike another Kemper offspring I know.

He came in here demanding that I fire her... well, to not hire her in the first place, despite the fact that she was given a significant portion of the company. Zach is just bitter because we're not equal anymore. I own more of the company that holds his namesake. But the truth is, I was a massive part of making this company what it is today, while he just inherited it. I won't deny that he's a decent sales person, but a leader he is not.

He's too busy seeing Jessa as a secret, as a flaw in the father he looked up to. I suppose I don't blame him for having conflicting feelings about his dad. But to project that anger onto Jessa isn't fair or right.

Jessa seems... sad, or broken in a way. I got the sense that the cottage, these shares, the job, are the lifeline she needs. I have a penchant for helping broken people, and I can't help myself when I know some of her history. There's a huge part of me that knows that this is what Collin would have wanted. He didn't give her those shares and disrupt his family for nothing. If he were still here, he would have wanted Jessa to be taken care of, so in his stead, I will make sure that Zach doesn't push her out and she has a place to work.

There's a light knock on the door frame and I look up to see Jessa. She looks anxious as she fidgets and tugs down her sun dress.

"Come in."

She takes her seat from earlier. Bouncing her knee as she looks around my office again. "Is this where you tell me it isn't going to work out?"

"No."

"Okay," she says in a breathy tone.

I push over the papers to her with her employment contract. "Take your time to look over this, what your duties will be, and the salary. If you have any concerns, let me know. It's a combination of marketing, design, and administrative duties."

She looks over the paper, carefully reading. Her mouth parts as she looks up at me. "That's the salary?"

"Yes, if you have any issues, I can discuss with Huck, but you will also need to consider dividends from your shares."

"No, this is far more than I anticipated."

"Should we bring it down then?" I ask. She blinks at me a few times before smiling and shaking her head.

"No, this... this is good."

"Take the evening to look over it and bring it in tomorrow. For now, would you like a tour and rundown of the company?"

She smiles and it's odd, when I first saw her I didn't think she looked much like Collin. But when she smiles, I can definitely see it. Collin was an optimist, a dreamer, and a friend. I sigh as I look at his daughter and remember the man who treated me like a son of his own. I rub my jaw and nod my head. "You've already been around the office, let's go to the warehouse."

She stands up straight, rubbing her face before following me out the door to my car. "The warehouse is only ten minutes away." She nods and I have to temper the urge to get her car door for her. She's quiet and contemplative as silence fills the cab of the car. I'm not sure what to say besides things that pertain to the company. I have to push back this nagging feeling that wants me to ask her if she's okay. It's honestly not a question even worth asking, of course she's not okay. I don't think anyone would be in her situation, so I bite my tongue as we pull up to the warehouse.

"Kemper's is a wholesaler, so we basically provide sports equipment, merchandise, and memorabilia to retailers, schools, and a few professional teams."

"So you don't have any chain stores?" she asks, and I realize she's taking notes on her phone.

"We have two in Florida, but other than that, it's all wholesale." She makes a noise of agreement and continues following me through the warehouse. "We deal with manu-factures across the world to get the gear made and we distribute it."

"What about large chain stores?"

"Those would be our biggest competition, we will never be able to compete with Nike or Under Armour. That's why our main focus has been on the athletic equipment itself and offering American made products."

"What are some of the things you make in house?"

"Baseball bats, skateboards, surfboards, and water bottles are the biggest ones we can manufacture."

"So you started this company with Collin?" she asks, and I keep my face blank as she references him by his first name.

"No, Collin already had the company up and running, but it wasn't growing as he wanted. I had money to spare and wanted to stay in athletics so it worked out for the both of us." She tilts her head like she wants me to continue, but I don't. Mostly because I don't know how much I want to give her in reference to my history.

"You cared about him?" she says softly and I clear my throat.

"Collin and I were close." I almost say he felt like a second father to me, but swallow that down really fucking quick.

She sighs, but doesn't ask me any more questions as we walk through the warehouse and I show her different goods. "We would be looking for you to possibly do some re-branding on our USA line, as well as emails to our current clients and marketing to potential clients."

"I can definitely do that."

"On top of that, I may have some administrative tasks throughout the day, so you will report directly to me." She nods, her thumbs still moving as she keeps notes in her phone. "Do you have any sports you enjoy?" I ask, shifting the conversation.

"I played field hockey in high school," she says, shrugging her shoulders.

I walk her down the hall to where we keep the hockey sticks, baseball bats, and field hockey sticks. "Here's our selection."

She picks one up and touches the handle before putting it back. She doesn't comment as we continue throughout the warehouse. Warehouse workers introduce themselves, and it's clear they know who she is. Jessa seems uncomfortable, but takes it in stride. It's nearly the end of the day, so I drive us back to the office.

It's only when we're a minute away that she speaks. "So everyone in the entire company knows I'm Collin Kemper's bastard child from a one night stand."

I swallow and sigh. "They just know that Collin had another child. They don't know the details."

"But you do?"

"Collin told me some things before he passed."

"He didn't reach out to me when he was sick," she says sadly. It's confusing, matching up the man I looked up to for over a decade with his actions. It's a tough pill to swallow, and really there's nothing for me to say, so I stay quiet. Jessa breaks the silence, "I would have come, had he called."

"I'm sorry." It's the only thing I can come up with. I know

it's not my place to apologize, but I can't feel anything but disappointment in how Collin handled this situation.

When we pull up to the office, everyone is packing up for the day. We head inside so Jessa can gather her things.

"I'll see you tomorrow?" I mostly ask because I'm not sure if she plans on coming back or not.

"Yes, I'll be back tomorrow," she says, throwing the strap of her purse over her shoulder and grabbing her portfolio and leaving the building.

I groan and grab the ball out of the top drawer, tossing it in the air and catching it. My hand slightly tenses with each squeeze. After all these years, my hand still fucking hurts. I want to throw the ball through the giant window in my office, but I refrain.

Penny drops off a few documents and looks at me expectantly.

"What?" I ask her.

"She's nice."

'Okay?"

"I think..." I look up at my cousin who rolls her eyes at me. "I think she needs a friend, and I plan on being that for her. I think she's sad."

"Of course she's sad."

"Maybe..."

"Listen, Penny. She's an employee, she's a shareholder. I'll be kind to her, not just because I'm her boss but because she's Collin's daughter. Is there anything else?"

"Damn, don't chew my head off, or I'll call Aunt Maggie."

"Seriously, you're going to call my mom when I tell you to mind your own business?" I ask.

"Yeah, maybe. I'm just saying. Everyone in the office is already gossiping about her; it's going to be hard. We have to make more of an effort. I'll make sure to ask her to lunch."

"That will be great. Is there anything else?"

She clears her throat and shakes her head as she leaves. She stops at the door frame and looks back at me. "Will you be at family dinner on Sunday?" I really need to make sure that there are no more family hires at this fucking office.

I wave her off and nod my head. She smiles before disappearing down the hall. It takes me a while to get the will to leave the office, to go back home where I feel so alone. I'm leaning in my chair and contemplating going to Avalon. Another night with meaningless sex sounds pathetic.

I groan as I pull the manila envelope from my desk and open the folded document holding the letter from Collin I haven't read. Nothing like reading a message from your dead best friend to sway you from going to a sex club. With the paper in my hands, I read his last words to me.

Aiden,

We built something wonderful together and I'm sure you're wondering about my decisions with my children. I hope that you understand I'm trying to right my wrongs. It's something I should have done a long time ago. You always felt like a son to me, so please, as my last wish, make sure my children are cared for. Be the mentor to them as I was to you. Guide them when they need you, but let them make mistakes too. I know this is a lot to ask of you, but you were my best friend. I trust you with the most valuable things I leave behind in my life. My children and my company. I know you'll make me proud.

-Collin

I have to resist crumpling up the paper and throwing it in the trash. What the actual fuck, Collin? All these weeks I spent visiting him in the hospital and he never said anything like this. He told me about Jessa, that he wanted to make sure she was taken care of. Not that he had expectations of me. He didn't even tell his wife and son about Jessica until he was reaching his final hours.

It's a hard realization when someone you put on a pedestal winds up not being the person you believed them to be. I'm trying to consolidate the Collin I knew: who was my mentor, business partner, and friend. To this man who died with such a huge secret he only revealed in death. I'm trying to have compassion and understanding for everyone, but it's extremely difficult.

I'm sure the shock is hard for Zach and Abigail, but the pain in Jessa's eyes is unmistakable.

Part of me hates Collin for putting me in this position, and as much as I want to punch Zach in the face most days, I'll honor his wishes. Collin gave me a new life, and the least I can do is make sure his children can reach their highest potential, despite their father's failures.

Jessa

Liquid Courage

MY WORK at Kemper's is easy, fitting in at the office, though, is feeling near impossible. The only people I talk to are Penny and Aiden. And Aiden is all business. He hardly even looks up at me when I go into his office to discuss something, which hasn't been frequent. Everyone else treats me like I'm a scarlet letter. Like I chose to be the bastard child of their fearless leader who lied to everyone.

I'm so sick and tired of being judged based on my parents' sins. I used to be treated like a pariah because my mother was an addict, and now I'm forbidden because my father was an adulterer. It makes me wonder what I will become. Right now, I mostly feel like a failure and a victim. And I really don't want to be the fucking victim any longer.

Penny's ponytail swooshes against my cubicle wall as she smiles at me. "Hey, we're all going to get drinks tonight. You in?"

Maybe this is my in, maybe if the office is plied with enough alcohol—if I'm plied with enough liquid courage—I could make some headway.

"Sure, I'd love to," I reply to Penny.

"Great, it's right down the street, so we can walk. Everyone usually leaves around four-thirty on Fridays."

I look at my phone, another slew of notifications I ignore as I check the time. Only an hour left till everyone leaves for the day.

"Great, come grab me and we can walk together?"

Penny nods and smiles back at me before she walks away and heads back to reception. I can handle this, I've got to at least try. I've got to come out of this shell that I've built around myself. I didn't used to be this uncomfortable in social situations, but I feel like I've been beaten down too many times and it's just made me disappear.

I don't want to be lost and floating through life anymore— I want to be me again—even if I'm not completely sure who I am.

I can't stop my nervous fidgeting as I watch the clock slowly tick away. I am slowly working my way through Kemper's current catalog of branding, stickers, emailers. Quite frankly, it's a complete mess. Nothing matches, there's nothing that indicates a clear brand message, and I'm trying to bring it up with Aiden. I only have the lacrosse and base-ball materials left to go through, but it's going to have to wait for next week.

For the most part, I'm liking the job. I like that I'm going to be able to make a difference here. I don't see this as a permanent place for me, but for now, I'm grateful. If only I could find my place in the office. When I peek my head out the top of my cubicle, it looks like mostly everyone has already left for the bar. I wait for Penny to say she's ready to go though. I'm not going to leave early on my first week. Aiden's door is open, and he has his glasses on as he stares at his monitor. I don't imagine he's coming; he doesn't seem like the type to go out and drink with his employees, but I could be wrong.

Why does part of me hope that I'm wrong? It's probably just because Aiden is so kind to me. Not just in a being my new boss kind of way, but like he actually cares about me being comfortable here.

I stare at him a little too long. He rubs his thumb against his chin, his five o'clock shadow in full force, and I bet it feels just the right amount of scratchy. More than likely I shouldn't be thinking about how attractive he is, and I certainly shouldn't be staring at my boss. Maybe if he could tone it down a little bit, I wouldn't feel so distracted.

My creepy behavior is quickly averted when Penny comes into view.

"Ready to go?"

"Yeah, let's head out." I shut down my computer and grab my purse. This time my sunglasses are already on as we leave the office and walk down to the bar.

"The place is called Mutiny, it's a cute little spot. Do you have any other plans this weekend?" Penny asks.

"No, just hanging out at the cottage."

"You should explore some. There's a lot of great nightlife, but it depends on what you're in to."

I feel like if I told Penny what I was in to she would stop being my friend, so I just shrug my shoulders, and she smiles.

"Maybe one weekend I'll take you up on that."

"If you like to dance, there's the best Cuban place a few miles south, or if you like more techno music, there's a place called Rogue. Then there's Avalon, of course." She laughs as she says it.

"What's Avalon?"

"It's—" She opens the door to the bar, and I hear her whisper the word fuck. It's then that I realize Zach decided to come to after work drinks, even though he hasn't been at the office all week. "Sorry, I didn't think he'd be here."

"It's okay, Penny. It's not your fault."

We go to the high top table. I sit next to Penny and Sharon in accounting. James, Lucy, Ed, Huck, and Tabitha are also present. Zach stands at the end of the table with Lucy and Tabitha who seem to hang onto every word he says. James seems involved in their conversation, while Ed, Huck, and Sharon are left out. I guess it makes sense, seeing as Sharon and Ed are in accounting and Huck is in HR. All the others are in sales, it seems to be cliquey for sure.

"Hi, Sharon," I say as confidently as possible.

"Hey, Jessa, how is your first week?"

"It's going really well. I think I'll really like making some new designs and getting to know the business better."

She nods and takes a sip of her cocktail.

"Do you have any kids?" she asks.

"No, and no secret ones either." My cheeks heat, and I nearly smack a hand over my mouth, realizing how fucking stupid I am. Sharon surprises me by smiling and laughing lightly.

"And here I thought you were a meek little thing."

Penny interrupts on my behalf. "Jessa is so nice, I wish more people in the office would give her a chance."

Sharon sighs and takes a long sip of her drink. "Sorry, I didn't mean to be standoffish. The office can be a little cliquey and well none of us knew how to approach you."

"It's all good. Really, I'm just happy to be talking to you now. What about you, do you have kids?"

Sharon raises her hand waving for the bartender. She orders some fruity blue concoction for the three of us. "Yeah, I have two teenagers; it's a fucking nightmare."

"Boys or girls?"

"Boys. It's disgusting and cruel," Sharon says and Penny laughs.

"Her son gave their family computer a virus recently from watching porn."

Sharon swats Penny, who laughs loudly, catching the attention of the cool side of the table. We're met with unpleasant looks, and Sharon rolls her eyes.

"Fucking sales douchebags," she mumbles under her breath, and I have to hide the laugh behind my cocktail glass.

I finish the first drink sooner than I intend to, so do Penny and Sharon. I think about leaving now and calling it a night, but then Ed starts talking to me and telling me about his daughters and how much he loves numbers. Then Huck talks about how he surfs on weekends or dives and finds lobsters. It's the first time I feel like I'm just Jessa and not their former boss' love child. I'm enjoying myself maybe more than I should, or more than my bank account can allow, but I need this.

We're on our fourth round when I excuse myself to go to the bathroom. It's when I'm sitting on the toilet and staring at the bathroom door that I realize I'm drunk.

Fuck.

The cottage is a forty-five minute drive with no traffic, that will be a huge Uber bill. It's not like I haven't slept in my car before, I could sober up and then go home. But I should see the rest of the night out first.

After I wash my hands and look at my half-lidded eyes in the mirror, I give myself a little pep talk. I will not say anything embarrassing in front of my new coworkers, and I will get home safely.

When I get back to the high top, nearly everyone has cleared out. It's just me, Penny, and Sharon.

"Well, girls, I'm gonna call one of my sons to pick me up. At least they can do that, seeing as I had to see my son's PornHub search history." She picks up her phone and texts her son before leaving cash on the table and giving us a wave as she leaves the bar.

"One more," Penny says. I nod, because I feel light, like I have no problems, and I don't want this feeling to end.

Penny doesn't order the same cocktails but two shots. We shoot them back quickly, and I have to stop myself from throwing up. I'm extremely proud of myself when I hold it down.

"So, give me the real Jessa."

"Huh?"

"I know you're from Virginia, you played field hockey, and who your dad was, but besides that nothing."

"Because we just met each other."

"Fine." Penny waves me off. "I'll start. I'm the family fuck up." I open my mouth to speak, and Penny waves me off again. "I was always falling for the wrong guys and changing who I was. I didn't go to college because my high school boyfriend was in a band and I wanted to be with him. So by the time I left him, it felt too late. The boyfriend after that was a lawyer, and he wanted me to be pretty and shiny. He paid for things, but he was... rough." Penny looks off in the distance. "This job was something I needed, and well, now I'm working on figuring out who I am without a man. Oh, and I really like dancing, spending the day at the beach."

I blink at Penny's drunk confession, and I don't know if it's the alcohol or how Penny makes me feel so comfortable, but I lay it all out for her.

"My mom was an addict. I won a partial scholarship because we were low income, but I still have a shit ton of debt. At school I started... um... dating my professor." Penny gasps, and she rests her hand on her fist like my story is riveting. "I really thought we were going to be endgame. It was great for a while; he taught me so much about myself... but apparently, I surpassed his age requirement. I caught him with one of his students a few weeks ago. I packed up my shit and went on a self-exploratory road trip. I was driving down here to meet my dad when Zach invited me to the funeral."

"Fuck," Penny says with her mouth gaping open.

"No kidding."

"How old was he?" Penny asks.

"Forty-three," I say quietly, hoping she doesn't judge me.

She whistles and takes a sip of the cocktail that magically appeared in front of her. When I look in front of me, there's one for me too, and I take a sip.

"What did he teach? No, wait. Let me guess." Penny taps her chin in thought. "Photography."

My mouth drops, and she cackles and downs her drink. "How?"

"Oh, who wouldn't fall for the introspective, hot, older man. I don't blame you. Hey, maybe this job will be your new start."

I smile at her and drink my cocktail. "I hope so."

"Fuck, we need to get a ride."

"Oh, that's okay."

She waves me off. "It's fine, I'll call my cousin. I'm sure he's still in the area."

"Your cousin?"

She doesn't answer as I hear her talk on the phone. "Jessa and I drank too much at Mutiny, can you come pick us up?" There's a long pause before Penny starts talking again. "I know, yeah. Yeah. Yeah. Are you picking us up or am I getting abducted by a random stranger?" She nods her head and smiles. "We'll wait out front."

The bartender hands us our tab, and I wince, starting to calculate my first paycheck and what's in my bank account. I decide then that this is my last Friday night out until my check clears.

One of the valets is flirting with Penny when a very familiar white car pulls up and honks. I blanch when I realize who it is.

"Penny, is Aiden your cousin?"

She laughs and waves me off. "You seriously didn't know?"

I shake my head as she opens the back door, scooting in, and I follow her. Aiden doesn't say anything, and I feel embarrassed but also still slightly drunk. I do my best to keep my mouth shut as Penny starts talking.

"Thanks for picking us up. Ugh, I'm so tired." I watch Aiden roll his eyes from the mirror.

"Put your seatbelts on," he says in a deep voice from the front.

I've never put a seatbelt on so fast in my life. Penny acts like Aiden is being bossy but puts hers on nonetheless.

"Your apartment is literally two blocks away," Aiden says to Penny.

"Hmm," she says, waving him off. He isn't kidding, it takes just three minutes to get in front of a small apartment building. Penny has her purse in her hand as she swings open the door. "See you Monday, Jessa!" She walks on wobbly feet, using her keycard and waving to the car before going inside.

Aiden doesn't drive off, and I swallow thickly.

"Are you going to sit in the back like you're being chauffeured or are you going to sit up front?"

"I can call a ride, you don't need to drive me all the way home."

He gives me a stern look in the rearview that I read as a 'get in the front seat and shut the fuck up.' So I unbuckle my seat, open the door and get into the passenger's seat.

"Do you need the address?" I ask.

"No."

"Right. Of course you know where it is." I might say it with more snark than intended, but I'm fortunate that Aiden doesn't say anything.

"So, Penny corrupted you?"

I shrug my shoulders and look out the window. Because if I look at my brand new boss, who is driving me home because I drank too much, *I might fucking die.*

"I think I needed a release and for people at the office to treat me like a normal person."

"Have people been rude to you?" he asks, his tone is even, and I shake my head.

"Just cautious, I think."

"Hmm."

The street lights are blurry as I look out the window. "I think I hate my dad," I blurt out. I'm met with silence, and I close my eyes. I'm not sure if it's the cocktails or sheer power of will, but somehow I fall asleep.

Aiden
Sex Clubs and Daddy Issues

IT ALMOST FEELS like a blessing that she falls asleep on the car ride home. Drunk confessions of what kind of person Collin was isn't something I want to get into tonight.

Frankly, driving to fucking Clearwater wasn't on my list of things I wanted to do tonight either. But there was no way I was going to let her or Penny get home in their current state. I can't even blame Jessa, I know how Penny can be, and I'm sure Jessa's desire to fit in left her drinking more than she normally would. At least I hope so, this behavior can't become a consistent occurrence. I scold myself for the line of thinking, like I have any say as to how she lives her life. But there's something festering inside of me when it comes to her, and I find myself constantly shutting it down.

Jessa's head is leaned against the window, her dark hair pressed against the glass and spiraling down her side. I can't help wondering how such a beautiful woman can feel so displaced. From my minimal interaction with her, it's clear she lacks confidence and is timid when it comes to asking for help or direction.

I shouldn't be thinking about how good it would feel to

give her direction. I'm her boss and that's it. The direction I give her is solely in the workplace and that's all. Besides being an employee, she's my dead best friend's daughter, and she's clearly going through something. The latter doesn't help with my predicament of wanting to make everything better for her, but it will need to be in a mentor type of way. Collin's last wish was for me to guide his children the same way he guided me, and finding his daughter attractive or just like the type of woman I like, is not what he would have wanted.

She sleeps unphased, her lips parted as she breathes softly as we cross the bridge and make our way to the cottage. I wish I could get out of this situation without waking her up, but that's not a possibility. When I reach the cottage I park in the driveway and stare at the house for a moment.

I'd taken Collin's death in stride, but when I look at this house it all hits me. He's really gone, and I find myself angry with him in a way I've never felt before. Angry that he died, that he left me with such a heavy weight, left his children to handle his lies when he couldn't. But there's also a part of me that just misses him. His boisterous laugh, going to sports games with him, how he made me feel like I wasn't a fuck up. Collin was a lot of things, but to me he was the person who stopped me from spiraling. I owe him everything, and I can do this for him. I can follow through on his last wishes.

I grip Jessa's upper arm and shake her slightly. Her lips close, and she scrubs her eye with the heel of her palm.

"Just a few more minutes, Daddy," she says.

My heart sinks in my chest and my cock stirs. *What the actual fuck.*

"Jessa," I say her name louder and with a stern tone. She blinks her big brown eyes and finally understands where we are. She rubs her hands down the sides of her face, and if it wasn't so dark in the cab of the car, I imagine I would see a blush across her cheeks. "We're here."

She clears her throat and opens the car door. "Thank you for driving me home, Aiden."

I nod at her. "Do you need a ride to work on Monday?"

"Oh no, I'll get my car before Monday."

"If you can't, will you let me know?"

She nods her head and digs her keys out of her purse. "Thanks again, Aiden." She walks off and I watch as she turns the key in the lock and enters. There's a part of me that wants to get out of the car and make sure that she locked the door after going in. But that's not my place, none of this is, and I can't help this nagging feeling in my chest. I can't remember a time I've felt this uncomfortable around a woman, and I'm not sure why.

Maybe it's because she just called me daddy and I have no fucking clue how to feel about it. *Lie.* I know how I feel about it, I'm just not going to fucking admit it to myself.

I watch as she turns off the lights in the cottage then reverse out of the driveway and head to the one place I always go when I feel out of control.

⁂

Is it fucked up that a sex club is my center? *Probably.*

It's the one place I feel like I can be myself, which is pathetic when I think about it. I've had a few relationships, but Avalon and my relationships have never been able to coexist. I've tried dating women from the club, but it always felt like the relationship was purely sexual, nothing deeper. I wonder if I'll ever find a balance between the two, someone who can embrace all the sides to me. Or maybe I haven't truly dug down deep enough to figure out what I need in a relationship, or I haven't cared enough to try.

The idea of settling down hasn't hit me until recently. I guess watching someone die will do that to you, make you dissect your own mortality. I just want a woman I can take to baseball games, the beach then bend her over and spank her and finger her pussy till she's crying—it shouldn't be this complicated.

I take a seat at the bar. Nothing happens at the front of the house, all clothes must stay on, this part of the club is for conversation and drinking.

The front is decorated with black and golds, the bar top glows a bright white and contrasts against my palm. I wave at Tex who doesn't even ask for my order, just pours my favorite whiskey and places it on the table top before me. I look around the bar, I know everyone here and I can't decide what that says about me. There are a lot of couples who come to play with others, and individuals I've seen here multiple times. Is Avalon starting to lose its luster?

I sure fucking hope not, because that means I'll need something else for this energy, for these thoughts. Right now, all I can handle is work, Avalon, and sports. I see Carmen and her husband Leo at the booth. I've joined in on punishing and rewarding Carmen a few times, Leo likes to be cucked. But when I look at her now, she doesn't do it for me. I realize how dramatized Carmen's sounds and reactions have been in the past, and how much I don't like it. I think I feel a little used in their dynamic, like Carmen is getting pleasure, Leo is getting off on it. Sure, I enjoy myself, but it feels surface level; I want something more. I need something beyond this physical dominance I can enjoy for the night, but I'm not sure what that dynamic looks like outside of these indulgent walls.

I guess Avalon isn't the place I should be looking for a genuine connection, but it's all I got. Especially as I try to rid myself of the image of Jessa sleeping in my car and calling me daddy.

It's not a term anyone has called me before. Sir and a slew of other terms. But daddy, I never considered myself that type. But I liked it more than I'm willing to admit. Maybe if I can test it out tonight. See if it's the term, the meaning behind it, or my worst fear, the fact that I might like it from Jessa's lips.

I drink another thick sip of whiskey when Carmen and Leo approach me.

All conversation goes through Leo as he clasps a hand on my shoulder. "Hey, Aiden."

"Leo, Carmen." Carmen gives me a small smile. I tilt my head at her and realize immediately that this isn't what she wants tonight. It's quite pathetic that I can read her cues better than her husband. The way she looks at him, she wants him to step up, I don't think she minds the sharing, she definitely got off when we were together. But I think she wants a connection with Leo. The sad thing is, I don't think he gets off unless he's watching. Not wanting to be in the middle of their marital drama, I shake my head and pull my phone out of my pocket. "Shit, I've got to go. I'll see you guys next time."

Leo nods, and I watch as Carmen gives me a wider smile. Maybe all she wants is her husband for the night. But the fact is, their marriage is none of my business. All I know is that if I were in Leo's shoes I'd never want to share. I've been happy to facilitate in the past, to get my own needs met, but maybe trying to fill this void isn't what I need anymore.

Leo and Carmen head to the back and I take a sigh of relief. If this isn't what I want anymore, what will fix this itch, and do I even deserve it?

I nod to Tex to just add the drink to my tab when I leave. It seems that not even Avalon can help clear my head tonight, all it's doing is making my thoughts louder.

It's well past one when I get back to my place. Maybe I should get a pet or something, that way this place wouldn't feel so vastly empty.

My bedroom feels worse than the living room, so I lie on the couch and look at the ceiling. I wonder what it is that I'm feeling. I'm turning forty next year. Am I worried about being alone forever? Does it feel like time is passing me by too quickly? Or is it something more that I don't know how to describe even in my own consciousness.

My front door slams and I'm jolted awake. I grab the baseball bat I have sitting by the coffee table and grip it between my hands as I walk into the foyer.

I'm about to swing when I see my brother Lincoln standing there with his arms in the air.

"Jesus fucking Christ, Aiden. What are you going to do, bash my fucking brains in?"

"What are you doing here?" I say to him, pointing the end of the bat at him.

"We're supposed to go to the range you prick."

I scrub my face and put the bat against the wall. "Sorry, I forgot."

"Thankfully you didn't crack my goddamn skull open."

I wave my brother and his dramatics off. "Let me just go get changed."

"Yeah, if you went to Avalon, do us all a favor and wash the scent of pussy off ya too." He snickers as he says it, and I regret not knocking the daylights out of him at that moment.

I take a quick shower and get dressed. There's a crick in my neck from sleeping on the couch and I'm rubbing out the tension as I walk down stairs.

"Some broad ride you hard last night?"

"Shut the fuck up, Linc," I say his nickname with a little disdain. Out of all my brothers, Linc likes to ride me the hardest. To be honest, I think it's all a cover up to hide what a fuck up he thinks he is. It must be a Carlson family trait, the more I think about it.

"Touchy, touchy. Let's go get you some coffee, princess." The bastard gets me coffee and a donut and I feel some of the frustration leave me.

"Can't we go to the batting cages instead?"

"Oh, if you're a good boy we can." Yeah, I really should have beat his ass with that baseball bat.

When we get to the range, my dad, Jeff, is there as well as my two other brothers, Benjamin and Gavin.

"Hey, Son," my dad says, and I sit down next to him as my brothers bicker over the line up and start placing bets on who is going to score the most points. My dad puts an arm around my shoulder. "How ya doing, kid?"

"Fine," I reply, and he squeezes my arm.

"Collin was a good man, I know it's a lot."

"I'm fine, Dad."

"Told you he was being a little fucking bitch today," Lincoln says. Benjamin laughs next to him as he puts his golf ball on the tee and lines his shot up.

"Something else got your panties in a twist?" Gavin says, grabbing the pitcher of beer and pouring himself a glass.

"Yeah, the fact that I'm related to you fuckers."

"Oh you love us," Benjamin says as he brings the club back and hits the ball in the air. We watch it fly across the field.

"No, actually. Mom and Dad should have stopped at me and never given me siblings."

"And have our parents live with that kind of disappointment, I don't think so," Gavin says, taking another deep gulp of his beer.

"Leave Aiden alone. He just lost a friend," Dad says, trying to intervene.

My brothers lay off for a little while after getting scolded until it's my turn to drive. "Don't fuck it up," Linc says as I swing, slicing the driver through the air. I pretend the ball is my brother's face as I hit it further than anyone else.

"No fucking fair," Benjamin bitches. My dad gives me a wink as he lights up his cigar. I should slap it out of his hand, but the man makes his own choices.

I sit back down next to my dad, and he squeezes my shoulder. "Proud of you Son," he says quietly so my brothers can't hear and all I can think about is whether his pride is deserved.

Jessa

Baseball Bat Dicks

I HAD to pay forty dollars to get a ride back to the office on Saturday, but there was no way in hell I was going to ask Aiden or Penny for help—I'm already embarrassed as is. I have a feeling that I said something horrific in my intoxicated state, and I'm dreading going to work today. How did I manage to make everything even more uncomfortable than it already is?

When I open the glass door to Kemper's, I'm greeted by Penny who waves and smiles. "Hey, Jessa. Good weekend?"

"Yeah, you?"

"Spent most of Saturday sleeping, but other than that it was great."

Sharon walks by with a cup of coffee in her hands. "Morning," she says with a smile. Even if I made an ass out of myself, at least I made one new friend in this office.

Tabitha drops off a stack of papers to Penny's desk. "Put in this purchase order as soon as possible," she says before spinning around. Penny rolls her eyes but takes the stack and smiles back at me.

"Is she always so rude to you?" I ask Penny. Sharon scoffs

and glares at Tabitha's retreating back. Her hips swishing in her tight pencil skirt and her blonde ponytail bouncing with each step.

"She thinks sucking Zach's dick gets her special treatment," Sharon says, and Penny snickers.

"Oh, I didn't realize."

"Yeah, so definitely don't expect her to invite you to any sleep overs any time soon," Penny says, and I nod. Tabitha doesn't seem like the kind of friend I would want anyway. I really like Penny, and Sharon is funny in her own way. It's better than having no one in this office, or everyone treating me like I have a disease.

Huck and Ed both give me friendly head nods as I walk to my doom—my cubicle. I sit down, turn on my monitors, and do my very best to not look into Aiden's office. Just the idea of him talking about Friday night makes my stomach hurt. He took a risk hiring me. I mean, sure I have a stake in the company, but that doesn't mean anything other than that. I need this job and I've made a complete ass out of myself the first week.

After staring at my screen, working through all the lacrosse marketing, I finally glance up to look at Aiden. He looks calm as he speaks on the phone. More than calm, he looks in control, and it's desperate and pathetic how much I'm into it. Maybe it goes beyond him being my boss that's triggering this gut-wrenching anxiety over what I might have said on the car ride home. He looks up at me while he speaks and he holds my gaze for a moment. God, the man has the most beautiful green eyes. He rubs his chin while he looks at me before retreating his gaze. I just stared at him like a freak.

Fucking awesome.

I'm creating a branding kit for the lacrosse line when Penny comes up. "Lunch?" she asks, and I shake my head. My stomach hurts too bad to eat right now, not to mention my depleting bank account. I need to start packing lunch, at least for the next couple of weeks. I have about four hundred dollars left in my account; it should be enough to pay for my phone, food, and gas until I get paid, or at least I hope. I do have my credit card, and I'll charge any excess to that, but I hate using it unless I absolutely need to.

"Not hungry today, maybe tomorrow?"

"Sure. Jessa, are you okay?" Penny asks, and she glances over at Aiden's door. "Did something happen when Aiden dropped you off?"

"You could have told me he was your cousin," I say calmly. I'm not trying to make her feel bad, but if I would have known, I would have absolutely slept in my fucking car even if I did roast alive. I can see the headline now, 'An adult woman cooks herself inside of her car instead of facing absolute embarrassment from her boss seeing her drunk.' Better yet, they could title it Florida Woman Dies of Stupidity.

She shrugs her shoulders. "Sorry, I forgot that you were new and didn't know."

"Everyone else in the office knows?"

"Oh yeah, I had a similar unfriendly welcome to the company," Penny says. It makes me feel a little better, that the cold shoulder isn't specifically me, this office is just a tough crowd. "But seriously, was he a dick or something?"

"No, he was kind. I'm just feeling embarrassed."

"Don't, seriously. Are you sure about lunch?" she asks, her bright blue eyes searching mine. She gives me a small assuring smile as she waits for my answer.

"I'm sure, thanks Penny." She nods and walks off.

The day is completely dragging, it's one of those days where you think an hour has passed, but when you look at the time it's only been about twenty minutes. I would rather do just about anything than feel the tension I do today. Aiden hasn't come out of his office once, not to ask me or anyone else for anything. Maybe it's narcissistic to believe it has something to do with me, but I can't squash the feeling.

I finished the lacrosse branding kit and decide to start working on baseball so I can show him both at once. I open the pdfs with the sticker files and my mouth drops when I see the first image. It's so extremely phallic looking that I don't even know how this image was created. What's worse is when I look at the words in a circular font around the baseball dick. 'Rays' Kids' day - sponsored by Kemper's.'

I swallow and look at the clock, it's nearing the end of the day. I've got to bring it up, right? Surely this is a mistake?

The chime of the front door alerts me to employees leaving for the day, and I know if I don't bring it up with Aiden, I won't be able to sleep tonight. I'll just fixate about it all night and worry about how it will be received. I print the document out and it looks like it's just Aiden and me left at the office—fantastic.

I swallow and try to stop the trembling of my hands when I lightly tap on the door frame of his office. "Aiden?"

He looks up and blinks twice. "What can I help you with?"

I take a deep breath and sit at the chair in front of his desk. "Did you approve all the marketing for our baseball materials?"

"Usually, why?" I slide the paper over to him. "What's

wrong with it?" I point to the cock looking sticker, and his eyes widen.

"It looks like a dick. Has this already been printed? I can make a design really quickly."

"Kids' day at Tropicana Field is tomorrow. I'm supposed to drop them off and go to the game." He swallows.

"Okay, and these stickers are on what?"

"The wooden baseball bats they're giving to the kids."

"How many are there?"

"Five-thousand," he says softly.

"Fuck," I whisper.

"Fuck is right," he says, staring at the cock baseball bat and balls.

"Where are they?" I ask.

"The warehouse."

"Can the stickers easily be removed?"

"Yeah."

"Okay, then we can fix this."

"What?" he asks, looking back down at the horribly designed stickers.

"Do we have a laser printer?" He nods, and I smile. "Great, okay. We need to go to Staples and get, well, a ton of labels, print them off at the office and go to the warehouse and replace them."

"Jessa, it's nearly five."

"We can't give kids a baseball bat with a dick sticker with our name on it." He groans and scrubs his face.

"This is going to take all night."

"I'm ready to prove you made the right decision hiring me. Can you run to staples? I'll design something right now."

"I'll call the warehouse and let them know we're coming. Are you sure?"

"I'm positive," I say, smiling at him. I pull up Staples' website and find the product we need, I screenshot it and send him a text. "Tell the employee this is what we need, and we need enough to do 5,000 labels.

"We could just take the labels off. It's a loss in marketing, but we can just take them off," he says pragmatically.

"I'm happy to do that with you too. But I think we can fix this. We can try. And we have part of the day tomorrow before you need to drop off, right? We can see how many we can fix tonight and then it can be all hands on deck at Kemper's tomorrow."

Aiden looks at me like I'm the smartest person he's ever met, and he nods his head. "I'll be right back. I'll pick up food on the way. Any requests?" My stomach grumbles then from skipping lunch, and I shrug.

"I like just about anything."

"I'm so happy you caught this. Seriously, amazing job." My cheeks heat, and I give him a small smile that he returns. Aiden grabs his keys, and I head back to my desk. He makes sure to lock the door behind him, which I appreciate since I'll be alone in the office as he heads to the supply store and I work on a new design.

It's probably stupid, but I feel proud of myself too. I feel valuable in a way I haven't felt in so long. I match the specs from the sheet I found online, and I'm finished when Aiden comes back to the office. He fills the printer with the labels and I set off printing the exceedingly large number of stick-ers. The machine whirls and prints them out.

"Everyone left from the warehouse, but Kenny told me

where everything is." I nod as I watch the labels print one by one. "I can't believe I approved that sticker. It's when Collin was fading out and I was on auto-pilot. What a stupid fucking mistake."

I can't help it as I touch his forearm. For a man so confident, he seems really hard on himself. "It's okay. We caught it in time. Shit happens." He smiles and doesn't shrink away from my touch, but picks up a sheet of my labels.

"Your design is a million times better."

I shrug my shoulders but can't help but smile. "Maybe once this crisis is averted I can show you all my ideas. Right now Kemper's branding is all over the place. I've broken it down by company branding and each sport. It's still a huge work in progress, but it's just an idea."

"Yeah, I'm excited to see what else you've come up with."

He fills the machine with more labels. Once they're finished, I grab my purse and Aiden grabs the labels and our food as we get into his car and head to the warehouse.

Aiden insists we eat before we get started, and I'm thankful as I devour the chicken over rice he got me from the Halal truck. I open the peach Snapple and nearly down it in a few goes. The warehouse is pretty fucking hot, and I take off my cardigan, my arms on full display. Aiden briefly looks up at me before shaking his head and then glares at the mass of boxes we have to work on.

"How should we do this?" he says.

"Maybe we can work on taking stickers off first?" He puts an empty box between our chairs and opening a box on the table. He grabs his phone and puts on some music, which makes me smile. We work in silence for a good twenty minutes, just the sound of the music on his phone and the clanking of small bats hitting the box every few seconds.

"So," he breaks the silence.

"So."

He laughs and just grabs another bat, taking the sticker off and sticking it on the table. "Are you liking Florida?"

"Besides the humidity, yeah. People are definitely a little different here, but I think I like it."

He laughs and shakes his head. "I've always lived here, so I don't really know any different. Where were you living before?"

"Virginia. Seems traffic is just as bad anywhere you go." He makes a noise in the back of his throat.

"Do you miss it?" he asks.

"No, it was just a place for me. I think I'm still trying to find somewhere to call home." We keep de-stickering bats quietly for a few moments. "Can I ask you about Collin?" He nods and I take a deep breath. "What was he like? I mean, I met him twice, but I didn't know him."

Aiden clears his throat before he speaks. "He was the life of the party, he loved entertaining people, telling jokes, and being the center of attention. He had the loudest and most identifiable laugh I'd ever heard; it made you want to laugh along with it. I'm sure you already know how big of a sports fanatic he was, we have that in common, and it was the majority of what we spoke about. But there were a few times Collin confided in me, but even I didn't know about you till the end. I think that a lot of people have a hard time remembering Collin as this larger than life loving person and also having a secret daughter."

"What was he like with Zach?" I ask and wonder if I'm crossing a line.

"Are you sure you want to know?" Aiden asks, looking at me. His face is soft, like he knows telling me is going to hurt me, but I'm a bit of a masochist as I nod my head yes. "He was the best dad you could ask for. Gave Zach the world, went to all his sporting events, took him on vacation, told him to follow his dreams. If anything, he probably spoiled Zach too much, that's why he's such a prick now."

I can't help the laugh that escapes out of me and Aiden just smiles and shakes his head. I pick up the next bat and when I take the sticker off I wince and gasp.

"You all right?" he asks and I look down at the drop of blood.

"Splinter," I wince and put my finger in my mouth. He stands up and taps the table for me to sit on it. I oblige almost immediately and he seems surprised but pleased. Since I'm wearing a dress, he stands to the side of my thighs, his muscular leg touching mine, and I do my best to ignore it. Which is impossible because it's a very nice thigh. I watch his face as he takes my hand in his callused fingers. I wonder how his fingers are that rough when he works at an office. I can't help but look at his large hands encompassing mine as he squeezes my finger, and I wince.

"Sorry," he mumbles. "It's in there deep. Let me get the first aid kit."

"I'll be fine," I say, even though it does hurt.

"It's not. Let me go get the kit." Aiden walks off, and I try to get the little bitch out of my finger while he's gone with no luck. He returns with the kit and digs out a pair of tweezers, disinfectant and a Band-Aid.

It takes him a good three minutes until he gets the offensive piece of wood out. "Little fucker," he mumbles as he puts the splinter down and unconsciously brings my finger tip to his lips. "All better." He must not even realize he does it, as he puts the disinfectant on and a plain skin-tone Band-Aid. "You're on sticker duty. I'll take them off, you put them on."

"I can keep taking them off." He gives me a stern look as I raise my hands in mock surrender. "All right, I'll put labels on."

"Good—" He stops himself mid-sentence and sits back down, continuing to take off labels.

I cannot start to have a crush on my boss. I look down at my bandage-covered finger and realize it's too late. A simple kiss on my finger, and a tiny bit of praise has me done for—it makes me feel pathetic—but I can't stop the lingering feeling growing in my chest if I tried.

Aiden

Kissing Pretty Girl's Fingers

I KISSED HER FUCKING FINGER.

What the fuck was I thinking? I wasn't thinking, I just acted and it was so natural. I mean she just saved our asses. I can only imagine the outcry if we had handed these out at the game tomorrow. It really looked like a giant fucking dick, and Jessa saved us from that embarrassment. I'm thankful to her, but also in awe. She noticed the problem, came up with the solution and is willingly here, with me, making this right.

Not only is she here and not bitching, she's smiling often, she's talking to me openly. So when she got hurt, I felt guilty, and I wanted to make it right. I kissed her finger and nearly called her a good girl.

I cannot feel this way about my dead friend's daughter. The daughter he wants me to mentor and take care of. Certainly Collin didn't have it in mind that I'd be kissing her finger or thinking about how cute she looks with her dark hair in a bun on the top of her head.

Part of me wants to tell her to go home and I'll spend all night doing this myself. It will at least stop me from looking at her and noticing things about her. Things I shouldn't be fucking noticing: like she fidgets a lot, touching her face, her dress, and her hair. Or that I can tell immediately when she's flustered by the tint on her cheeks. I shouldn't like the way she looks at me either, with her big brown eyes fanned by full lashes. I definitely shouldn't like the way she looked at me after I kissed her fucking fingertip.

She puts the stickers on in silence while The Kinks play in the background. I check the time and we've been at it a few hours, but it feels like the dent is small. I'll wait until I get any hints that she's tired and we'll call it a night. We will have a few hours with the whole staff to correct these. I figure if we can get halfway, we will be able to fix all of them.

Jessa's phone is buzzing on the table, and she ignores it.

"Do you need to get that?" I ask her, and she shakes her head.

"Nope. But I could use something else to drink. Do we have anything else here?" she asks, and I'm immediately on my feet. What the hell is going on with me. I go to the fridge and bring us both a bottle of water. "Thanks," she says softly as she takes off the lid, and I watch her throat move as she swallows a large gulp.

The silence begins to get uncomfortable and I wonder if I made it this awkward when Jessa speaks. "Is this something they do every year?" she asks, waving a bat before putting a sticker on it and throwing it in the box.

"Yeah, I think we've sponsored it for a good eight years now. We always do a promotional product for the event."

"Did we make these?" she asks, and I give her a small smile.

"Yeah, saves cost and Collin was always adamant that it should be a Kemper's product."

"Makes sense," she says. "He loved this company?"

"I wish you had the chance to really get to know him," I say, truly meaning it. It's got to be hard to hear about your own father second hand. Not only that, but to continually hear what a good man he was, when he wasn't to you.

"Me too. Want to know a secret?" she says and I nod. "I was already on my way to Florida when I got the text from Zach. I wanted to get to know him."

"I'm sorry."

"Me too," she says. "I'm still hoping Zach comes around, but I'm losing hope."

"I could talk to him," I say, and I want to smack myself. Who the fuck am I to offer that to her, and I know how stubborn he can be? If he's going to come around, it's going to be on his own terms.

"I appreciate it, but I think this is something I need to figure out on my own." She tosses another bat in the box before speaking again. "What about you, do you have a lot of family?"

"Too many family members if you ask me."

She laughs. "Like Penny?"

"Penny is nothing compared to my brothers." She tilts her head like she wants to know more. "Being the oldest of four is definitely something. We all like to pick on each other, still do, even though we're grown ass adults."

"Do you have any nieces or nephews... or kids of your own?" she asks. I wonder if she's gauging my relationship status and I know I shouldn't like that, but I give her the information she needs.

"No, to my mother's chagrin, all of her sons are hopelessly single and childless."

She hums and there's a question I've been wanting to ask.

"What about your mom? Any other siblings?"

"No, my mom passed a few years ago, and thankfully she didn't have any other children." She leaves it at that, and continues working on the bats. It's nearly one in the morning when we get halfway through the box and I decide to call it a night.

Jessa looks absolutely exhausted, and the idea of her driving the forty-five minutes home to Clearwater eats away at me.

"I live right down the street and have a guest room if you'd like to crash there."

"I couldn't impose," she says, and I shake my head.

"You just saved my ass, and the company's. You can have whatever you want, plus I don't like the idea of you driving so far so late."

Her brown eyes explore mine before responding. "Okay."

"Okay."

Her eyes are wide when we get to my house, and I try not to feel proud that I've impressed her. She keeps her opinions to herself as I take her to the guest room. "Do you want a shirt or something to wear?" I ask her and she nods. Should I give her one of my old Rays shirts with my name on it... no... and I certainly shouldn't enjoy the thought of her wearing my name. She thanks me, and I leave her alone for the night. Thankfully I'm exhausted enough to not dwell on it as I pass out, knowing that tomorrow is going to be long as fuck.

※ ※ ※

When I wake up, it feels like any ordinary day as I get ready, I wear casual clothes for the game later and head downstairs to get a coffee. I'm greeted by Jessa sitting at the bar top, her legs crossed as she sips her coffee. She's still in my fucking shirt.

"Oh, morning," she says blushing. "I'll go get ready."

I indulge and look at her legs one more time. I feel like a pervert for wondering what she has on under the shirt, and I know wholeheartedly I shouldn't be looking at her legs and enjoying what I'm seeing. "I'll take you to your car and you can go home and get ready."

She arches a brow at me, taking a sip of her coffee, and I wonder if I've been caught looking at her inappropriately. This is all so not okay. I should have just driven her to Clearwater, but no, I decided to make things even more inappropriate by having her sleep here, in my clothes. She puts the coffee down and glances at me in a soft way, like she's taking my appearance in. I shouldn't like it as much as I do.

"But the bats?" she questions, and I can't help the tug in my chest. Why does she have to be so caring and perfect? She's beautiful. I've thought so since the moment I met her, but the more I learn, the more I like, and the more guilt starts to consume me.

"The rest of the office can put in some work. Make sure you dress casually, you're spending half the day at the game with me."

"What?" she asks.

"You made this happen, you're coming to the game with me."

She smiles and hops off the stool, the shirt bunching at the top of her thighs, and I have to hold back a groan. I don't watch her ass or my name on her back as she walks down the hall to the guest bedroom. Why the fuck did I invite her? I knew it was crossing the line, and having her bare feet pad across my kitchen floor feels too domestic, in a way I didn't think I'd ever like. I'm not sure what these feelings are festering inside of me, but I shut them down immediately.

Thankfully, no one is at the office to see me drop Jessa off to her car. I called Kenny at the warehouse, and he's bringing all the bats over here so we can finish. Some of the warehouse crew is even coming to help. We should be able to knock the rest of these out quickly.

"You're sure you don't need my help?" she asks, while opening her car door.

"I'm sure. Just be ready for the baseball game." She smiles and leaves, and it's wrong but all I want to do is make her smile more when she comes to the game with me today. She's easy to be around, easy to make happy. But she seems so innocent, not only that, but she needs to be off limits. We can't start something for a multitude of reasons, no matter how beautiful and adorable I think she is.

Jesus Christ, I feel like a school boy, not a nearly forty-year-old man.

Penny comes in first, and while my cousin can get on my nerves, I can't deny that she has a heart of gold. She might have been adopted by my aunt, but the girl fits into our chaotic family so well. She's immediately removing labels at her desk.

"Seriously, Aiden, it looks like a huge, fat cock, how didn't you notice?" I glare at her and she laughs. "Sorry, it's just really bad. You were gonna hand out these cock stickers to children."

I ignore her teasing and I just know my brothers are going to make fun of me as soon as she tells them this story. "Just make sure everyone gets a box when they come in. All hands on deck."

"Of course, good thing we have Jessa, huh?" she says with a smirk on her face. I wave her off and head to my office where I continue ripping off these fucking stickers and putting the new ones on. I ignore all the grumbling from employees outside my office, but they all put in the work. That is, everyone except Zach, who is dressed for the game. I'm sure he's assuming he's going to be sitting next to me, when in fact, he will be with the rest of the employees in the higher section.

"Hey, Aiden," he says, leaning against the doorframe. "Serious fuck up with the stickers, huh?"

"Yeah," I say dryly and go back to taking the stickers off. "Luckily, Jessa caught it." He makes a frustrated noise, and I try not to snap at him.

"What time do you want to leave for the game?"

"I'm taking Jessa."

"You're what?" he asks incredulously.

"She saved us big time. She's going to do the drop off with me, and she's sitting with me in my seats."

"You mean my dad's seats?" Give me strength to deal with this little fucker.

"The seats he gave to me, because he wanted them to go to someone who would appreciate them."

"This is seriously such fucking bullshit. She shouldn't even be here."

"Get the fuck out of my office," I say. His eyes are wide as he looks at me. I'm so over his shit. I put up with his antics when Collin was alive out of respect, but honestly, he needs to be put in his place. He isn't even that much younger than me, so his immaturity is seriously unfounded.

"Seriously, you've known her for two weeks? You're giving me an attitude about that gold-digging bitch?"

"Zach, I suggest you get the fuck away from me before this becomes a bigger issue." I glare at him and clench my fist. My hand hurting from all these fucking stickers. I'd risk hurting it again to punch him in the face right now.

"Fucking ridiculous," Zach complains as he stomps away like a petulant child. But as he's storming away, I see Jessa's wide eyes. She was there the whole altercation, and I feel mortified. She quickly turns away and starts with her bats that she shouldn't even be working on with how much she's done.

With the whole staff—sans Zach—it only takes us about three hours to finish all the bats. Kenny packs them up in the truck, and I tell the office to enjoy themselves at the game, and I'll see them tomorrow. Jessa seems shy when I tell her to meet me at my car.

"I could drive and meet you there."

"No, hop in," I tell her. She huffs, but opens the passenger door. She's wearing cut-off jean shorts that show too much thigh. Thighs I should not be staring at let alone for the second time today. She doesn't have a Rays shirt on; we'll have to change that. Her hair is in a long ponytail and green sunglasses cover a portion of her face.

"I've never been to a baseball game," she says when we park at the stadium.

"Well, you're in for a treat." She smiles and takes in the stadium as we park and meet Kenny at the receiving gate.

Their marketing manager, Lewis, is there and thanks us for the donation as they take them to the exits to give to the kids after the game. Giving kids wooden bats during the game isn't a great idea, I can only imagine the injuries or the amount of wooden bats flying in the stands.

I take Jessa to the fan shop first, and she looks around. "Do you need a hat or something?" she asks and I shake my head.

"No, you can't come to a Rays game and not wear a shirt."

"Oh, Aiden, that isn't necessary."

"Honestly, I insist. Which one do you want?" She blinks at me a few times. "You pick, or I will," I tell her, and she swallows.

"Can you pick?" she asks.

Fuck.

I look through my choices, and with how hot it is, I grab a white t-shirt with a V-neck and the logo front and center. She smiles as I grab the shirt and take it to check out. Once I pay, I hand it to her.

"Thank you," she whispers.

"You're welcome. Let's get you changed and get some hot dogs and beers." She nods and nudges my shoulder before heading to the bathroom to get changed.

When she emerges from the bathroom with a red bra clearly visible underneath her white t-shirt, I realize how exactly fucked I am. I'm not sure what's worse, sitting next to her and having this knowledge or if I just would have sat next to Zach's miserable ass.

Jessa

White T-Shirts and Red Bras

I DON'T KNOW why I want to play with fire so bad. But I can't help myself. It's been a while since I've felt this way.

Sure my ex, Sean, made me feel special and wanted, but I've realized now how early on that faded out. Our relationship was over before I caught him cheating, and I should have seen the signs way before I left him. We didn't play as much as we used to and he stopped caring for me the way he did in the beginning—in the way I'd grown accustomed to. I'm not sure if I'll ever have the dynamic I had with Sean, and it's a concession I could make for the right person. But there are attributes in a man that I find compelling, and that are parallel with what I want romantically and sexually.

Deep down, I know that Aiden shouldn't be that person for me. He's my boss, and I've only just met him. But have you ever just felt so alone that any smidge of affection and human connection becomes nearly polarizing? I don't know how to explain it, but Aiden does that for me.

The way he stood up for me against Zach had my heart racing, and not to mention all the tender moments we had last night. It doesn't help that I slept in his shirt and went to sleep smelling like his clean laundry, or that he's buying me things. I always feel like a bitch when I say gifts are my love language, but it is, and well, Aiden is doing it subconsciously.

Maybe I should have told him not to choose the white one, but I liked him choosing for me, and he did it effortlessly.

I know I'm stirring the pot, but I don't care. This neediness within me isn't going to just magically solve itself. I know myself well enough, what I need to feel completely whole. I wish I was the type of woman who didn't care about men, and could live completely independently. But, that's not who I am and all I want is for someone to take care of me. Maybe I'm latching on to what a genuinely nice person Aiden is, but it's all I have right now, and as pathetic as that is, I'm going to hold on to the one good thing I have.

Even if it's only a friendship, or even just flirting. I'll take what I can get. Any friendship, kindness, or care I can soak up right now, I'm greedily taking it.

I immediately watch Aiden's reaction, his pupils dilating and his throat bobbing as he takes in the tight-white shirt and the red of my bra deliberately shining through. I've noticed him looking at my legs twice today. I know that there's some level of attraction on his end. And maybe I'm being devious, but is it so wrong to want an attractive man to look at you like you're the sexiest thing he's ever seen?

"Beers?" I ask as he blinks up at me.

"Uh, yeah. What do you like?" He glances at me one more time, and his eyes stick to my chest longer than any boss ever should. It lights a fire under me. I've felt hopeless and unwanted recently, and all I want is just a smidge of affection. I surely won't deny it from this beautiful, attentive man.

"Maybe a seltzer?" He nods and we stand in line.

"What do you want on your dog?"

"Just ketchup." He scoffs but smirks as we go up to the teller. Does he know how attractive it is that he asked me what I wanted and ordered it for me? Maybe Aiden is willing to play with fire just as much as I am.

He carries all of our food as we walk to our seats. I'm in awe at the dome top as we keep walking further and further down. When he takes a step in an aisle, we're only four or five rows behind home plate.

"Something tells me that these are really good seats."

"Basically the best seats you can get," he says, sitting down. When I follow suit, he hands me my seltzer and hot dog.

"Is the cover thing on all the time?" I ask, pointing to the roof. He smirks and nods his head.

"It's always seventy-two and sunny at Tropicana Field." He looks around the stadium and I can't help but feel that this place means more to him than he's letting on.

He drinks his beer and eats his hotdog. "So where is everyone else in the office sitting?" I ask, and wonder if the game was paid, for why he felt he needed me to sit next to him.

"Up there," he says, pointing to the left corner.

"Peasant section?" Aiden tilts his head back and laughs.

"I guess so, but their beer and snacks are covered. Could be worse."

I click my tongue and take a bite and chew before speaking again. "So you're like a cool boss."

He shrugs, being modest. "I try. I took on a lot of responsibility the last few years when Collin got sick, and I enjoy it."

"You're good at it." It's the first time I see a blush creep on his cheeks. It's adorable, and it makes me want to test his limits even further.

Suddenly a teenager is holding a baseball near Aiden's face. "Mr. Carlson, would you mind signing my ball?" he asks. Aiden looks at me apologetically as he sparks a conversation with the young man. He signs his ball and shakes his hand before turning back to me.

"So... are we going to talk about that?"

"I used to play professionally." I motion my hands for him to continue. He shifts in his seat. "I played for the Rays for ten years, hurt my hand and retired. I had money to invest, and instead of turning to partying, Collin convinced me to become a part of his business and that's what I did."

My mouth parts, and I look at him appreciatively. "So you weren't kidding when you said you love sports."

"No, I love them all, but baseball will always be number one."

"Well, I didn't realize I was sitting next to a true expert. You'll have to teach me," I say, looking up at him. His gaze travels to my mouth when the word teach escapes my lips. I involuntarily bite my bottom lip and smile at him.

"I'll teach you whatever you want to know," he says back and all I can think about is the lessons I'd love for him to teach me.

We're interrupted by another one of his fans who he speaks to and signs their memorabilia. I take this time to eat my hot dog and calm my ass down. You wouldn't think this stadium is air conditioned with how on-fucking-fire I feel right now.

I take a sip of my seltzer, making a mental note to savor

the drink. No way am I going to be a mess in front of Aiden again.

"Sorry about that," he says, turning back to me.

"Don't be, you've been retired for how long now?" I ask.

"Eleven years."

"That just goes to show what an impact you've had. Eleven years later and people still remember you. You should be proud of that."

He scrubs his chin, and I can hear the scratchy texture of his nails against his face. I like his facial hair a little grown out, I realize. "I guess."

"You're a great boss, you own a company, and you had a successful athletic career. You have a lot to be proud of, Aiden." His pupils dilate at my pride over his accomplishments, and it makes me wonder if no one tells him how great he is. Maybe I should do that more, he seems to like it, and it's deserved.

His face is so close to mine, and all it would take is me shifting my body weight closer and we would be touching. I want it, but I'm not sure if Aiden does. Even if he's attracted to me, starting an office romance or fling isn't something to take lightly. But the more time I spend in his orbit, the more I learn about him, the more I want.

Wanting something is dangerous, it sets you up to be disappointed, but I can't help but feel like Aiden would be far from disappointing.

The game starts, breaking our eye contact, and I turn to watch. Asking Aiden questions here and there. He answers me in a calm tone and doesn't treat me like an idiot.

"So wait, if they get hit with a ball they just get to go to first base?" Aiden nods his head. "I guess that makes sense?"

He laughs and some man is screaming about ice cold beer down the steps. Aiden holds up his hand and gets his attention.

"Need anything?" he asks, his face close to mine.

I blink rapidly and shake my head.

Suddenly, the people in the seats around us are shouting and the woman next to me forces me to break eye contact with Aiden. She taps my shoulder and points at the big screen. I see Aiden and me, we're inside a heart and in pink bubble letters are the words 'Kiss Cam.'

"Oh," I say looking back at Aiden.

"They will just go to the next person, don't worry about it." I nod at him, but wish desperately that he would. Of course, I look back at the screen and now it's announcing that he's a retired player and everyone around us is screaming for us to kiss.

If it was just us? If our co-workers weren't at the stadium too, I might just go for it. But I can still be a little bold, I decide.

I lean forward and place a kiss on his prickly cheek. His eyes are wide as he looks at me while I back away. There's a mix of boos and claps around us. I guess they were hoping for more action than that. I don't blame them, I'm just as disappointed. I sit back down, knowing that my cheeks are pink, but I don't back down looking at Aiden.

I'm not sure I expect a scolding, or something, but he just looks at me. That is until the beer guy comes up and Aiden asks me again if I want anything, which I shake my head no to.

Did I just fuck this all up?

Have I been reading him wrong, is he truly just kind and

giving? I swear it felt like he was flirting with me, and the way he looks at me screams that he's attracted to me.

"Good call, with the office here," he says, and I take a drink and nod my head. Just like that the conversation is over.

The rest of the game feels like I'm walking on eggshells. Do I just play it off? It was just a kiss on the cheek; Europeans do that shit to complete strangers. Or do I own up to the fact that there's something here. Something I want to put my finger on, maybe I really need to tamper down this crush and find a different outlet.

When I was with Sean, we would go to a club in DC every now and then. It was invite only, but people came solo all the time, people like me who need an outlet. Maybe there's something like that here. A place where I can get what I need, and try to not maul my boss in the process.

"You good?" Aiden asks, interrupting my thoughts.

"Yes," I reply, smiling at him. "Thanks again for the seats. It's been special, even more so knowing you played on that field." He nods and drops the conversation there.

I definitely misread the signals—someone shoot me.

I see a few girls with their faces painted, and I look around. Maybe it's stupid, but it looks adorable, and I want a fucking glittery butterfly on my face.

A woman sits three people down, and I have to stretch over Aiden to touch her arm. "Sorry to bother you, but where did you get your face painted?"

She smiles. "Just two sections over, I guess it's for kids' day."

"Do you mind if I go?" I ask Aiden. He shakes his head no and stands up.

"I'll go with you."

"Oh, you don't have to come with me." He gives me a stern look, and I shrug my shoulders and we walk in silence to the face painter. It's all kids in line and my full-grown-adult-ass. I can't help but to fidget with my shirt. "We don't have to wait in line."

"Jessa?" he says.

"Yeah?"

"Get your face painted."

"Okay," I say, looking up at him. He doesn't complain as we wait. The woman doing the face painting smiles at me and pats the chair.

"What can I do for you, sweetheart?"

"Maybe some butterflies?" I ask and she nods. Picking up her paint brush, I close my eyes as she works. And even though my eyes are closed, I can feel Aiden staring at me. I just can't discern if it's in embarrassment, affection, or confusion. I really shouldn't have kissed his cheek. This is what I get for being bold.

I just... need direction.

I sigh as the face painter finishes up. I blink my eyes open as Aiden looks at me. "Pretty," he says with a smile. We're definitely back to square one, where I feel confused about how Aiden Carlson feels about me.

Jessa

You're Not My Daddy Anymore

THE WORK WEEK continues with no mention of the kiss cam, and Aiden goes back to being a hermit in his office. Is it wrong I wish there was some other tragic phallic-looking sticker ordeal to spend more time with him?

No... bad Jessa.

If he were interested, he would have said something at the baseball game. He didn't, and he's my boss. It's time to look for affection somewhere else. Of course my phone rings, and I'm so fucking frustrated I finally grab it and go out of the office.

"What?" I answer the phone.

"Come home, baby, Daddy didn't mean it."

"Tell me, Sean. How do you fuck your student and not mean it?" I say angrily.

"Don't be like that. I know you need me, Jessa. Where are you even living? You left most of your things here. I know you're coming back to me."

"I'm not coming back. I don't want to be with you, and I'm living somewhere else."

"Come back home now and I won't be mad," Sean says

with all of his arrogance. It's what initially attracted me to him, and now I hate it.

"No, Sean. We're broken up. You're not my boyfriend, and you're certainly not my fucking daddy anymore."

"Don't make me lose my temp—" I hang up the phone and slide down the side of the building, my ass connecting to hot as fuck concrete, making me jolt up.

There's a slight gasp to my left, and I'm mortified to see Penny standing there with a vape to her lips.

"Um, I can act like I didn't hear anything," she says sheepishly, and I wave her off.

"It's fine, I'm not embarrassed about what I like."

She smiles at me and leans against the wall next to me. "You know, if that's what you're in to, there's a place called Avalon." I tilt my head at her, and she continues. "It's a sex club, pretty posh, membership only. But they are having an event this weekend to try and get some new members."

I blink at her. "And you know this because you go?"

"I haven't grown a pair of lady balls big enough to go yet, but you should check it out. Nothing like getting over an ex like getting under someone new."

I smile at her and nod. "I think it would help. I mean I'm over Sean. I think I was way before I found him cheating, that was the thing that just pushed me to leave, you know?"

"But you miss the lifestyle?" she says, more curious than anything.

I shrug my shoulders before speaking. "I like being taken care of in that sense. It's been hard being on my own."

"Then you should go! If no one catches your eye, you can just leave. But who knows, maybe you'll meet someone interesting."

"Maybe I'll check it out."

"You'll have to report back if you do," Penny adds in and I laugh.

"Of course."

"Now, can we go get a sandwich? I'm fucking starving," Penny whines and I laugh nudging her shoulder.

"Yeah, let's go."

I'm at the copier, minding my own fucking business when I notice Tabitha strutting her stuck-up ass around the office and heading toward Aiden's.

For someone who seems to be into my half-brother, she sure does spend a lot of time trying to get Aiden's attention.

It irritates me.

Luckily for my irrational jealousy, he isn't in his office, and Tabitha storms off, her nose high in the air as her heels click and her ponytail swishes behind her.

"She gone?" a soft voice says behind me, scaring the shit out of me.

"Fuck," I whisper to myself as I clutch a hand to my chest.

Aiden laughs and his hand squeezes my shoulder before retreating. "Sorry, didn't mean to scare you."

"That's okay," I say softly, holding on to the copier as the papers shoot out. "Not a fan of Tabitha?"

He gives me a look like he wants to tell me the truth, but then remembers that he's my boss. "She complains a lot," is all he says, and I click my tongue against the roof of my mouth.

There's a dark bitchy side of me that wants to say maybe she would stop complaining if she wasn't with someone like Zach, but I swallow it. I hate being that person, but I can't say that it's a total lie.

"Maybe we should give her more bats to take stickers off of, and see how much she complains then," I say, and Aiden smirks at me. He shakes his head and looks down at the documents coming out of the printer.

"Are these your branding ideas?"

"Yeah," I say in an airy tone. I don't even recognize my voice.

"I'm excited to see them. When did you want to go over everything?" he says, not disturbing my papers, and my heart starts beating rapidly under my rib cage. It's a mixture of fear and excitement. I think my ideas are great, but what if he hates them? There's also the fact that I'll be in his office with him, staring at his hands, watching his expressions and thinking about how dreamy he is.

Why couldn't I have had an ugly boss?

"I have time on Friday," he says, and I nod my head.

"Friday works."

"Looking forward to it," he says with a smile, as he heads back to his Tabitha-free office. I really wish Aiden would start being a dick to me. His kindness is giving me mixed signals, and I'm not sure how I'm going to make it through this meeting without combusting.

※ ※ ※

Did I sleep last night? Certainly fucking not. The thought of this presentation has been running through my head all night. Being in Aiden's office with him, and the dirty thoughts I keep having about him don't help.

The thought of leaning over his desk to reach for a stapler and his hand creeping up the back of my thigh. Fuck, I even thought about him fucking me bent over the desk with his office door wide open, Tabitha staring with wide-eyed jealousy. Yeah, this isn't helpful. At least I have Avalon to look forward to on Saturday, so maybe some of this pent-up tension will get released then because my vibrator sure as hell isn't getting the job done.

I put on more makeup than usual, covering my under eyes and giving me a hopefully brighter appearance than I feel right now.

When Aiden calls me into his office, I feel like every nerve ending is firing off, but I grab my portfolio, ready to impress him as I sit opposite his desk.

He gives me a soft smile, and maybe I'm deluded, but I haven't seen him smile that way toward anyone else in the office.

"Let's see it," he says, holding out his hand and accepting the papers.

"My idea is Kemper's standard logo is fine, but needs to be incorporated more into each division. Right now, there's nothing in the baseball line that matches with the skateboard line. And while that's great because there are major differences between products and buyers, we still want people to remember the Kemper name. There needs to be some uniform representation in the branding."

He smiles again, flicking through the pages, and I feel proud of them. Is this the work I want to do for the rest of my life? Hell no. But I feel proud of the direction and the work I put in, and when I look at Aiden's face, I can tell he is too.

"You've done a great job, Jessa," he says, looking at my designs and marking up which ones he loves or isn't sure about. "I'm—Collin would have been proud of this," he says, swallowing and looking back down at the files.

It feels like everything falls back to his relationship with my father and the current situation we find ourselves in—me being his employee. He leaves me notes and tells me again how proud he is of the work I've done. There's something soft in his eyes as he says it, and I still feel like something is lingering between us, but I let it go. I need to find an outlet for these feelings instead of imposing them on him. If he felt the same there would be a clearer sign.

It's Saturday night and I've RSVP'd for Avalon's open event. It's black tie, and I have my tight-black dress on. It hits me in all the right places, and I feel confident even if I'm still nervous. I have small gold hoop earrings with butterflies on them and my hair is in loose curls down my back. I feel beautiful, and my new tan from living on the beach doesn't hurt either.

I'm not usually someone who is into casual. Not that I would ever judge someone who is, but for me and what I'm looking for in a sexual dynamic, there needs to be trust, and you can't just earn that overnight. Avalon does offer a sense of security that going out to a club or bar doesn't offer. Picking up a stranger, you lose the safety that somewhere like Avalon offers. Not to mention most people here have some idea of kink etiquette and the chances of finding someone who matches my interests are higher.

I wouldn't be able to pay the membership fees right now, but I wonder if there are any discounts for single women. I'm getting way ahead of myself, per usual. But, I at least have tonight. I think Penny is right that being with someone else will really put the nail in the coffin that was my relationship with Sean.

Avalon isn't far from the office, and it's around sunset when I arrive. The entrance is a mix of black and gold, not in a cheap way. It feels lux and formal with dimmed lighting. I sign in at the front of the desk and check my purse and phone into their secure lockers. I almost feel naked without my phone, there's nothing to hide behind.

My heels click on the black marble as I join the woman— Clara—who will be providing our tour.

"After the tour you can sign up for membership or ask questions. You can engage in everything except sexual activity, since we need STI screening for our members. But touching, if welcomed by one of our members, is permitted."

There are two couples along with me on the tour, and I can't help but feel out of place. I'm not sure if I could join a couple or not. No, I know for a fact I couldn't. I wish I was that bold, but I would want to be the center of attention and that's not possible when you have to take two people into consideration.

"Avalon prides itself on being a clean, safe, and unique place for you to indulge in your fantasies. We take our members' privacy and safety above all else. If you decide to sign up, your information will remain confidential and cameras are not permitted on the premises." She walks us through the halls and there are a series of closed doors.

"There are individual rooms you can rent with other members or pairings, but our biggest features are the areas for voyeurism, exhibitionism, and experimentation." As we walk farther we're greeted by a massive room, decorated the same as the foyer with black and gold. There are pairings of people and groups all throughout the large space.

Most of the seating are sectional-like black couches and chairs, with people engaging in various sexual acts and scenes. I'm fascinated as I watch a woman who is on her knees between a man's legs. They are both fully dressed, but she just touches him and looks at him like he's the only person in the room.

Fuck, I need that.

She looks up at him like he's the center of the universe and this deep longing is yanking in my chest. When he cups her face gently and then wraps a fist in her hair, I can't help but to be undeniably turned on. It's a mixture of envy, arousal, and intrigue that keeps my eyes locked on their performance. He's gentle, but firm with her, everything that I like. When I get a good look at the man, my first thought is that he isn't as attractive as Aiden. Jesus Christ, I have it bad. I need a man to take the reins and let my brain shut off just for a little while. I force myself to look away from the couple and re-engage with the group.

"This is the main area, clothes optional, and mostly anything goes for activity," she says, continuing to usher us through the space. I can't stop glancing back at the woman on her knees, but I'm forced to as we enter an area with a stage that is currently vacant. "We have multiple shows a night, some are paid professionals who give training or explain certain kinks. We also have days where members can sign up and perform on stage."

The couples in my tour group are chatting animatedly as she takes us to a few more rooms. They have a wax room and some others set up for specific bondage and impact play activities. Some of the rooms smell like leather and cleaning products which makes me scrunch my nose, but I understand the need for everything to be sanitary.

Clara makes sure to reiterate the rules for the night as she drops us back off at the main area. I get one free drink for attending the event, and I order myself a lemon drop. I take the cocktail and take a seat at one of the sectionals.

Even if nothing happens for me tonight, just being around like-minded people helps. The woman who was kneeling for the man earlier is gone, which is a shame. I could have happily watched them all night long. It's early in the night so most of what's happening around me is kissing and gentle touching, conversation making up most of the noise in the room.

There are multiple security officers around the room and I take note of where they are, just in case. I'm wishing I had my phone so I could hide away in my corner, when a man comes and sits down next to me. He's a little younger than what I would go for, but his suit seems expensive and his smile is charming.

"May I take a seat?" he asks even though he's already halfway to sitting down.

"Of course." I gesture to him and he takes a seat.

"Lincoln," he says, holding out his hand, and I shake it.

"Jessa."

"I haven't seen you here before," he says, and I smile at him, though it feels forced.

"I'm here for the tour and to possibly join."

"Is there anything I could do to sway your decision?" he asks with a smirk. It's then that I really look at his face. Something about him seems so familiar, but I can't put my finger on it.

"I have pretty strict rules being a visitor," I joke, and he smirks. That familiarity rings in my head, and I still can't place it.

"There are so many ways to make you come without fucking you, sweetheart," he says, and I swallow thickly.

"That's true." I can't decide if I'd be interested in him or not, he seems a little too cocky for what I'd usually go for, but I am just here for a good time. "What would you suggest?"

"I could—" Suddenly Lincoln is being gripped by his lapels and no longer sitting across from me. The man who grabbed him whispers in his ear and Lincoln smirks at me before waving goodbye. "I could just head over and get a drink. Nice speaking with you, Jessa," he says as he walks away. I trail his descent with my eyes, but quickly turn to face the man who made him leave in the first place.

Aiden.

He sits down next to me and there's a huge elephant-sized silence between us before he speaks. "Sorry for my brother," he says, clearing his throat. Of course that's who he reminded me of, in a more boyish type of way.

"He wasn't bothering me," I say, and Aiden rubs his jaw.

"Should I tell him to come back?" he asks, and I want to shake the man in front of me.

"No, I don't think Lincoln and I have the same interests."

Aiden unbuttons his jacket and sits back, taking a more relaxed stance on the couch, his arm behind my back and his ankle resting on his knee. I'm not sure what should be more attractive to me: the fact that Aiden is here and potentially into some of the same things as me, the way he ripped his brother from speaking to me, or how fucking hot he looks in a suit.

"And what are your interests?" Aiden asks, taking a sip of his whiskey and licking his lips as he looks at me. My gaze travels from his lips to his eyes and he smirks at me.

"I have multiple, but I think it would be more fun for you to guess," I say, feeling bold and picking up my cocktail and taking a sip. Maybe I wasn't wrong, and Aiden wants this as bad as I do, but he doesn't know if the risk is worth it or not.

Maybe it's because I'm impulsive or needy, but I don't really care for the repercussions at the moment.

"I think that's a dangerous game, kitten." He eyes me hungrily and shifts his pants. I can't help the small smile that takes over my face with his use of a pet name.

"I like a little danger sometimes," I say, knowing how stupid I sound, but I hold back my own grimace.

He smirks and leans forward into my space just a little more than what would be considered friendly.

"I think you're looking for someone to take care of you, who tells you what to do, who takes your pleasure into their hands." My breathing hitches, and I nod my head. "I think you want even more than that, but I don't think we should get into that right now."

I look into his deep-green eyes that are so full of want, and honestly, it takes everything not to just crawl on his lap and tell him not only do I want those things, but I want to make someone feel good, needed, and cherished too.

Licking my lips instead, I respond, "And what do you want?"

"I want a lot of things I shouldn't have."

"Shouldn't being the keyword?" I ask and he nods his head. He takes out his wallet and leaves a tip for the waitress —who hasn't even stopped to ask us if we want anything—as he stands up and fixes his jacket.

"Lincoln isn't what you need, you're right. I don't know many people suited at Avalon for what you're looking for. You probably shouldn't spend the money on the member- ship," he says, walking away. I'm quickly on my feet and following him. I grab his arm and he spins around on his own accord as there's no way I could manhandle him even if I wanted to.

"Aiden," I start to speak, and his hand is around my throat and my back is pressed against the wall. His touch isn't threatening or rough, more like he's trying to ground himself and the only way he knows how to do that is by touching me. It's tender, and it has me pressing my thighs together as my eyes meet his.

His thumb is rubbing my jaw in a tender caress as his hand is lightly holding me still. "This can't happen," he says, and I blink at him a few times.

"Why not?" I ask, feeling a little petulant.

"I made some promises I intend to keep."

I roll my eyes, loathing my dead father for cock-blocking me at the moment. "He's dead," I say, and I don't mean for it to come out so coldly, but it does. Aiden's hand dropping from my throat instantly when the harsh words are out. The warmth of his hand and body leaving my own as he blinks at me before walking away.

"I'll see you on Monday," he says in a low tone before heading out of the club's doors.

This was definitely not the evening I had in mind.

Aiden

I Want This

AVOIDING the person who is also supposed to be assisting me is a nightmare. I don't know what the fuck I was thinking. I just saw Lincoln near her and acted like a fucking asshole. I acted like she was mine to tell me what to do. I very nearly gave her everything we both wanted.

Part of me regrets it and the other part of me is frustrated at her for continually tempting me. Her bringing up Collin was the sobering thing I needed to walk away. What would he think if he was still alive and I met his daughter at a fucking sex club?

Jessa is a mystery to me. I have an idea of what she's looking for based on slip ups here and there and the fact that she was at Avalon. But her ability to be the person to make these dangerous moves is taking me for a loop. I would have thought she would be a timid submissive, someone who waits for someone to come to them.

I'm not sure how strong I am to hold back any more either.

The way she looked at Avalon, *fuck*. I can't even think

about it without getting hard at my desk. This infatuation isn't going to stop, unless I keep my distance, even when I don't want to.

A clearing of a throat at my office door has me looking up to see Penny.

"Everything's all set for Friday," she says.

"Has everyone RSVP'd?"

"Yes, it looks like everyone is coming." Great, now I'm going to be trapped on a floating vessel with no escape with her.

"Perfect, thank you, Penny." My overly observant, extremely nosey, but with good intentions cousin gives me a look before clicking her tongue.

"Is everything okay, Aiden?"

I give her a tight smile and nod my head. "Everything's fine."

She looks at Jessa sitting at her desk and then back at me. "Okay then." She looks like she doesn't believe me, but thankfully she drops it before leaving my office and going back to reception.

Just when I think I'm about to get some reprieve, another blonde head pops in. I control my internal grimace as Tabitha doesn't knock and just sits in the chair across from my desk.

"Sharon says she won't expense my dinner with Hampton Athletics," she says, sliding over the receipt to me. My eyes bulge when I look at everything that was consumed and I blink at her.

"Tabitha, this bill is nearly two-grand. What the fuck?"

"Collin was always big on keeping the customer happy, that's what I did."

"They're not even a big client."

"Okay, so how do I get this expense?" she says, looking at me petulantly, which I can't fucking stand. I know that if I say no the whole sales team is going to lose their shit.

"We will expense this, but no additional expense reports except your mileage for the rest of the month."

"You've got to be kidding." Her mouth is agape, and it's in that moment I realize why she and Zach are fucking: they're both a massive pain in the ass.

"No, you can't expect to be spending large amounts like this for client dinners."

"This is bullshit, Aiden. Collin wouldn't blink an eye."

I sigh and scrub my face, about to tell her to leave me the fuck alone, when a soft voice chimes in from outside of the door. A light knock against the doorframe.

"I'm so sorry to interrupt," Jessa says.

"Then don't," Tabitha says. I have to hold back my irritation with her entitled tone.

Jessa gives her a far friendlier smile than she deserves before looking back at me. "I just got off the phone with the warehouse, there's been an issue. I'll transfer them over to your line."

"Thank you, Jessa. Tabitha, what I said stands, please let Sharon know." She huffs as she gets up and glares at Jessa before walking away. I'm about to pick up my phone when Jessa winks at me before shutting my office door. Instead of an emergency, there's a text from Jessa.

Jessa: You're welcome 😉

There was no issue at the warehouse?

Jessa: No, thought you could use some help.

Thank you.

I probably look a little too hard at her text message and the fucking winky face she sent me. I'm so totally and completely fucked over this girl, and I don't know what to do. She's right, Collin is dead, and he wasn't a father to her. But why can't I stop feeling guilty over how beautiful and sweet I find his daughter to be?

Would it be the worst thing in the world to see where this goes? There are few facets, the first being we work together, and the second is my obligation to Collin. But the overwhelming urgency to give into what we both want, which I feel is something we've both been craving. There's a part of me that knows Jessa is what I've been missing. The woman who can properly combine the two worlds in which I've been separating myself.

Despite my better judgment, I open my office door, if only to have a direct view to watch Jessa work throughout the day. Maybe I should move her to a different cubicle. But then I wouldn't be able to watch the way she taps her pen against her lip as she thinks, or the way she shifts in that fucking chair.

I sigh, opening a browser and ordering her a new chair that will arrive next week.

I'm so incredibly fucked.

❋ ❋ ❋

"It's hot as a witch's tit out here," Sharon complains, causing Penny and Jessa to laugh. Jessa's eyes crinkle with joy, and I like her looking happy more than I'd like to admit.

"I don't know that me or my hair will ever get used to this humidity," Jessa says, taking the hair tie off her wrist and pulling her hair up into a ponytail. Her dark hair slightly curled and sticking to the sides of her face. It's a casual work event for the Fourth of July and she's wearing a white and blue striped dress with a pocket that has red stars on it. I feel pathetic paying attention to what she's wearing, but then again, I notice a lot about Jessa. Especially because it shows off just the right amount of thigh.

It's even worse when I look up to find her brown eyes meeting mine, she saw me checking her out. I either need to give in and see what this is between us, or I need to find another way to get her off my mind. Because this is getting to be too much—I can barely focus at work somedays. Not even because I'm watching her, but I catch her eyes on me often, and I enjoy it more than I should. I just know this is all going to explode in one way or another.

The line moves and Sharon starts fanning herself dramatically. Jessa gives me a soft look before looking back at the boat.

We rented the yacht with three other companies. So we're not at capacity, but the boat is filled with far more people than our office and warehouse staff.

"I'm so ready for a cocktail," Sharon says and Penny hums her agreement.

"If anyone needs an Uber tonight, it's on the company," I say, making it clear that everyone needs to get home safe. If anyone even seems wobbly I'm sending them in a car, I couldn't live with something horrific like that being on my conscience. I might not genuinely like all of these people, but I care about them in my own way. Jessa tilts her head at me, and I hope she doesn't think this is about picking her up that one night. Her cheeks are pink before she speaks.

"Do you guys do this every year?" Jessa asks.

"Oh, we've done a tiki ride, a BBQ, and a crab feast. This is our first year going on a big boat like this," Penny answers. We're all standing in line to get on the boat and Jessa is dangerously close to me, so close all I want to do is touch, but I don't.

"This is so awesome. I've never been on a boat like this," Jessa says excitedly.

"I booked it," Penny says with a shrug of her shoulders.

"You did a good job, Pen," I say. I expect Penny to be the one beaming at me, but it's both her and Jessa, and I almost can't handle their happiness over a similar compliment.

We're finally on the boat and we're greeted by the blessing of air conditioning as we enter the main space of the venue. Appetizers are being handed out and the bartenders are working overtime to get their drinks sorted.

"Come on, let's go get drinks," Penny says, grabbing the two other women and dragging them to get cocktails. I swear Jessa gives me a longing look as she walks away, but I'm probably reading into every single thing she says and does.

I make sure to talk to everyone from the office as well as the other companies we split the yacht with. That was Penny's idea, and she seriously deserves all the credit. I wind up sitting at a table with Zach, Tabitha, and James. But Jessa's back is to mine as she sits at her table, it's like my body knows where she is at all times.

Tabitha has already had a little too much to drink, her eyes are glassy and her hands are all over Zach as she babbles on about something I can't even pay attention to.

"You should have fifty percent, honey," she says to Zach and that's what gets my attention.

"I'm sure Aiden would hate it if we were on an even playing field? Huh?" Zach says in a joking tone that's laced with ill intent.

"I wouldn't care, if it was your father's wish."

Zach scoffs. "My dad sleeps with some crackhead and now we all have to pay the price?"

I clench my bad hand under the table. I've left a lot of my anger issues in the past, but fuck me if Zach isn't bringing them right back up to the surface.

I could sense movement behind me but don't turn right away. It's only when I see her striped dress retreating in my peripheral vision that I know I need to follow her.

I blink at Zach who has Tabitha laughing. It takes every ounce of me, but instead of getting into it with him, I walk away instead.

"Oh come on, Aiden, it was a joke." I wave him off and just keep walking, headed outside where I find Jessa crossing her arms over the railing and looking out to the retreating sun.

I'm cautious as I take the spot next to her, folding my arms. When I look down at her, I see the tear streaks running down her eyes.

"Fuck." I unconsciously put a hand on her shoulder. "Do you want me to yell at him?" I almost ask if she wants me to hit him. I might risk my hand and jail time to erase this look of defeat from her face.

She wipes her rogue tear and shakes her head. "I just…"

She sighs, and looks back out at the sunset. She cleans her face again before she looks at me. "I just don't understand how he can hate me so much. I didn't do anything."

"No, you didn't. This has nothing to do with you, you know that, right?"

"It feels like it's about me."

"Zach is insecure and jealous. Fucking Collin," I say under my breath. If he wouldn't have kept her secret, then there wouldn't be all this resentment.

"Thanks for coming out here, I know you've been avoiding me," she says.

"I haven't been avoiding you."

She rolls her eyes and leans against the railing as she looks at me. "You've done basically everything you could possibly do to avoid me since Avalon."

I rub the back of my neck as I look down at her, her eyes no longer filled with tears as she waits for my response.

"I don't know how to act around you."

"I need you to be honest with me, Aiden. You can tell me that there's nothing here or that you don't want this and I'll stop. I'll stop flirting and tempting you, and I'll just be your co-worker. But I will move on. Or you can admit that you want to see what's happening here. No guilt about my dad— we can deal with the working together part when it comes to that. But I don't want you to be uncomfortable at the office or feel like you can't talk to me."

She just completely laid it all out on the table for me, and if the choice is to risk it all or never find out, I think I'm willing to risk it all.

There's a loud crack, and as we look to our left, a set of fireworks is going off for the holiday. It breaks the tension of the moment and gives me some time to figure out what I want to say back.

When she smiles while viewing the fireworks, I know it's worth the risk. She wasn't wrong when she said Collin is dead. I shouldn't let his opinion factor into this, especially when he's made some fucked-up decisions. The workplace part is the bigger issue, which we can likely avoid dealing with, at least for a little while.

Without touching her, I place my hands outside of her on the railing. Her back only a few inches away from my chest as I lean in to whisper against her ear.

"I want this," I tell her. I swear I can feel her shiver at the words.

She turns away from the fireworks so she's looking at me, her back pressed against the railing. "Dinner at my place on Sunday?" she asks. Our gazes meet, and it's like my heart is beating frantically out of my chest. I want to touch her, kiss her, give her whatever she wants. But now is not the place, and we definitely need to talk about some things before this goes any further.

"Aren't I supposed to be the one asking you on the date?" I joke with her and she smiles.

"You were being too slow. Do you like seafood?"

"I do." My fist is gripping the railing so tightly I'm sure my knuckles are white.

"Perfect," she says in a breathy tone, her eyes lingering on my lips before she meets my gaze again.

"Should I bring anything?"

"I don't have any whiskey, so bring your favorite." There's another crack of a firework and employees start piling out onto the deck to watch the show.

"Sunday," I say, letting the skin briefly touch hers before removing my hands and pulling back to stand next to her.

Fortunately for all of us, Zach and Tabitha choose another spot to watch the show, and I get to stand here and admire the beautiful girl I'm done holding back from as I watch her glow against the lights of the glittery explosions.

Jessa

Daddy Kink 101

SUNDAY? Why the fuck did I say we should have our date on Sunday? I mean, I thought there was a chance we might be hungover Saturday, and I didn't want to risk it. But it's nearly 2 p.m. on Sunday and my nerves are shot. All I can think about is Aiden is coming over here to the cottage that I still don't completely think of as my home yet. There's too many goddamn lighthouses in here for me to consider it mine.

What is he going to want to know? How far will things go? Is he going to be concerned that I've only been out of my last relationship a few weeks, even though it was over long before that? Will we start something and he'll suddenly decide it isn't worth the risk or that he feels too guilty because I'm Collin's biological daughter?

I opted for a sundress because they're my favorite and I've noticed on more than one occasion that Aiden seems to be a big fan of my legs.

I can tell he has a dominant energy to him. Usually men who are in charge of people have that aura about them. That doesn't mean that it transfers sexually, but seeing him at Avalon, he's definitely got something that he's in to.

Great, now I'm on a spiral of us being compatible. I can switch, kind of. I don't mind taking control or initiating, but I much prefer to be told what to do, to have my pleasure in someone else's hands.

Shit.

I'm overthinking all of this. It's been nearly two days of overthinking and my stomach hurts. I've prepared our dinner for tonight, and I know my stomach is going to hurt too bad from nerves to even eat it. *Awesome.*

There's a knock on my door, and I'm up immediately, opening it with what is probably too much enthusiasm.

Aiden looks sheepish as he gives me a smile, a whiskey bottle in his hand. "I know we said four, but I couldn't wait any longer."

"Thank God, me either." I step to the side and let him into the home. He looks around in a nostalgic way before following me into the kitchen. I grab him a glass for his whiskey and take some white wine out of the fridge for myself. "Do you want to sit outside for a while, or are you hungry?"

"Outside is nice."

He leads the way, opening the sliding door. The breeze feels nice today, along with the awning protecting us from the sun. We both take a seat on the lounge chairs next to each other. I wish they were connected, but then again, this is probably better. I shouldn't get too attached if we start talking and realize we aren't a match.

I take a sip of wine before Aiden looks over me again. "I

like your dress. You look beautiful." I can't help the heat that takes over my chest.

"Thank you."

"I guess we should just talk about it?" he suggests, and I'm so thankful he says something first.

"Yes, I'd like that."

"I think it's clear we're both attracted to each other and something's here. But maybe that we're both weighing the risks?" he asks and I nod my head.

"For me, the only thing I'm worried about is work. I don't want anyone to hate me more than they already do."

He makes a noise in the back of his throat as he shakes his head like he's remembering Friday night. "I think if we start something, maybe we keep it quiet at the office."

"And outside of the office?" I ask.

"You'd be my girl everywhere we went. On dates, around my family. I know things are already tense for you at work, and I don't want to be the cause of any more of that tension." Am I a psychopath who only notices he's wanting me to be around his family? I fixate on that for a moment before I speak.

"I think I could do that, could you?"

Taking a sip of his drink, he moves from his relaxed position sitting on the side of the chair. I follow his movements. The way we're sitting, my knees are just touching his as he looks at me.

"I could. It wouldn't be my favorite thing."

"Why?"

"Because you're someone worth showing off, Jessa," he says and I'm licking my lips, ready to close the distance and kiss this man.

"I think you're worth showing off too." His smile is more of a smirk as he shakes his head.

"There's probably more we should talk about, if we're getting involved." I swallow and nod my head in agreement. "We don't have to get into everything, but I think I'd like a better idea of your expectations."

I tilt my head at him. "Like why I was at Avalon?" I ask questioningly.

"Among other things." I feel nervous and start fidgeting with the end of my dress. His large hand clamping down on top of mine before he squeezes. "We don't have to get into all of this tonight. It's our first date, I just didn't know if it was something you wanted to talk about, and it doesn't mean that anything has to happen tonight either." I appreciate his chivalry, but if this man doesn't touch me tonight in some shape or form, I may scream.

"I don't mind, but you'll share too?" I confirm, and he nods. I clear my throat and take comfort in the weight of his hand overtop of mine. "I've really only had one serious boyfriend. His name is Sean, and he was my professor." I gauge his reaction and he doesn't have any. "He introduced me to the lifestyle. I went to a few places like Avalon with him, but not often. Most of our dynamic was at home. Looking back, I realize that I just went along with what he said, because he was the expert—or so I thought—I was learning what I enjoyed. But I think I have a better grasp of what I'm looking for sexually and in a partner."

He squeezes my hand gently for me to continue. "I like being submissive, though I wouldn't consider myself inca-pable of taking control. I just don't like to do it frequently. I like impact play, being watched, being praised, but most important for me is receiving affection."

"Do you like rewards and punishments?" he asks in a deep tone that makes me shiver.

I nod my head and drag my teeth over my lip. "But I would ask that withdrawal of affection or touch is never a punishment."

He balks at me. "What the fuck?" I knew things with Sean were less than perfect, but I overlooked them because I was so afraid of being alone. I don't voice that, I just continue speaking.

"Outside of the bedroom, I love flirty play and banter, but if I do something wrong or something that bothers you, I'd rather talk about it then and there and not bring it into our sex life."

Aiden blinks at me like I'm telling him the sky is green. He swallows and rubs his free hand along his jaw.

"I'm going to be honest, kitten. Your ex sounds like a complete fucking prick."

"Considering I caught him sleeping with one of his students before I left, I'd have to agree."

He groans, taking a sip of his whiskey and putting it back down on the table. "I go to Avalon for a few different reasons, but I've never really combined my proclivities at Avalon into my dating life."

"What do you do at Avalon?" I ask, eager to know. I've been wondering since I saw him there in the first place.

He grimaces slightly. "I like a lot of the things you're asking for: being in control, bringing pleasure and praising my partner. I have been involved with a few couples at Avalon before as well."

"Oh, are you bisexual?" I ask him.

"No, mostly fucking the women in front of their husband or partner. I have been touched by a man before, but I firmly enjoy women."

"That's not something you'd want to do with me, right?" I ask, unsure. Sharing is not something I want. I want someone solely dedicated to me. I'm a greedy, selfish girl, and I openly admit that.

"Fuck no. I've never shared when I've been dedicated to a person and it's not something I need. It's mostly who was available at Avalon."

I nod and appreciate his honesty. A lot of men wouldn't be so forthcoming with the information he's telling me.

"So, you've never brought a girlfriend to Avalon before?"

"No."

"And you haven't really done the things you like at Avalon outside of the club?"

"Not really, no."

"But you'd like to?"

"Yeah, I'd like to have it all. Even if it makes me a selfish asshole. I'm still grappling with how exactly Collin would feel about this. But, I feel like finding out what could be between us outweighs any guilt I have over that."

I swallow, holding back what I want to ask for. I've basically resigned myself to not even bringing it up. I don't need to call him daddy. He doesn't need to be that, I can live without it. He's already feeling guilty for being close to my biological father, adding that into the mix could fuck it all up.

If he can give me everything else except that title, I'd be happy, happier than I ever was with Sean. Aiden looks at me like I'm special, and it seems like our interests align. It's also so fucking nice to be spoken to as an equal, not like I'm lesser than in the partnership. It's become more and more clear that I still have a lot to learn about what a good dominant truly is.

"What labels would make you feel comfortable moving forward?" he asks, and I know I should just blurt it out, but I don't.

"I think just saying we're exclusive, not seeing anyone else and learning one another is enough."

"Is that really enough for you?" he asks with an arch of his brow.

"What do you mean?"

He shakes his head and looks out to the beach. You can see a little sliver of the water from here. "That night I dropped you off, you said something, and I wasn't sure if I should bring it up."

My heart is racing out of my chest and if my stomach hurt earlier, it feels like battery acid is in it now.

"Oh?" I ask, hoping that he will spell it out for me.

"You said daddy, and I know you definitely weren't referencing your absent father."

When did it get so unbearably hot outside? It feels like my skin is on fire, and I just want to jump out of it.

I clear my throat and I want to yank my hand away from his, but I don't. I use it as a grounding point and stare at our combined hands as I speak. "I called Sean that. I like it and what it symbolizes in a dynamic, but it's not something I need."

"But you enjoy it?" His tone is far from judgmental, if anything just pure curiosity. I look up and his green eyes look so soft and captivating as I respond.

"I do enjoy it."

"I've never been called that before, but I think I'd like to see how I like it. What are the things you like most about it?" He's not laughing at me or judging. If anything, he's going out of his way to understand what I like and need. Was Aiden created in a lab? Because I don't think any man should be this perfect.

He squeezes my hand, and I smile looking down at our hands and looking back up to him. "I'm not into age play if that's a concern, not that I would ever yuck anyone's yum, it's just not for me. For me, it's a matter of security and you being my person, knowing that you'll take care of me and make sure I'm safe. I guess it's pretty cliché considering how I was raised. They say you want whatever you didn't have as a—"

"Baby, I didn't ask you to psychoanalyze yourself, I just want to know what you would want from me and what would make you happy."

I blink at him. The term baby sliding off his tongue so easily makes me wet. "I like it when you make choices, when you take control, when you tell me what to do. I'm also a very affectionate person, and I need an annoying amount of attention."

"I can do that."

"You can do that?" I parrot and he nods his head. "And what do you like?"

"Honestly? I think I'm still figuring it out. I like being in charge." He gives me a smirk before putting his other hand on top of mine. "I like impact play, making a mess of my partner and giving them so much pleasure they can't think straight."

"Sounds like a daddy to me," I say jokingly, but he looks at me like it's not a joke at all, like he could potentially like it just as much as I do. He licks his lips and looks down at our hands.

"If I do something you don't like?" he asks. My first thought is 'impossible.' My second thought was about all the things I didn't like Sean doing and I didn't stick up for myself. I need to be different, I want this to be different so desperately.

"Outside of the bedroom, I'll tell you directly. Inside of the bedroom no or stop is direct with me. I don't use those words freely. If I say no or stop, I mean it." He looks at me seriously, taking in my words. "Same for you?" I ask..

"Same for me, I can do that."

"If you don't like being called daddy, it's not a deal breaker for me." He licks his lips again and looks down at mine.

"I don't think that's going to be a problem."

He's on me in an instant. Leaning forward, his hands leaving mine as one tangles in my hair and cups the back of my head. His other grips the lounge chair for support. His eyes meet mine, like he's checking in and this is what I want. I bite my lip and nod my head—it's the only communication he needs as his lips touch mine. His lips are soft and warm as he gently kisses me. This is a first kiss, an exploration of our chemistry and learning each other's reactions.

Aiden is patient and in no rush to shove his tongue down my throat, he's delicate with each press of his lips. My hands are pressed against his chest and my chin is tilted up toward him. His hand on my head is firm, but not rough. I want to tell him that I'm not made of glass but at the same time I'm soaking up his gentle reverence.

His soft kisses end far too soon as he separates from my

lips, Standing to his full height, he holds out his hand, which I eagerly take. We still have some time before dinner as he leads us out toward the beach for a walk.

"I don't want to rush things. I want to do this right," he says. I must make a noise of protest, because I want more kisses and touches. His hand squeezes mine, and he leans down and kisses the side of my hair. "It's important that I do this right," he says, and I can't argue with that tone or how fucking adorable I find this man. I've never felt like I'd be valuable enough for someone to pursue in this way, and I can't deny the feeling is both overwhelming and heart-warming.

"I want to do this right too. But that doesn't mean we can't kiss or do other stuff," I say. You can't blame me, not really. He looks so damn good with the sun shining against his skin, he just kissed me like I was precious, and is basically agreeing to be my dream man.

"We'll see where we stand after dinner." He smirks and drags me along the beach, I nearly forgot about dinner with all the extremely adult conversations we had. Is this what a healthy relationship looks like? Fuck if I know, all I know is this dinner better knock his pants off—literally.

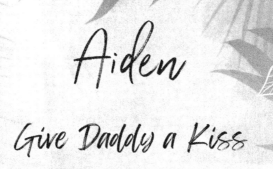

Aiden

Give Daddy a Kiss

THE DINNER JESSA made for us is un-fucking-believable. Honestly, this whole night feels unreal. I've never been vulnerable like that with a woman before, and it's given me a level of comfort with Jessa I didn't expect so early.

Could I dom her in the bedroom without a single conversation, there's no doubt in my mind. But with her, I want something more, I want a dynamic that works behind closed doors and out in the open. Finding that delicate balance isn't something that's going to happen overnight. That's why this night needed to slow down. I could have taken Jessa right to her bedroom and spent hours there with her, but this isn't just about carnal urges—for either of us.

"Do you want dessert?" she asks as she puts my plate in the sink. I nod my head and she hands me a small, clearly homemade cupcake. "It's from a box," she says quickly. I take a bite and smile at her, which she returns.

"Tastes perfect to me," I tell her and a dusting of pink takes over her cheeks. It's still early enough in the evening that I don't feel like I need to leave right away, and I can tell

Jessa wants me to stay longer as well. "Want to watch something?"

"Yes," she says quickly with a smile. "What do you like?"

"I like a little bit of everything, and I'll never make you watch sports unless you want to."

She smirks as she leads me to the couch, her taking a seat first and me following, there are a few inches of space between us, and I make a note to close that gap as soon as possible. "I think I have a good compromise," she says. She tucks her legs under herself as she pulls out the remote and finds what she wants to watch.

I haven't felt this nervous around a woman in years. I think part of it has to do with how badly I don't want to fuck this up. If we started something and it went horribly, this would all be for naught. And maybe a part of me is jealous or feels a little uncomfortable with the thought that I'm the inexperienced one in the lifestyle that she's used to.

Not that her ex seems like a fucking prize. It's clear, some of the things he did to her were so fucking wrong and never how I would treat a submissive. Plus, the person is supposed to be your partner before you add any additional dynamic into the mix. I want to make this right for her. I want to give her what she needs, and I can't help the glimmer of hope that I'll get everything I've been seeking in return.

She puts on a show called *Friday Night Lights.* I'm focusing more on her than the show, but she smiles up at me. "You know, I think you kind of look like Coach Taylor."

"Oh yeah?"

"Maybe a little nicer though?"

"You think I'm nice?" I smirk at her and she nods. "I don't have to always be nice." I mean it, I've worked through a lot of anger and frustration. I do my best to be kind to others and keep that part under wraps. But if she wants a little mean with the nice, I can do that too. Though I prefer a softer approach, I can play whatever role she wants.

Her throat bobs. "I like you nice, but maybe sometimes," she says, shrugging her shoulders.

"You're pretty far away on the couch there." She immediately scooches over so that my arm is wrapped around her and she's leaning slightly against me as we watch this ridiculous football show.

I feel like I'm on a date in high school, the nerves ripping through my body, sitting on the couch with the girl watching a TV show.

Jessa explicitly said she wants someone who can take control. I'm trying to consolidate that I can be both the man I am at Avalon, at the office, and at home. Why am I having such a hard time combining all the facets of who I am?

I'm tired of thinking so hard, so I just act.

"Jessa?"

"Hmm?" She sits up, her hair falling to one side as she blinks her dark brown eyes at me.

"Sit on my lap." My tone is gentle and clear, and she listens so beautifully, climbing onto my lap, her legs parting on each side of my thighs. Her sweet sundress pushes up her toned thighs as she does. My hands rest on the flesh I've been recently obsessed with, kneading the muscle with my thumbs.

"I thought you said slow," she whispers, her hands running a line from my shoulders to my chest.

"This is slow."

"Okay," she says, her eyes meeting mine.

I'm not sure where I summon the audacity and authority but the next words out of my mouth were ones I never thought I would say. "Give Daddy a kiss."

The change in her body language is instantaneous as she melts into me, her core sliding against my growing cock, making her dress rise even further. My hands are on her bare flesh as her hands slide behind my neck. Her fingertips toying with the loose hair behind my neck as her lips meet mine.

She lets out a feminine sigh as she kisses me slowly. Like we have all the time in the world, like she can't get enough of my taste, or like she's trying to memorize the shape of my lips like I am hers.

One of my hands leaves her thigh to hold her neck, my thumb guiding her jaw to where I want her mouth. She lets me control the speed of the kiss and where I want her body, except for the slight movements of her hips seeking friction against my groin.

I deepen the kiss, needing more of her taste and touch. Her tongue works alongside mine in a simplified way. It's leisurely and soft, not an overwhelming or rough dominance. The kiss feels like our date, feeling out how we're going to work and if we're compatible. The longer we kiss, the more I realize Jessa could easily be a person I give everything to and it's both exhilarating and terrifying.

She's sliding her covered pussy against me, and I grab her ass with both of my hands to make her grind down harder on my cock that so desperately wants out of my shorts.

We said slow, I'm not rushing this, I remind myself, even though all I want to do is push up her skirt and thrust up into her wet cunt until she slumps over in pleasure.

Jessa's lips leave mine for a moment to look down at

where we're touching. Her lips part and her eyes meet mine before our lips are back on each other. Our kiss turns more frantic, like neither of us could possibly get closer to each other. The friction of our clothes is a barrier we both want to remove, but we know we shouldn't. I'm trying to remember why we should take this slow as her warm cunt rubs against me.

My grip on her ass is tight. I know if I looked her ass would be white from my fingertips handling her. But she seems to love it, and it only makes me harder and want her more. The noise that rips out of my throat when she lightly tugs on my bottom lip is deep and loud. It only makes Jessa more greedy as her hands tangle roughly in my hair.

"You want me to make you feel good, kitten?" She nods and kisses the side of my face and jaw. "Be a good girl and spin around on Daddy's lap." It shouldn't feel as natural as it fucking does calling myself that, or telling her what to do. Or the way this is all escalating, but it does, and all I want is more of her.

She looks up at me, her big brown eyes blinking as she smiles and she softly says, "Yes, Daddy."

I nearly come in my fucking pants. I've always enjoyed being in control, asserting my will over someone else's pleasure. But Jessa doesn't just want that, she wants everything, and fuck if I don't want to give it to her.

Like the good girl that she is, she grabs my thighs and turns herself around. Her soft ass pressed firmly against my straining dick as her legs fall outside of my own. I'm shimmying her dress up her legs and slowly dragging my hands up her thighs in anticipation. Her head rests on my shoulder, and I know she can feel my heart racing against her back.

"Are you wet for me, baby?"

"So wet," she says breathlessly.

I kiss the side of her face and push her dress up to her waist. My hand travels from her inner thigh and glides over the lace covering her wet pussy. I groan against her hair when I feel how wet she already is from grinding on me. Her hips buck into my hand, eager for me to touch and give her what I promised, but I take my time with her, slowly gliding my hand back and forth over the lace.

"Please," she asks, with her cheek pressed to mine.

"My girl wants to come? You want me to make you feel good?"

"Please, Aiden," she says, her hips canting forward into my hand.

Not wanting to turn her into a begging mess the first time we're together, I oblige, slipping her panties to the side as I run two fingers up and down her dripping pussy. I can't help but make my approval known by kissing her throat and sliding a finger inside of her. It doesn't take long for me to use two fingers and the heel of my palm against her clit. I want her to come quickly, so that I can make her do it all over again.

She lifts her legs, using her feet to dig into the couch which only pushes her ass tighter against my cock. She wraps her hand around the back of my neck as she seeks purchase, and I fuck her with my fingers relentlessly.

Her thighs shake, and her cunt clenches around my fingers, more of her wetness dripping down my hand as she moans and her weight falls completely back against mine.

Once her pussy stops pulsing against my hand, she slumps against me, her legs falling back down flat. I want to push it and see if I can make her come again, so I do. I don't stop playing with her pussy. My touch is gentle and more exploratory, not the rough finger fuck I was just giving her.

She doesn't beg me to stop, but her small whimpers and moans are everything I need to know about how sensitive she is right now.

"One more?" I ask her, and she nods her head even though her breathing is heavy. "You're so fucking good for me."

She moans, her head pressing against my shoulder as my thumb moves back and forth on her clit in a soothing motion. Her thigh jumps each time I rub on this one spot and I keep doing it over and over. Her hand is clenching my hair. No doubt she wants another release and for me to give her a break.

Not wanting to scare her off, or cross a line too far, I do just that. Putting two fingers inside of her and using my palm to rub her clit. Her hand leaves my hair and latches on against my wrist. She doesn't tug me away, and I can't help but feel like we're both fucking her and I love it. My face is against her throat, inhaling her scent, and I'm devouring every little noise she makes. Including the light gush of her cunt.

Wetness trickles down my hand and onto my shorts as Jessa moans so loud it rattles something in my brain. The warm wetness of her cunt is relentless as her needy pussy grips my fingers and she whimpers through her second orgasm. Her body twitches, and her hand goes limp against my wrist.

Her body is relaxed against mine and I push her dress back over her thighs.

"Turn back around for me, baby." Her body is tired, but with my help, she spins in my arms. Her head easily rests against my chest as I rub gentle circles on her back. We lie like that for a few moments before she pops up suddenly.

"I want to make you feel good too," she says, and I shake my head.

"I do feel good, trust me."

She clears her throat. "I haven't done that before," she says shyly, and I smile.

"Good," I reply, leaning forward and giving her a kiss. Happy that I have at least one thing up on the previous asshole she was dating. "I liked it," I reiterate.

"It felt amazing," she says dreamily. "Sorry for the mess I made on your shorts." Her cheeks are pink, from exertion and some slight embarrassment.

"I always encourage you to make a mess of me."

She bites her lip. "Only if you'll let me return the favor," she says before leaning down and giving me a kiss. "Can you stay a bit longer before you go home?" I nod my head and try not to think about where I would want to come on her, because that's definitely not something you should be thinking about on a first date. Have I seriously found the sweetest woman on the planet who also wants to do the nastiest shit with me in bed? It feels like I'm holding a golden ticket in my arms as she passes out against me, and I'm stuck sitting here watching a show about guys playing football. But truthfully, I wouldn't want to be anywhere else.

Jessa

I Want To Make You Feel Good Too

WORKING WITH AIDEN IS HARD, but in a wholly different way than it was before. Before it was more like walking on eggshells and hiding how attracted I was to him. Now, it's like I have to prevent myself from kissing him, or perching my ass on his lap while he works.

Having a man finger you so good that you make a mess of him and yourself is one thing, but the fact that he held me until I woke up, that makes Aiden Carlson absolutely lethal to my mindset and my panties.

I must have only slept for an hour after he made me come twice, but he didn't complain, he just let me rest and he held me. He didn't rush off, or demand for me to return the favor. He took care of me in a way that I wouldn't expect from someone who I'm just starting to date. I feel like Aiden is proving everything to me right now, that we are a good fit, that he respects my boundaries, and that he wants to get to know me in every sense.

So I'm basically a big pile of fucking mush all throughout my work day. It's been three days, and I'm already jonesing for some alone time with him. We've been mostly talking through texts and small exchanges at the office. Part of me likes us being a secret at the office, the other part of me wants to scream from the rooftop that he's mine and that he's completely off limits.

I might have a daddy kink, but I'm just as possessive, and the thought of anyone in this office, or elsewhere, thinking that Aiden is a free agent makes me have extremely violent thoughts.

Even though I know this is my idea and it's for the best—at least for now. Things always seem too good to be true in the beginning, and I hope that's not the case with Aiden because damn, he seems perfect. But it's better to tread cautiously, especially when I'm already having issues with my half-brother and some of the sales people in the office.

Tabitha heads into Aiden's office, and she shuts the door behind her, the motion making me feel sick and like I want to punch her right in one of her giant, perky-ass tits. I swear I never used to have violent thoughts like this. I don't think I ever had some seriously jealous moments over Sean, but this just feels so different.

Maybe I'm needy and slightly insecure. I don't give a fuck, I text Aiden anyway. I doubt he'll answer with Tabitha in there.

> I can't stop thinking about Sunday night.

> Aiden: Which part specifically?

I'm a little shocked he answers even though he's in a meeting with Tabitha, the dedication to responding to me fills me with selfish glee. *Fuck you, Tabitha.*

How good you made me feel.

Aiden: I want to make you feel good again.

When?

Aiden: Tonight, my place?

I want to make you feel good too, Daddy.

Suddenly the door opens, and Tabitha gives me a slight smirk before walking back to her desk.

"Jessa, can I see you for a minute?" Aiden asks, and I nod my head before following him into his office. He shuts the door behind us, and his arms are immediately wrapped around my waist when he pulls my body against his chest. "Are you trying to drive me fucking crazy at work?"

"Is it working?" He grinds his hard cock against my ass, and I hum in approval. "It is working then."

"I wanted to tell Tabitha to leave my office before she even sat down, but then you just had to make it a little more interesting."

I spin in his arms, grabbing a fistful of his shirt and bringing him down for a playful kiss.

"So, tonight?"

"Let me take you on a proper date and we can go back to my place."

I smile and nod my head. "I'd like that."

"Good, I want my girl to have everything she wants." He leans down and kisses me again. "Now, go do your job or else I'll have to take it out on your ass later."

I swallow and blink at Aiden. How he can be so sweet

one moment, and then just the right amount of domineering the next, it does it for me.

"I hope so," I say, kissing his rough cheek one more time before leaving his office and sitting back down at my desk.

I've barely caught my breath when Penny comes bouncing by my desk. "Hey, got some time to grab lunch?" Her voice isn't as peppy as usual, and I wonder what's going on with her.

"Sure," I say with a smile, grabbing my purse and following Penny outside. She's quiet as we walk to the food truck. I notice that while still beautiful, she looks tired, and it's the first time I've ever seen her anything less than perky and upbeat. "Penny, are you okay?"

She blinks at me, and I watch in mortification as she starts to cry. I drag her out of the food truck line and sit at one of the wooden picnic tables with her. I place a gentle hand on her back and she tries to breathe normally. "This is so fucking stupid, I can't believe I'm just breaking down like this." She wipes her eyes and is slowly calming herself as I rub small circles on her back.

"We can talk about it if you want, or if you just want to sit here. Whatever you need." She gives me a watery smile and wipes the rest of the tears off her eyes, trying to protect her mascara.

"Have you ever loved someone you couldn't have?"

I shake my head and just keep rubbing her back, trying to bring her any comfort that I possibly can. Whatever she wants to trust me with is up to her.

"Why can't you be with them?" I ask curiously. She's never mentioned being interested in anyone when we go to lunch or happy hour.

She scoffs. "Because it's so stupidly complicated I can't even get into it."

"But you both want to be together?" I ask, and she nods her head. "Then I'm sure you can figure out a way to make it work."

Penny starts crying again, and I rub her back. It takes her a few minutes to calm down again, and I can't help but to wrap my arms around her and squeeze her into a comforting hug. Penny and I haven't been particularly affectionate with each other, but it's clear she needs it right now. Her body relaxes against mine and she breathes evenly.

"I'm so sorry for ruining lunch."

"Hey, you didn't ruin anything," I say, pulling back and rubbing her arms. "Do you want to go home early? I'll cover for you at the office."

"Really?" she says with a smile that doesn't meet her eyes.

"Of course, what are girlfriends for?"

She leans forward and hugs me, sniffling lightly. "Thanks, Jessa." I hug her back as she clears her throat. She skips lunch, and I guess I am too as she walks to her car and leaves for the day.

I wish I could help her more or knew more about her situation, but as soon as she's comfortable, she'll talk about it. My heart breaks for her as I head back to the office. I close out Penny's computer and situate her desk.

Tabitha comes over with a dolly and a stack of boxes.

"Where's Penny?" she asks.

"She had to leave early today," I say, and Tabitha groans.

"I need her to drop these off at the high school."

"I didn't realize Penny did deliveries," I say, skeptical of Tabitha.

"Sometimes she does. These need to get there before their practice, and I don't have time," Tabitha says, and I know I should tell her to go fuck herself. But there's this nagging voice in the back of my head, the one that always wants people to like me.

"I can do it," I say, and Tabitha smiles.

"Oh, thank you," she says and just walks away. The thank you seems so insincere, but whatever. I think I can fit all these boxes in my car.

I walk down to Aiden's office and knock on the wall. His face is passive at first, but when he sees me, he smiles. "Hey, Jessa."

"Hi." I grin like an idiot and forget why I came here for a moment. "Penny wasn't feeling well so she went home." His brows furrow, and I continue. "Tabitha needed some boxes dropped off at the high school, and I offered to do it."

Aiden sighs and scrubs his chin. "You can't let her manipulate you," he says, and I sigh in return. Not wanting to get into how I need to be liked in the office, instead I just shrug my shoulders.

"It's not a big deal, but might just push our dinner a little?"

He shakes his head. "No, I'll go with you."

"You sure?"

"Positive," he says, looking at my exposed legs in this sundress. The look is heated, and all I can think about is how much I want him to always look at me like that. "We'll leave at four-thirty."

"Okay, perfect. Thank you."

He smiles, and I go back to my desk and try to think

about anything besides Aiden's smile or his promises for tonight.

We take Aiden's car because his is cleaner, newer, and there's no concern of it breaking down on the way to the school. He only let me put one box in the car, while he loaded the others, I enjoyed that more than I should.

His windows are down, as well as the sunroof, his dark hair blowing slightly with the breeze. He looks so ridiculously hot in his sunglasses. He wore a dress shirt today that's rolled up to his elbows and the top two buttons are undone. I swear I think I lose a few brain cells staring at how gorgeous he is.

That's until he smiles and places his hand on my thigh as he drives. Now I'm completely done for. He gives my thigh a tentative squeeze and for the rest of the ride his thumb rubs my skin and toys with the hem of my dress.

We don't speak in the car. He plays music instead and it just feels so easy. A part of me is shouting that nothing is ever this easy, but I shut that stupid bitch up. I'm not going to let anything take away an ounce of giddiness I feel when I'm around Aiden.

He rolls up his windows when we get to the baseball field and gives my thigh another squeeze before we both get out of the car. He groans as I pick up a box, but he leaves it alone as we walk them out toward the field. Aiden and a few of the players walk back to his car to get the rest of the boxes as I wait at the dugout.

The coach is young, probably only a few years older than me.

"Can't thank you enough for dropping those off. We ordered a little too late this year for summer camp."

I wave a hand at him. "It's no problem at all, just glad the boys have everything they need."

"Kemper's helps make it possible with their donations every year." He gives me a smile and break eye contact and look at the field. "I've never met you before though, are you new?"

"Yes, been here for a little over a month now."

"That makes sense. I would have remembered you for sure. Tabitha is pretty, but you... you're—"

Suddenly, an arm wraps around my waist, and Aiden kisses the side of my head.

"You good, baby?" he says.

"Coach here was just telling me how much they appreciate Kemper's." He looks distinctly at where Aiden is touching me before he clears his throat.

"Do you think you could hit a ball or two for the kids? Not every day they meet a professional player," the coach asks, and as Aiden turns around, a group of boys are nearly begging him with doe eyes.

"All right, just a few."

I smile at the thought of watching him play dressed like the hot CEO that he is right now. I stay in the dugout and watch as all the kids, Aiden, and the coach take the field.

Aiden's wearing dress shoes, but he seemingly doesn't give a shit as he digs them into the dirt and plays with the grip of his bat. Hitting the tip of it on home plate and taking his stance. Conceptually, I know he played professionally, but when I watch him swing the bat and send the ball all the way past the fence toward the football field, my mouth drops.

The kid who is in the dugout with me whispers, "Holy shit." And I can't help but agree with the sentiment, just in a completely different way.

Aiden doesn't run bases, just directs the pitcher to throw again, and he does. Aiden only strikes out twice, but the rest of his hits seem to impress the kids.

"Does Mr. Carlson's girlfriend want to hit one?" one of the kids shouts.

"I don't know how to," I say loud enough for the kid in the dugout to hear.

"Your boyfriend is one of the best hitters ever and you don't know how to hit?" the kid says judgmentally. I don't tell the little turd that I only just started officially dating him this past weekend.

Aiden raises an eyebrow at me and holds the bat.

"Fuck, fine," I say, climbing my way out of the dugout, glad that I wore sandals and not heels today.

"Have you ever gone to bat before?" Aiden asks, and I shake my head.

Aiden looks at the pitcher and says loud enough so most of the team can hear, "Do you have any softballs?" One of the kids nods, and the ball twice the size of a baseball comes rolling to the pitcher. "Throw underhand," Aiden says sternly to the kid throwing the ball. As he takes my hands and shows me where I need to hold the bat. He stands behind me and shows me where my elbows need to go and even uses his leg to make my feet spread apart more. "Now, you just need to time your swing right." Aiden must hold up a hand for the pitcher to throw, because suddenly this ball is being hurled toward my face and I don't know how to react. I don't swing.

A kid tosses the larger ball back to the pitcher, and he

waits for Aiden's go ahead. "I got you, I'll tell you when to swing," Aiden says softly in my ear. The pitcher nods and the ball is thrown again. As soon as Aiden says swing, I do. The connection to the ball rattles my hands and arms, but I connect nonetheless.

The ball bounces close on the ground, and goes straight into the hands of the pitcher.

"Good job," Aiden says with a smile, handing the bat to one of the kids who have now lined up asking for signed baseballs. He's patient and kind, giving the kids smiles, and words of encouragement.

I think falling for Aiden Carlson might be one of the easiest things I've ever done in my life.

Aiden

Check Please

AFTER WE LEAVE the summer camp practice, we head to my house first, where I park and round the car to open Jessa's door.

"I thought we were going to dinner," she says in a tone that indicates she would be okay skipping a meal and going straight to my place.

"It's right down the street, it's easier to walk there instead of finding parking."

"What are we having?"

"Is Italian okay?"

"I love Italian," she says, Without any hesitation she puts her hand in mine as we walk down my driveway and on the sidewalk.

Affection has never come so easy to me, and I'm not sure why. I've had girlfriends. I feel like I've been in love before, but the beginning of a relationship has never felt as effortless as this. I'm not sure if it's because we've been upfront about our intentions with one another or because of the anticipation and getting to know each other. All I know is that I want to make Jessa happy, and seeing her happy brings me a joy I'm still wrapping my head around.

"You were so good with the kids back there," Jessa says as we're walking.

"I like kids," I say with a shrug of my shoulder.

"Do you want kids someday?" she asks and I clear my throat, wondering if this is the moment that it all comes crumbling down.

"I haven't completely decided, but I've been leaning toward no," I say to her honestly.

She sighs in relief and nods her head. "I've felt the same way. Everyone is always saying I might change my mind. But I can't help but feel that I like exploring and doing my own thing too much to have children. I wish I had siblings so I could have nieces and nephews that I could dote on and then return back to their parents."

"I have three brothers, but they all seem just as hopeless as me when it comes to finding a long term partner."

"You are far from hopeless," she says, squeezing my hand. "Honestly, the whole time you were on that field I was wondering how you were ever single in the first place."

I shrug my shoulders and look down at her. "I wasn't always so patient, I used to have a temper. It's something that I've really been working on since I got involved at Kemper's."

She squeezes my hand and wraps her other around my bicep.

"I've only seen your kindness since we've met. Even at the funeral, you were the only person who was kind to me. You didn't have to be."

"I absolutely did. I know it's hard to talk about Collin, but he would be so pissed with how Zach is acting."

Talking about Collin always makes her uncomfortable, so we move on.

"What about your mom?" I ask.

She sighs. "My mom had her own issues, but she did love me the best she could with what she had. I think seeing Zach and everything he grew up with makes me feel like I could have been saved. But she did love me, she did try, but at the end of the day her addiction won."

"I'm sorry," I say, wrapping an arm around her shoulder.

"It's been five years now, it still hurts. But at the same time she isn't suffering anymore. I know that now, she truly was suffering." She shakes her head. "What about your family?"

"Well, I told you I have three brothers." She nods her head and smiles. "My parents are still together, they live on the bay. I usually go there every other week."

"Have you always been close to them?"

"Not always, my last year playing and a few years after I retired were hard." She squeezes my bicep again as we reach the restaurant. I give them my name and we're seated under the shaded patio.

"This is nice." She looks over the menu. "Do you have a favorite dish?"

"I can order for us," I suggest and she closes the menu with a smile. "Anything you don't like?"

"Not a fan of oysters, clams, or mussels."

"How un-Florida of you," I joke. The waiter takes our drink order, and I order appetizers and main dishes for the both of us. "How are you liking the cottage?" I ask her.

"It's nice. I'm grateful to have it, but it doesn't feel like home yet."

"Is it all the lighthouses?" She laughs and nods her head while she plays with the end of the table cloth. I've noticed her fingers always seem to be busy. She's always touching or fidgeting with whatever she has nearby.

"Or the little bits I learn every time I open a drawer and find pieces of information about the man I'll never know."

"If you ever have questions about him, or want to know anything, I'm here."

"I know and I appreciate that. It just... I don't know, hurts?" she says. Her brown eyes search mine as the waiter drops off her wine and my whiskey.

"I really wish I knew what he was thinking. I know Abigail would have left, and I guess he was trying to protect his marriage. It's not an excuse, he should have done better. You deserved more."

"Thank you," she says quietly and takes another sip. "I think the conversation has gotten too heavy, what do you think?"

"You're right. You did good with the bat today. You're going to need to get a little bit better though."

"Oh yeah?"

"My family usually plays softball or kickball when we all get together."

"Aiden, are you inviting me to meet your family?" I can't pick up if she's terrified, or likes the idea.

"When you're ready."

"What about let's take this slow?" She arches an eyebrow at me. But it's playful, like she doesn't like the idea of moving slow as much as I don't. I just don't want to fuck it up, there's too much at stake.

"I think I've underestimated my self-control."

"Thank God," she says smiling behind her wine glass.

"Oh, were you hoping for something tonight besides dinner and good conversation?"

"Whatever you're willing to give, or whatever I can give," she says innocently as our waiter drops off three appetizers.

I'm saved from having to reply as we eat the bruschetta, prosciutto, and the mushroom dish I didn't know how to pronounce to the server.

Once we're finished with the first course, she smirks at me, knowing that she's affecting me as much as I do her.

"Whatever you can give? Huh?"

"This definitely isn't one sided, Aiden. I plan on giving, often. I just want you to control how you receive it."

I have to clear my throat and sip more of my whiskey as I just enjoy looking at her. She wore a simple olive green sundress today and it looks perfect against her complexion and dark hair. Though I can't help thinking about taking off.

Last week was easy, it was all about her, but somehow I find myself nervous over the idea of the night being about me. I haven't played that particular game before, but I'm eager and more than willing.

I'm having lingering feelings about how far we can take this and how soon. I have this idea in my head that certain things can only happen at Avalon and doing them at home crosses some sort of line that we shouldn't be crossing.

But we're definitely not at the point where I can invite her as my plus one... are we?

"You're making me regret not just taking you right to my house."

"Honestly, I was starving, but I wouldn't have minded either."

"You didn't eat lunch?" I ask her, and she sighs as she looks at me.

"I was going to but that's when—" She stops herself. "It wasn't intentional, I'll make sure to do better."

"Good girl." I smirk at her and the waiter drops off our food at the same time. Jessa's cheeks are pink. I'm sure in slight embarrassment that he probably heard the tail end of our conversation.

We both eat and the air feels electric, both of us buzzing with excitement and want. If Jessa is anything like me, she wants to do everything but also doesn't know where to start. I know I told her we should take it slow, but fuck if I don't want to just go from zero to one-hundred with her. No matter how terrifying it is, she makes me feel a way that I never knew existed, but now every time she makes me feel like her protector, or that I'm someone special to her, I want another hit of that feeling.

The rest of the conversation sticks to being completely PG. She tells me about where she grew up and college and I do the same.

"Would you care for dessert?" the waiter says and Jessa is already shaking her head.

"I think we're good, just the check please," I say and Jessa downs the rest of her wine. I do the same as we pay and leave.

It's slightly colder than it was earlier, and I hold her close as we walk back to my place. I'm not sure why I'm so nervous as I unlock the front door and we go to the living room and sit next to each other on the couch.

I put on something on the TV that I can't even pay attention to when Jessa breaks the silence.

"Aiden?"

"Hmm?"

"Can I be good for you?"

I push her hair behind her shoulder, my thumb lingering on her racing pulse point as I nod my head. "You're always good for me." Her hands are both on my left thigh, and she's rubbing the smooth texture of my pants as she looks at me again and licks her lips.

"I want to show you how good I can make you feel." Her eyes search mine for direction and I remember her words from earlier. How she wants to be good for me but on my terms, that's what will get her off in the process. Just like bringing her comfort and praise gets me off, her gifting me control because she feels safe with me is what gets her off.

"Are you going to get on your knees for me, kitten?"

"Please, Daddy," she says in a soft voice, making my dick twitch. She's already sliding off the couch, and I'm parting my legs to make space for her.

Her hands glide up and down my thighs, and I just enjoy her touch for a moment until I realize her knees and shins are on a cold, hard, tile floor.

"Do you want a pillow for your knees, baby?" She nods and smiles as I grab a throw pillow and she places it under her knees. "Wouldn't want my girl uncomfortable when she's making her daddy feel so fucking good, would I?"

"Thank you," she says as she continues rubbing my thighs. She rubs her cheek against my thigh and her hand slowly explores my hard cock outside of my pants. I swear I nearly come when she places a chaste kiss on my covered cock. "So big," she whispers.

"Take my cock out of my pants," I tell her. She looks up at me from under her lashes and tenderly unbuckles my belt.

She undoes the top button before peeling the zipper down. She rubs her face against the cotton of my boxer briefs before she delicately takes me out of my pants.

Her touches alongside my length are tender, leaning toward reverent. She kisses the underside of the head and swipes her tongue over the tip and slit. "I knew you would be big," she says, kissing the side of me again.

"You like being on your knees for me?"

She swirls her tongue under the head and looks up at me with her big brown eyes. "I want to make you feel good," she tells me. I gather her hair around my fist and stroke the side of her face.

"You do make me feel good. You want to slide my dick down that sweet little throat?" She parts her lips, slowly wetting my length, and she continues to take more of me down her wet and willing mouth. "That's it. You're taking Daddy's cock so good. Look at you." She continues swallowing me as she looks up at me for approval. "So good, show me how deep you can go."

She accepts the challenge, her grip tight on my thighs as she takes my cock deeper and deeper down her throat. The sound of her spit sloshing and dripping all over my dick.

"That's it. You're making a mess of my cock, aren't you? You know how much I love you making a mess of me, baby."

She hums around my length, and I can't help but buck my hips and thrust into her mouth. She moans and the sound is muffled but like music to my ears.

"Touch your pussy while you make me come." Her right hand slides from my thigh and travels down her body where she touches herself and I'm desperate to watch. "Take your dress off," I demand, and she takes me out of her mouth with an audible pop. She immediately grabs the hem of her dress and throws it over her head. She's wearing a simple pair of pale pink panties and a bra that matches. I lick my lips. "So pretty. Get up on the couch so I can play with your pussy while you suck Daddy's cock." I'm still amazed at how natural the title has come to me, something I didn't know got me off, but it does more than ever.

Jessa rests her arms on my legs as she leans down. Her ass rises in the air as I slide my hand down her spine and lightly smack her ass before putting two fingers into her dripping pussy while she moans around my length.

"My pretty baby likes that, huh?" She moans her agreement and I can't help it. The way she's sucking my cock the way I like and her cunt dripping around my fingers is what breaks me. "I'm going to come, don't swallow."

She doesn't make any acknowledgement, just sucks my cock with more enthusiasm than before. I'm fingering her pussy fast and can feel her clenching around me as I fill her mouth with my release, a curse leaving my lips as my hand fists her hair. With one last thrust she parts from my dick and pulls up. Her eyes are glassy and there's a sheen of sweat around her temples, but she looks proud of herself.

"Are you on birth control?" I ask, and she nods. "Were you a good girl?" I ask, and she opens her mouth showing me my come on her tongue. I don't know what takes over me as I take her mouth in mine. The salty tang of my cum entering my own mouth before I push her on her back wasting no time and pushing my cum inside of her pussy, pushing her panties out of the way. She moans and fists my hair as I use my fingers to push it even further inside of her.

"Make a mess on my face," I tell her before sucking on

her clit and fingering her pussy, feeling the mixture of her wetness and my cum. My cock is already getting hard again just from thinking about it.

I don't toy with her. I suck her clit hard, and I'm relentless with my fingers' pace as she comes around my hand and wets my chin with her release.

She's panting and shaking as I look up at her. Her eyes are closed and she looks so fucking blissed out that all I can think about is I want to see her like this every day.

"Jessa?"

"Just a second," she says softly, and I knead her thighs. Waiting for her to come back online. She slowly blinks and sits up.

"Are you okay? Did I go too far?" I ask her in worry. I've gone so much further at the club, but in my living room it seems like the rules are different. I wish I could stop grappling with this concept that I'm different people in different places. I'm just Aiden, and Jessa seems to want to get to know all facets of me. She smiles and shakes her head, climbing onto my lap and wrapping her arms around my neck. I try to ignore the fact that her nearly bare pussy is on my half-hard cock as she holds me.

"You did so good. Thank you," she whispers.

Great, now I'm going to be addicted to this woman's praise.

Jessa

I Think We're Best Friends

I WAS HOPING that I would see Aiden this weekend, but he already has a trip planned with his brothers, so I'm trying to branch out—it's time to make Florida home. Penny was more than eager to hangout, she said this weekend was going to suck for her if she didn't have something to do anyway. Since I live on the beach, she's coming to me. I've already gotten snacks and drinks, and I'm just sitting at the island tapping my fingers on the countertop. My phone rattles on the counter, and I smile, hoping that it's Aiden calling.

Nope. It's Sean.

I've had enough, this is getting so out of hand. I pick up the phone, and in the most authoritative voice, I tell him off. "Sean, you have got to stop calling me, it's over."

"Jessa, what have I told you about taking that tone with me?" I'm immediately put off by the way he talks. I thought I liked how controlling and domineering he was when we were together, but it's become clear I like a softer approach.

I want to hurt Sean, I realize.

"I'm with someone else now," I say and there's a long pause over the phone before he speaks again.

"No one can give you what I do. No one is going to put up with your shit the way I do, baby girl."

"That's where you're wrong, Sean. Stop calling me." I hang up, and it's about time I hit the block button. It feels so good to finally take that step, it's my way of completely putting him in my past and not allowing him to disturb this peace I'm creating for myself.

Before, I would probably feel guilty, or like I'm in the wrong for blocking him, but I know this is the right thing. I'm creating a new life for myself, one where I'm not the victim and I get what I want and need.

My phone buzzes again, and my heart sinks, thinking maybe I fucked up and didn't block him properly. I smile when I see the name on the screen.

> Aiden: Hey, baby. Just wanted to let you know we got to the beach house. Miss you, can't wait to see you when I get back.

I probably look deranged as I stare at my phone.

> Me either. Penny is coming over soon. Have fun with your brothers.

> Aiden: Are you going to tell Penny?

> Maybe, if it comes up?

> Aiden: I trust Penny, and you. I want you to feel like you aren't keeping secrets from your friend. As long as you're comfortable, so am I.

> Fuck, you're perfect.

Aiden: Not even a little bit, but you make me
want to be.

You make me want to be a lot of things too.

There's a knock at my door, and I grab my phone and answer it. Penny has a pitcher in her hand and a huge smile on her face.

"Come on in."

"This place is so cute!" she says as she puts the pitcher on the counter and I look at my phone one last time before giving Penny my full attention.

Aiden: Be good, I'll talk to you tonight.

I'm always good. Penny just got here. Don't
get in too much trouble with your brothers.

I must have a massive grin on my face as Penny gives me a curious look. Aiden was so right, I need a girlfriend to talk about all this shit. I'm not sure exactly how comfortable I can get with Penny when it comes to certain intimate details, but I know she's trustworthy.

"Who are you texting?" she asks with an arch of her brow.

"Aiden," I say, trying to control my face.

"I knew you two had a thing!" she says, snapping her fingers and pointing at me.

"Does the whole office know?" I ask, my stomach sinking in a moment of fear.

"I doubt it, we work with a bunch of selfish assholes. Their head is too far up their own asses to pay attention to anything.

I take a breath and grab two stainless tumblers for us. Penny starts pouring our drinks.

"Do you not want people to know?"

"Just not the office, for now."

She nods and takes a sip of her drink, her eyes squinting a little bit. "I might have made these a little too strong." I take a sip, and she very much made them too strong, but we don't plan on leaving the cottage today.

"Am I stupid for thinking we can hide it from the office?"

"Pfft, no, it's probably hot. Sneaking around, hoping no one will find out."

"Sounds like you have experience."

She shrugs her shoulders and takes another sip. "Are we hitting up the beach or what?"

"Let's go."

❋ ❋ ❋

Letting Penny make our drinks is a mistake, it's only four in the afternoon and we're ready for a nap. We needed a break from the heat so we're both sitting on the couch with old *Grey's Anatomy* episodes playing in the background.

Penny breaks the silence first. "I bet Aiden fucks like he might die if he doesn't make you come."

I sputter, dribbling some of my water on my chin. "He's your cousin," I say, not responding to her very true statement.

"His *adopted* cousin. And tell me I'm wrong and I'll drop it. I know the man goes to Avalon."

Thank goodness I didn't take another sip of water as I blink at her.

"How do you know he goes to Avalon?"

"I have my ways."

I squint at her and tilt my head. "You're a little freak under that pretty little package aren't you?" I say and Penny barks out a laugh.

"Takes one to know one."

"I'm not into anything too out there." I'm scooching on the couch closer to her for this interrogation and she laughs.

"I heard you tell your ex he wasn't your daddy anymore."

"Right," I say, wondering if she wants more details. It's hard to explain to people who don't get it. Who think that the kink is just all about having issues with your parents, when really it's about the relationship dynamic and having someone who takes care of your needs in a reverent way.

Penny stops me from my spiral with a hand on my arm. "Hey, I'm not judging, far from it. It might not be my thing, but I get it. I don't judge you, Jessa."

It might be her strong drinks, or I haven't felt this close to another woman since freshman year, but I wrap my arms around her neck and hug her tight. I don't let go for a ridiculous amount of time, and when I pull back, Penny's eyes are watery.

"I think we're best friends now," she says, and I have to clear out the tears from my own eyes.

"I think so too."

We order a pizza and spend the rest of the night sitting on the couch, exchanging stories and laughing so hard my face hurts. I don't think I realized how much Sean isolated me, how much he wanted me to be just his. His control went beyond the bounds of the dynamic I wanted and as I make these realizations I see how different Aiden is.

I know that the relationship is new and I shouldn't get my

hopes up. But Sean would never encourage a night out with a girlfriend. Aiden told me he trusted my judgment to tell Penny and to have a good time.

I must have a dreamy look on my face as Penny throws a pillow at my face. "You've got it bad."

I laugh and nod my head. "Yeah, I guess I do."

"Are you going to meet his family?" she asks.

"He mentioned it," I say and Penny's eyes bulge. "What?"

"I've never seen Aiden bring a girl home."

"Oh," I say, shocked. He said it so casually, like it wasn't a big deal.

"Has he mentioned The Bahamas?" she asks, and I shake my head. "Then I won't spoil the surprise."

"So rude," I joke with her, and she laughs. "So I guess you're sleeping on the couch?"

"Yeah, and tomorrow, we're throwing all these light-houses in the fucking trash."

"I've been thinking about making this place more like home."

"Tomorrow," she says sleepily, and I agree before heading off to bed myself. My heart is full and I'm about to go to sleep when I get one last text.

> Aiden: Night bbbabbbyy.

I laugh, because I'm guessing Aiden has had a bit to drink today too. I send him a string of emojis and go to sleep.

Aiden

Why Wasn't I an Only Child?

WHY DID I think going to the Sarasota house with my brothers was a good idea? Lincoln is sad drinking, Benjamin and Gavin are dancing to some song talking about being slutted out.

"Why did we come here again?" I ask as Lincoln rolls his eyes.

"Those little twin fuckers thought we needed a brothers trip."

"How are they so happy?" I ask Lincoln.

"Because their IQs are so low, it helps not to feel the crippling weight of life's struggles."

"What the fuck is wrong with you?" I ask him, and he slings his beer back.

"Nothing," he mumbles before sighing. "How's your new girlfriend?"

"Good," I smile.

"Mom wants you to invite her to The Bahamas."

"Of course she does. I'll think about it."

Lincoln blinks at me a few times and looks at me like I've

grown five heads. "You've never brought a girl for Labor Day weekend."

"So?"

"Damn, she's got you fucked up."

"Is little Aiden Waiden finally settling down?" Gavin asks from where he's dancing. He looks like an idiot, but he doesn't care. Honestly, the twins have a lightness to them I wish I could have. Maybe it's being the youngest, but they never seem to take things seriously.

"Our big brother is pussy whipped. How does it feel?" Benjamin asks curiously.

"Will you three just leave me the fuck alone?" I have my phone in my hand and Benjamin starts making kissing noises.

"He needs to call his girlfriend."

"No I don't. She's with Penny anyway," I say, getting annoyed with the attention being on me, seeing as I'm the one with the least amount of problems right now.

"She's with Penny?" Lincoln asks questioningly.

"Yeah, so?"

Lincoln shrugs his shoulders, and the twins start inventing a new drinking game. At least I get to go home tomorrow, might as well join in the fuckery while I can.

"Okay, you roll the ping pong ball and whatever cup it lands in, that's what you have to drink," Benjamin says.

"What the fuck did you put in those cups?" Lincoln asks. Valid question.

"All of them are alcohol, except maybe one or two," Gavin responds.

"We finish this game and you'll let me go to sleep?" Lincoln asks. The twins nod and we accept the challenge. I'm tired and on the wrong side of drunk, the kind that's more tiring and gives you a headache. It could also be my brothers annoying me that's making my head throb.

Lincoln goes first and gets beer, the twins get some variety of beer as well and when I get to my cup the sting of tequila makes me want to vomit, but I push through. We go three more rounds and by the time we're done the twins are more hyped than when we started and Lincoln and I are exhausted.

"Cigar?" Lincoln asks.

The ocean brings a quiet that wasn't inside with our brothers as we light our own cigars.

"I am happy for you, ya know?" Lincoln says.

"I know." I hide my smile with my cigar.

"You deserve to be happy. I'm excited to meet her. You know, outside of Avalon." Lincoln smirks, and I have to roll my eyes. I watch my brother's movements, and he hasn't been the same lately.

"You deserve to be happy too, Lincoln."

"I'm not sure the rest of the family would agree."

I'm confused as I look at him and he waves me off. "You should invite her to The Bahamas. I know it's a while away, but that just gives you more time to be together."

"I'll ask her." I wonder if Jessa even has a passport, I guess I need to ask her sooner than later. We haven't even completely slept together yet, so it seems like we're moving fast, but at the same time it feels natural.

"I'm going to go for a walk," Lincoln says. I give him a wave and go inside. I text Jessa before going to sleep. I should bring her down here sometime. I guess it's not all that different from her house on the beach, but I'm sure she'd like it.

It's odd how much my mind wanders to Jessa and how much I like it. I find myself wanting to invest my time into making her happy, and the happier she is the more fulfilled I'll be. The idea of keeping her safe and comfortable makes me feel needed. I guess I never knew how good it felt to both be wanted and needed, but I think I'm addicted.

✻ ✻ ✻

I could have probably waited until tomorrow morning to see Jessa at work, but I didn't want to, and I worry that it's too late. It's almost ten at night when I pull up in front of the cottage, and I'm debating this being a bad idea. I shove that feeling deep down to the insecure part of myself I'm trying to vanish.

With a ridiculous amount of self-confidence, I knock on her door. She opens it timidly, but as soon as she sees me, a huge smile takes over her face.

"Hey."

"Hey. I know it's late, but I wanted to see you before work tomorrow."

"Do you want to come in?" She opens the door for me and I walk in. What I see is not the normal lighthouse-coastal design I'm used to seeing. It's more feminine and less beachy.

"The place looks nice."

"Penny helped me," she says as I look around.

"Did you two have a good time?"

"Yeah. She knows, and she's happy for us."

"My brothers are too, in their own way."

I wanted to touch her as soon as she opened the door, but I somehow held back. As she stands there with her sleep shorts and a tank top with no bra, I can't help myself. Gently wrapping one hand around her throat and using the other to touch her clavicle, feeling her heart race.

My lips meet hers, and she sighs in relief, her body language relaxing as she returns the kiss. I don't make it too heated, we do have work tomorrow, and I just had to see her, touch her in the way I want and can't at the office.

"I missed you," I whisper to her between kisses.

"Aiden?" she says in a raspy voice.

"Yeah, kitten?"

"When are we going to have sex?"

I clear my throat and kiss her one more time. "Are you feeling impatient?"

She nods her head and kisses me again. "We need to do that before you bring me to Avalon."

I'm surprised and back up a little from her, though I don't remove my hands.

"What?"

She blinks at me. "I assumed that we would go together."

"I mean I thought about it of course, but I just wasn't sure if that was something you wanted."

"Aiden?"

"Yeah," I reply, and she smiles up at me.

"You can always ask me if I want something or need something. Just as I will for you. Like what do you need right now?" She tilts her head as she looks at me. What do I need right now? Of course I always want to be with Jessa sexually. But right now? All I want to do is sleep, preferably next to her.

"Can I spend the night?"

Her smile widens. "Come on." She drags me by the hand

to the master bedroom which now looks like it's a woman's bedroom. The only thing that still has lighthouses is the fan.

"I can replace the fan for you."

"I'd like that."

"We could paint the walls too."

"Maybe."

"If there's any other work that you need, I can do that too."

"Aiden?" I break my train of thought as I look at her. "Get in the bed." Taking my shirt and shorts off, I get under the covers first and open my arms to her, and she immediately crawls in. Her scent engulfs me, and it's centering as I kiss the top of her head.

"How are your brothers?" she asks softly in the dark.

"The twins are always wild, Lincoln seems a little sad, but other than that we had a good time."

"You're the oldest?"

"Yeah, then Lincoln and then the twins." She rests her head in the crook of my shoulder. I have to ask her or it will eat away at me. "It's about a month away, but my family always goes to The Bahamas for Labor Day weekend, I was wondering if you'd want to come."

"You want me to meet your family?"

"Yeah, I do."

She props herself up so she's on her elbows as she leans in and kisses me, her long hair trailing down my arm. "I'd love to," she says, smiling as she gives me deeper kisses. Ones that can't be stopped, that come from a place of urgency and want. Maybe I'm being a sentimental asshole, but if this is going to be my first time with Jessa, I don't want it to be rushed or over dramatic, I just want her.

I flip us so she's underneath me, a whoosh of air leaving her as I hold most of my weight on my elbows as I kiss her face, throat, and jaw.

"I want you," she whispers.

"Don't worry, baby. Daddy's going to take care of you." She whimpers, her hand grabbing my cock from the outside of my boxers. Her other hand tangles in my hair as I lean forward and kiss her. My hand sliding from her throat, to her breasts, to under her sleep shorts.

I slide my fingers from her clit to the inside of her pussy, collecting her wetness and spreading it around her cunt. She increases her pressure around my cock as she thrusts her hips up into my hand. Jessa whines when my hand leaves her clit, and I can't help the slight laugh that leaves me.

"Such a needy girl for me, aren't you?"

"Only for you," she says back, I swear she knows how to give it back tenfold. I groan as I grab her waistband and remove her shorts. Her glistening cunt just waiting for me to give her what she needs.

Jessa is ahead of me as she's tugging my underwear off, and I push them down my legs. Her hands wander the expanse of my chest, and she licks her lips as I fist my cock and swipe the head along her wetness.

As I slide into her, her nails dig into my back and my hips thrust slowly in and out.

"Fuck, baby," I hiss as she clenches around my length.

"You can put more weight on me," she says breathlessly, and I do. Our chests touch and my hands tangle in her hair as I kiss her face and thrust into her. One of her hands slides down my back as she grips my ass as I fuck her.

It feels like every part of us is touching, and I can't help but wonder if this is enough for her. Does she need more to get off? "What do you need?" I ask her, and she moans as I thrust.

"Just you. Just this. Don't stop."

I don't. As her brown eyes meet mine, I realize that she's being honest and there's a plethora of ways to be with someone sexually and they're all perfect and amazing in their own right. I lean forward and kiss her and pick up my pace. I can feel my pelvis rubbing against her clit, and the little noises escaping her let me know she's close. I slide one of my hands under her left ass cheek, gripping it hard as I fuck her.

"Yes, just like that."

"You want to come, sweet girl?"

"Please, Daddy," she says, her lips parting and eyes closing as I fuck her through her peak. Her pussy clenching around my cock and her back arching as I give her everything and chase my own release.

My hips stutter and a puff of air and a low moan escapes me as I finish. We're catching our breath, and Jessa's hands don't leave my body as we just lie there. I keep my cock inside of her for as long as possible until it becomes too much.

When I slide out of her, she winces, and I spread her legs and admire the wet spot underneath her as I watch my come slowly drip out of her pussy.

"You like that?" she asks as I nod my head. "I do too," she says softly, and I drop her legs and lean forward to kiss up her body. "I do need to go pee though," she says shyly.

I laugh and shake my head. "Go pee, baby."

She gets off the bed dramatically and goes to the bathroom before coming back to bed completely naked where I wrap her in my arms again.

"I guess you got your answer to your question," I joke with her, and she laughs.

"Mmm," she mumbles sleepily.

"Goodnight, Jessa."

"Goodnight, Daddy."

Good-fucking-night indeed.

Jessa

Supply Closets Are For Breakdowns

AIDEN KISSED me goodbye before he left early to get changed before work, and I can't deny I'm so close to just saying fuck it and telling the office.

At least, that was before I ran into Zach. I'm picking the copies I dropped from our run in as he stares down at me. He doesn't offer to help me pick them up; he just looks down at me with disgust.

Once I have them all picked up and clutched against my chest, I blink up at him. "Zach, can we talk?"

"Fine," he says sharply. He leads the way to the room we call the bubble, because it's a conference room with all glass. We both sit down, and he glares at me. "Okay, talk."

I clear my throat and look at him. "I can understand you not trusting me, or maybe me reminding you of your dad and him being dishonest. But I've never done anything personally to you."

He scoffs and shakes his head but doesn't speak.

"I can't be held accountable for just being born. You do realize you had a father, right? That I had only met him twice. You're the one who had a mom and a dad who loved you and gave you everything. I know you're bitter about the shares, but don't you realize that out of the two of us you are the one who won here?"

"I'm bitter?" He laughs again. "No, I'm fucking angry. I'm angry at my dad for sleeping with your whore of a mother and hurting my mom. I'm mad that he didn't just fucking die taking his dirty secret to the grave. I'm pissed that you're constantly here and in my face, a constant reminder that my dad's a liar and a cheater. You ruined my dad's fucking memory, and I hate you, Jessa. We're never going to be friends, half-siblings, fuck, I don't even want you to be my co-worker. Your mom should have had an abortion and saved us all from this massive fucking headache." He doesn't even falter as he spews all this hatred at me. I do a good job of breathing and holding it in.

"I expect you won't ask me for a little chat again," he says, standing up and leaving the office. It's early, and the office is still relatively empty. Still, this is basically like getting a front row seat to my breakdown if I stay in this conference room. I don't know how, but I hold it together until I open the supply closet and shut the door behind me.

I slowly sag down the wall and wrap my arms around my legs and rest my face in my knees as the tears finally come.

They aren't tears just for the horrific words Zach spewed at me but for my own grief. The mother I never really mourned, the father I never got to know, and the brother I'll never have. I've never felt more alone than I do at this moment.

The people in my life who were genetically built to care about me and be my support system don't exist. I don't have a family, and it seems like right now is the moment it finally soaks in. There's no blood relation to me. I don't care about fostering a relationship with Zach anymore. That ship has definitely fucking sailed. What I want is to not feel so alone and lost like I do right now.

The door to the supply closet clicks, and I try to wipe my tears and not look absolutely pathetic as the figure steps in.

Aiden's face drops as he sees me.

"Jessa, baby. What's wrong?" I shake my head, fresh tears spilling down my cheeks, and I feel so embarrassed that he's seeing me this way. I can't speak just yet, and he doesn't make me. He just sits on the floor next to me and grabs me by the waist and sets me on his lap. His large hand rubbing up and down my back soothing me. My breathing evens out, and I slump against his body.

His cedarwood and vanilla scent centers me, and I'm so happy he walked in. I wouldn't have sought him out for comfort. But it's nice having his arms wrapped around me so at this moment I don't feel so alone.

"I... I don't have anyone, Aiden," I say with a sniffle.

"What do you mean? I'm here with you now." His eyebrows furrow, and I want to use my fingers to flatten them out, but I resist.

"My mom's gone, I never had a dad, and now I have a half-brother who wishes I was dead." He pulls back and analyzes my face.

"He said that to you?" I sigh and slink down further. "Jessa, what did he say to you?" His voice is lethal, and I consider not telling him.

"He said my mom should have had an abortion and we would all be better off."

"Oh, fuck no." He picks me up by the waist, and we're both standing. I grab his arm and tug him back.

"Aiden, it's okay."

"Fuck no, it's not okay." I'm worried he's going to do something physical to Zach as he swings the door open and heads toward Zach's desk. But he stops short of it and takes a breath before spinning to the opposite side toward Huck's office and walking in. "Huck?" He says it loudly so the whole office can hear. "I have a formal complaint about Zach Kemper."

Suddenly, Zach is on his feet and standing next to Huck's door. He glares at me. No doubt my face is puffy and red from crying.

"Aiden, why don't you mind your own business. This is a family matter. In fact, it's a family business."

I watch as Aiden holds his right hand tightly like he's rubbing the tendons there. The look of disgust he gives Zach is enough for him to take a step back.

"I don't care what it was about, you can't talk to an employee like that. No matter what problems you have, you're only a few years younger than me, Zach, so I don't know why you're acting like a petulant child. Collin would be disgusted." That last sentence has Zach risking his life as he gets closer to Aiden's face. Zach isn't as tall as him, but he still looks intimidating.

"You need to learn your fucking place." Zach sneers.

"No, I think you do. Jessa and I have majority shares. So I'd consider your next words carefully," Aiden says with authority. I look around the office, and it appears everyone is watching the altercation go down.

"Jessa and I are going to the Rays game," Aiden says to

break the tension. This is to my surprise as the work day has only started. "Huck, I still want that report. Penny, take all my messages. And if anyone else in this office wants to harass an employee, I'd think twice before doing so."

Aiden doesn't touch me as we leave the office, though I could tell he wanted to. Penny gives me a tight smile as we storm out. Aiden is walking fast, too fast for me to catch up. He finally notices and waits by the passenger door as he opens it up for me. I get in without a word said and he gets in the driver's seat.

We've been driving for a good ten minutes when I break the silence.

"Aiden?"

He sighs and puts his hand on my thigh and squeezes. "I'm sorry, baby." I take his hand in mine.

"I'm not mad, I just want to make sure you're okay."

"I will be," he says softly.

"It's early. What time is the game?"

"Noon."

I look at the clock, and it's only nine-thirty. "Okay."

"I shouldn't have just kidnapped you back there, but the thought of you in the office with that motherfucker, I just couldn't." Aiden might not be family, but in the moment I most needed it, someone cared about me. I use one hand to rub some tension from his neck.

"It's okay. I'm glad I won't be sulking at my desk all day."

"Do you want to get some anger out?" he asks with an arch of a brow.

"Okay." He squeezes my thigh, and we spend the rest of the drive in silence, both of us in our own heads and trying to work out what happened this morning. I'm still upset, as I should be, but having Aiden protect me in the way that he could as my boss, it means a lot to me. I'm not sure what is going through Aiden's head. He mentioned before he used to have a temper, and it seemed like Zach was pushing that button. I don't think I would have been too upset if Aiden punched him, but it wouldn't have gone well for him, and I don't want him in trouble.

Aiden pulls up to a sports complex.

"What is this?"

"Golf balls or softballs?"

I blink at him a few times. "Softballs."

"Perfect."

We get out of the car, and Aiden takes my hand and kisses the knuckles before we go to the front desk. "I need a softball cage," he tells the kid at the front desk.

"How long?" the kid says.

"An hour." The attendant looks at us, and hands us two helmets and two bats. Aiden hands me my bat and hands his back.

"The hybrid bat," he says, pointing to a blue and gold one. The kid trades out the bats for Aiden.

Aiden grabs us two sports drinks before he takes me out to the range.

"Are you okay if I hit a few first?" he asks, and I nod enthusiastically. Clearly knowing this is something he needs. He kisses the side of my head as he pushes a button and goes inside of the cage. As the mechanism whirls, he waits in his stance before he just pummels each ball that comes shooting out of the cannon. There's a clanging of the ball hitting the fence after each hit and then another jarring sound of the ball hitting the bat.

He doesn't say much, just stands there and continually hits the ball over and over. He must have been in there for nearly twenty minutes. I can see sweat starting to pull on the collar of his dress shirt, but he clearly doesn't give a fuck. I don't tell him to take a break or ask if he's okay. When he's ready to talk or have me in the cage, he will tell me.

Softballs bounce down the lane and collect in the container so that they will just shoot again down the range.

Aiden pushes the button that stops the balls and sighs. Unlocking the door and standing beside me, he takes a few sips of his drink and blinks at me.

"Do you want a go?" he asks, not telling me I have to but giving me the option.

"Does it really make you feel better?"

"It really does," he says. I nod my head, and he puts the helmet on my head. He adjusts the settings for the ball machine and gives me some instruction on my stance as I enter the cage alone. He stands behind me, his fingers interlaced with the fence as I swing and miss the first few balls.

"That's alright, you're swinging too soon. Wait for the ball to be just a little closer." I nod, my helmet making my hair flat and sigh as the next ball comes flying at me.

I think about the pain of loss and moments never had. How I deserved more as a child but need to move on. I take that anger out on the ball, putting all my weight behind the hit and swinging.

The bat connects, and it's not like the last time I hit a ball. This time the fucker goes flying. The force of the bat hitting the ball radiates down my arms, and it feels good. It feels like a release of negative energy.

So I keep doing it. Thinking about the things that have

hurt me or how Zach spoke to me today, and I hit the ball. I'm not proud of it, but I picture his face multiple times as I swing. His smug, stuck up, douchebag face meets my bat multiple times.

It's only when my arms start to hurt that I stop. I somehow nearly forgot that Aiden was there, but the smile he gives me when I turn around fills me up completely.

"It works, doesn't it?"

I sigh and push the button to stop the balls and take off the helmet.

"It works."

Aiden

I'm Her Daddy Now

WE GO BACK to my house so I can change and Jessa can take a quick shower before we head to the game. I feel better, but not completely.

It took everything in me to not smash Zach's face in. I can't believe the things he said to Jessa. I don't care how angry he is at his father or the situation, he can't talk to her like that. No one can talk to her like that. She looked so broken and hurt in the supply closet, I wanted to destroy whatever made her feel that way.

I was planning on selling my tickets for today, but I'm glad I didn't. It was an excuse to get Jessa out of the office and to not raise too much speculation. Though, I imagine there is more over the way I reacted, and honestly, I don't give a fuck. Maybe if the office knows she's mine, I won't have to worry about anyone fucking with her anymore.

"Ready?" I ask as she puts her damp hair over her shoulder, knowing it will probably dry on the way to the game.

"Yeah, we don't have to go. If you just want to stay home?"

I shake my head, needing something to do. If I sit around

this house, I'll be tempted to go back to the office and not take the high road. "No, but if you don't want to go, we can do something else."

She gives me a weak smile and shakes her head. "Let's go." She wears her dress from work, and I changed into a Rays' shirt and some breathable shorts.

She squints as we get in the car, and I look over at her. "Forget your sunglasses?"

"I left them on my desk and the other pair in my car."

"We'll get you a hat at the stadium," I say, squeezing her thigh, and she smiles at me. It's her actual smile, and I feel some more tension leaving my body.

We don't talk about the situation anymore as we park the car and walk hand in hand through the stadium. We're back in the same shop that I bought her the t-shirt from last time. She's looking at the hats and then she looks at me. Without her vocalizing it, I make the choice for her, picking the pink one with the blue Rays logo embroidered on the front.

"Thanks, Daddy," she says quietly so no one can hear, it's one of the first times she's called me that in a non-sexual situation. I enjoy it.

"You're welcome, baby." I kiss the side of her head, pay for the hat, and rip off the tag, putting it on her head and leaning down and giving her a chaste kiss. "Want to get something to drink or eat?"

She nods, taking my hand as we head to the concessions. "I think I want one of those big pink lemonades and a soft pretzel with cheese, please."

"You got it." I order and we head to our seats.

"You know, I think I could get used to coming to games with you."

"Don't forget about hockey and football season."

Her cheeks heat and she smiles before ripping her pretzel. "I don't know anything about either of those."

"That's why I'm here."

"Among many other reasons," she says, bumping me with her leg. The game starts, and I feel much better than I did earlier in the day, but there's still a lingering anger sitting in my chest. I hate feeling this way, like I can't let it go. It doesn't help that I can still sense that Jessa is hurting, even though I know she's having a good time right now.

"We should go to Avalon on Friday," she says, interrupting my thoughts. My arm is bracketed behind her. and she leans closer to me so the conversation is more private. Even though the seats are pretty bare since it's a mid-day weekday game.

"Friday?" It seems fast considering we just slept together, but I wonder why she wants to go.

"I think it would be a good release for the both of us," she says casually, picking up her lemonade and taking a sip.

"There would be rules," I say, as I panic over bringing her there, actually crossing this bridge of combining the two pieces of who I am.

"I love rules," she says with a smile, and I know she isn't lying. Jessa is truly a good girl; she isn't much of a brat. She doesn't act out for attention. She just knows if she's good she'll get what she wants.

"You wouldn't be able to talk to anyone else unless I give you permission."

"I can do that." She smiles. "What else?"

"I would be daddy there, not Aiden."

She licks her lips and nods enthusiastically.

"And no sharing," she throws in, and it's adorable how she thinks I would ever fucking share her with anyone.

"Absolutely not."

"What are you comfortable with doing there?" she asks, her hand on my leg. Fuck, I love how effortlessly affectionate she is.

"I like being watched, watching, playing out scenes, but I think mostly I would like to be watched with you. Having people see my pretty little baby."

Her cheeks take on an adorable shade of pink as she smiles. "I'm comfortable with people watching and being naked. Are you?"

"I'd prefer to be mostly clothed." She seems to be completely okay with that.

"Are you okay with others seeing me?" she asks and at first I wonder if it's a trick question, but then I really think about it.

"I've never been watched with someone I've cared about in this capacity before. I think I would need to see how I feel."

She kisses my cheek. "Thank you for being honest."

"Is there anything you would want if we went?"

She toys with the hem of my shorts as she thinks. "I really want you to spank me."

"Even though you've done nothing wrong?" I ask, just making sure we clarify. I don't want her to seek this relief because she thinks she's done something wrong.

"No, not as a punishment. I think it would feel good for both of us. I get off on it, and as long as it's something you enjoy."

"I would." I adjust myself, and she smirks at me, her hand still fumbling with my shorts.

"I think we're both still feeling a little tense. I've just..."

"What?" I ask her when she trails off.

"I've just been wanting that truly euphoric feeling of completely giving up control and even more so in a public setting. It's especially hard since we're a secret half the time. I don't know, I guess I want people to know I belong to you."

I blink at her a few times and suddenly there's people in the seats next to us cheering and pointing at us. When I look up, we're on the kiss cam again, and they even mention I'm a former player on the screen. Jessa looks at the screen and then back at me before licking her lips.

This time there's no hesitation as she tilts her head and her lips meet mine, my hand possessively on her throat as people cheer and aww at our affection.

It feels right, and we probably kiss far longer than necessary. But when I pull back and look into her deep brown eyes, all I see is devotion staring back at me. I'm not sure that I've quite earned it yet, but if she's giving it, then I'll take it.

"We'll go on Friday."

"Really?"

"Really, but tonight I'm taking care of you. Do you want me to take you home first to pick up a few things?"

"If you don't mind," she says, shrugging her shoulders.

"Not at all." I kiss her again, and she smiles. The rest of the game feels like a haze until the ball hits the batter's bat at the wrong angle and the ball comes flying behind the net of the backstop. Jessa shrugs away and I put my right hand and catch the ball. I immediately feel the pain radiate in my hand but don't let it show as I sit back down.

"Holy shit, are you okay?" she says, and I nod my head.

"Would have been much worse if it hit you."

"Baseball is fucking dangerous," she says, grabbing my hands. She doesn't question it, just starts rubbing the muscles in my hand. There's a kid three rows up, and I toss him the ball with my left hand.

"Here you go, kid." He has a beaming smile on his face, and Jessa kisses my hand before kneading more of the tension out.

"Do you want to talk about your hand? We don't have to," she says gently, and I sigh.

"I broke it. It's what ended my career. I was on the disabled list for a while, but the break extended to my joint, I basically have arthritis in my right hand. It doesn't always hurt, just sometimes."

She kisses my hand again and continues her massage. "I'm sorry, that had to have been hard."

I shrug and look down at her. "Honestly, I think it saved my life." Her brows furrow as we try to pay attention to the game and she massages my hand more. "I was living recklessly, angry all the time. I still was after the injury, but I think it made me figure out what's important. Honestly, I still think I'm figuring it out," I say to her softly.

"Me too," she says, leaning forward and giving me a kiss. "Can we get out of here?"

"Yeah, we're losing so fucking bad anyway," I say, taking her hand in mine as we head to the cottage to collect her things.

❀ ❀ ❀

When we're at her place, she's packing a bag, and I know it's probably too soon, but I don't care. "You want to pack some things to keep at my place?"

"Okay," she says with a smile, stuffing her bag with more items. Once she's packed, she goes to grab her phone off the charger, and it starts buzzing. "For fuck's sake, I blocked his number, and he's calling me from a burner or something."

"Give me the phone," I say, holding out my hand. She doesn't hesitate as she hands me the phone. Her obedience and trust in me is such a massive turn on. I'm not sure if I've earned it, but I'll accept it nonetheless.

"Hello," I say slightly deeper than my natural voice.

"Who the fuck is this?" he says back in shock.

"This is Aiden-fucking-Carlson, and I'm Jessa's new daddy. If you don't stop calling my girl, we're going to have fucking problems."

"Let me talk to Jessa."

"You will not call her again, and if I find out you do, I'll fuck up your life."

"Listen here, you asshole—" I hang up the phone, and Jessa blinks at me, her lips parted, and I worry that I've gone too far. But then she throws herself at me and I have to catch her, my hands gripping her ass as she wraps her legs around me and kisses me harder than she ever has.

"We're changing your number," I say, and she nods and kisses me again.

"You can have whatever you want, Daddy," she tells me. We don't make it back to my house, and I'm feeling a lot better about going to the office tomorrow.

Jessa

Breaking Rules

I FEEL like an even bigger freak at the office the rest of the week, besides Penny and Sharon. Honestly, that's all I need: Aiden, Penny, Sharon. Everyone else in the office can kiss my ass. It feels so good to have this outlook. The high road? We don't know her.

It probably has something to do with the way Aiden spoke to Sean the other day. I've never been so attracted to a man in my life than I was at that moment. The way he put Sean in his place, the way he claimed me.

During my lunch break, we went to change my number, and Aiden saw how out of date my phone was and upgraded me. I'm not one to refuse gifts. If Aiden wants to spoil me, I'm definitely going to let him. So I now have the latest iPhone, with a pink glittery case and a Popsocket to match.

I'm not sure what I'm more excited for, the sparkly phone or going to Avalon with Aiden tonight. I'm walking past Penny's desk, and she looks so solemn.

"Hey, Penny, is everything all right?"

She gives me a weak smile. "Yeah, I'm fine."

"Maybe we can do another girls night soon?"

That perks her up. "I'd love that, maybe this time we can go out."

"We can do whatever you like."

"Perfect, next weekend?"

"It's a date."

Her smile is genuine then. "Thanks, Jessa."

"Of course." I go back to my desk and it feels like the day drags on forever. It's always like that when you're excited for something. But somehow I persevere and get through the day. I've got to say, I don't think this is a job I want long term. I mean, I don't mind doing the design work, but there just isn't much of it. I'm in no place to be picky with work. I like seeing Aiden every day, and I think having a stake in the company means I should at least know how it works.

But this office is just toxic. I think I should make a plan to leave; maybe I should see what Aiden thinks. Part of me feels like a quitter after a few weeks, but I'm just not sure how much I can walk on eggshells and not like the job I'm doing.

It would be different if there was more design work, but after my altercation with Zach, it has me thinking about my next move.

Definitely not leaving the state. The cottage is growing on me, and things with Aiden are moving so quick, but in the best way. I think I could call this place home, but I don't think Kemper's is my career aspiration.

I enjoyed being more freelance and doing more design work. Even if I don't have many contacts here, maybe I could start that on the side until it takes off. I wonder if Aiden would be upset if I left. But if I left the office, there would be no point of secrecy, even if I'm the one who suggested it. Before I leave, I've got to make sure that Aiden and I are solid, and that whatever I move on to, I'm making decent money. It will be hard to beat my compensation at Kemper's, but I can't help but feel like it will be worth it.

I must have spent so much time in my head as Aiden leaves his office, giving me a wink before he leaves and heads to his house. I'm out of my seat in a moment, grabbing all my shit and nearly running out the door. Penny laughs at me, and I shrug my shoulders as I get into my car and drive to Aiden's house where we decided to meet. I'm worried the sundress I packed is too casual for Avalon, but I can't wear the same dress I wore the last time.

When I get to Aiden's house, the garage door is already open, and I pull my car through. Pulling out my bag and dress, I walk to the door. I feel stupid for a moment and decide to knock against the door leading into the house. Aiden opens immediately and greets me with a huge smile.

"Hey."

"Hey." I lean forward and he gives me a gentle kiss before breaking apart and looking down at me. "I thought we'd eat here before we get dressed to go."

"You're cooking for me?"

"It's just spaghetti and meat sauce, so don't get your hopes up." I smile and place my things on one of his bar stools before taking a seat on the other. He's busy browning the meat as I look around. I've obviously been here a few times, but I still admire how clean and nice his home is. I mean I knew Aiden had money—he was a professional athlete and he's part owner of Kemper's. He has money, but he isn't overly rich, you can tell by the way he carries himself and speaks to people. I'm eager to learn more about his family and how he grew up, but I already have an idea that his parents are down to earth people, even if they have money too. I wonder what it's like to constantly have money in your bank account and not have to worry about rent or how you're going to pay all your bills.

I mean I felt comfortable enough with Sean, but at the same time, I felt too dependent. When I caught him cheating, I had nearly nothing in my name, no place to go, because it was his house. I won't end up there again, leaving myself in a position with nowhere to land. The cottage and shares my father gifted me have afforded me that, and just thinking about it makes me sigh. I've been hating Collin Kemper in my head often these days. But if this is what he could do for me, giving me the cushion I needed to land on my feet? Then I need to forgive him. He's gone, this anger I'm holding onto only hurts me.

"Are you doing okay over there?" Aiden asks, his brows furrowed.

"Yeah, I was just thinking about Collin." His eyes widen, and he turns to throw the spaghetti into the boiling water.

"Is there anything you want to ask me about him?"

I shake my head and sigh. "I think I just need to learn to live with the memories I have and what he gifted me in his passing. I really needed this job, money, and a place to stay. He might not have known how badly I needed it, but nonetheless, even though he's dead, he gave me things I needed when I was at my lowest."

"You were already in Florida the day before when Zach texted you?" he says, we never really talked about what I was doing before and I think Aiden deserves to know everything.

I give him a deprecating smile. "I was already on my way to talk to Collin when Zach texted me about the funeral."

"Fuck. I'm so sorry," he says, while he gives me most of his attention, his peripherals checking on the food.

"I had caught Sean cheating and it was the last straw. I think part of me wanted to leave before that, but I had become so codependent. When I saw him with a student, it was the push I needed. I packed up my most important belongings and started driving. I stopped at a lot of parks and monuments on the way down. Probably stalling more than I realized, maybe if I hadn't been so scared to confront him I would have gotten here in time."

Aiden gives me a soft look like his heart is breaking for me, and I shake him off.

"I could have come sooner, Collin could have reached out sooner. There are so many possibilities in life, but I think I'm ready to just start living in the now."

"Living in the now?" he asks.

"Yes, enjoying my boyfriend's spaghetti and going on dates with him, decorating my cottage, and working at Kemper's. Living in the past isn't going to do me any good. I want to appreciate what I have now."

"I like that," he says smiling.

"What part, the boyfriend part?"

"Yeah, I like that part the most, but I like seeing you happy."

"You've become a big part of that happiness, you know."

"I'm hoping you still feel the same way after tonight," he says.

"Oh, I definitely will be."

✻ ✻ ✻

I shouldn't have worried about what I was going to wear, because Aiden bought me the most stunning, deep-red dress I've ever seen. It's tight fitting and shows off my figure amazingly. It has thin straps and a neckline that doesn't leave much to the imagination.

While I'm happy to be the one wearing it, Aiden seems to approve of his purchase as he keeps stroking the material on my back and right above my ass as we check in.

I have to stop myself from staring at him in his suit as well. Aiden dresses more casually at the office, seeing him look so professional just makes me want to obey him more. It gives him more authority, and it fits his body perfectly. He has to clear his throat because I'm staring at him when I should be listening to the receptionist.

I have to fill out some paperwork and sign a ridiculous amount of documents as Aiden's guest. Even though we discussed not sharing, since I'm not an official member I wouldn't be able to partake in any activities with anyone else anyway.

The receptionist gives Aiden the details about how I could be added to his account if we decide this is something we would like to do in the future together. The main entrance is just as I remember it. It's classy and feels almost like a prohibition era bar with the black and gold decoration.

This area is pretty void of people, and when I hand over my phone to reception, I realize that it's ten o'clock. I imagine the fun is getting started inside. A bubbling of excitement and nervousness is coursing through my veins. Everything Aiden and I have done so far has been relatively tame. I'm asking him to take more control tonight, our roles are stricter and our relationship is going to be put to the test.

Aiden rubs my back as we go to the bar and get a drink before we go inside. "If at any point you want to leave, you'll tell me?"

"Yes," I nod my head and take the lemon martini the bartender made for me.

"Yes, what?" Aiden asks in a demanding tone.

My eyes meet his and I take a sip before swallowing and answering with a smile. "Yes, Daddy."

"Good. Now, there may be people here that I know, is that going to bother you?"

I take a deep breath and groan a little bit. "I'll try to not let it bother me."

"If you're feeling any type of way, tell me, okay? Don't hold it in and let it fester. I'm going to take care of you and part of that is making sure that you're physically and mentally okay."

This is what having a daddy is supposed to be like.

I could tell him how perfect I think he is, or how every time he shows me such pure kindness I want to tell him I'm falling in love with him. I know it's crazy and fast, but fuck if he doesn't make it impossibly easy.

"Is your brother going to be here?"

"No," he says plainly. "Lincoln has been going through something—I don't know what. But he hasn't been back here since that night."

I nod my head, glad that his brother isn't going to see me get my ass spanked red. It sure would make The Bahamas trip uncomfortable. I take the last sip of my drink, and Aiden puts down some cash before helping me off the stool and taking my hand, leading me toward the back section.

"You remember all the rules?" he says, and I nod my

head. He gives me a look that says non-verbal communication isn't going to fly here, so I promptly answer him.

"Yes, Daddy." He kisses my temple and we walk into the main room. We decided beforehand that this is where we're going to stay tonight, baby steps and all that. There's more people here than there were last time, not that it truly matters.

Once I'm over Aiden's knee, I won't care how many people are in the room, that's part of the excitement for me. That he'll put me in such a state so even if we're in a room of fifty people, he's the only one I can focus on.

We take a seat on one of the long leather loungers, giving us plenty of room for what we have planned. One of the beautiful servers comes to take our drink order and Aiden orders us the same thing we had at the bar earlier.

"This is your last drink and then nothing but water, understand." I nod, and he kisses me softly before putting a hand around my shoulder and toying with the strap of my dress.

A lot of people are just talking or kissing, except for two couples right across from us, which seems like a swinger's situation. The two men are kissing each other while the two women are on their laps and kissing each other as well. Everyone looks extremely happy and eager for what the night will bring, and I can't blame them. I envy people who are that secure that they can enjoy being with other people like that.

I just simply can't, if someone even looks at Aiden with an overabundance of interest, I might go slightly feral. I make sure to mark my territory by placing my hand provocatively on his thigh.

The waitress comes back with both our drinks and two

glasses of water. She places the water on the table next to us and Aiden hands me my drink while he takes his. She gives us a kind smile until she's wandering around and asking anyone else if they need anything. I only take a single sip before I look up and an attractive couple is standing before us.

Aiden stills slightly next to me, and I catch on fast. He's interacted with them at the club before in a way I don't want to know about.

"Aiden, you brought a guest?" the man says.

"Yes, Leo, Carmen, this is my girlfriend, Jessa." I love that he throws the girlfriend in there. He doesn't leave what we are as a mystery to these people, making it known that I'm important.

Remembering my rules, I just give them a tight smile, and Aiden smiles at them too.

"Are you two open to playing?" Leo says.

Fuck the rules.

"No," I say sharply, and both Leo's and Carmen's eyes go wide.

"Oh, I see, that hasn't been a problem before," Carmen says, looking at Aiden and giving her husband a shitty look.

"Things have changed with my personal situation. I'll only be coming here with Jessa and will only be intimate with her while I'm at Avalon."

Hell yeah, you tell him. I rub his thigh more—more like marking him as mine—and Carmen tracks the motion. I'm not really sure what the expression is on her face. It doesn't read as jealousy, but it feels like longing.

"Are you sure?" Leo asks, and I'm about to stand up and punch this tool in the dick.

I'm sure Aiden was about to answer, and I already broke the rule once, *so fuck it*.

"Daddy said no," I say with authority. I swear Carmen's eyes are nearly out of her eye sockets as she glances between Aiden and me.

Leo looks at me and then his wife. "Didn't know that was your thing, Carlson," Leo says, digging fun at Aiden. I wanted to punch him earlier, but now I want to murder him and toss him in the ocean.

Aiden doesn't rise to the bait. Just raises an eyebrow and glares at Leo. "I think we've both expressed our lack of interest, have some class, Leo."

The man's face turns bright red, and he walks away, tugging his wife along.

"What a fucking asshole," I mumble, and Aiden chuckles.

"Be that as it may, you broke the rules, kitten."

I mean, he was already planning on spanking me, and I'm usually very good, so I doubt the punishment will be harsh. "What is my punishment?"

"No coming till I say so." I blink at him and part my lips. That's not what I was expecting, and I don't hate it, but I also don't think I can control my orgasm. He must see all of these thoughts rumbling through my head as he grabs my neck. It's always a firm enough touch, but it feels endearing when he does it. His lips meet mine and it works that fast, forgetting where we are, that people are going to be watching. I mean, it's all part of the draw, but it disappears and his touch remains the center of my attention.

But this connection we have is so magnetic and strong, that if I really needed to, I could tune it all out and just focus on how good he feels. How he tastes like whiskey, and his stubble rubs against my chin. Both of his hands are on me, and it makes me feel cherished that I'm the center of his world at this moment.

Aiden makes me feel so many things that sometimes I feel like they're about to pour out of me in a slur of unintelligible words. But when our lips part and his green eyes glance down at me and he speaks, that's when I know I'm truly done for.

"Bend over daddy's lap."

Definitely fucking done for.

Aiden

Spanking Can Be Catharhc For Both Parties

BEING the good girl that Jessa is, she immediately follows direction. I'm not even mad at her for breaking the rules, it was clearly out of a possessiveness—of me—and I can't deny that I enjoyed it more than I'd like to admit. Leo has gotten so pushy with me wanting to be involved with his wife, and I'm glad we finally squashed that. It's clear that Carmen is feeling some sort of way about it, and Leo is too fucking selfish to even notice.

Jessa slides over my lap, my right hand gliding down her spine and squeezing her ass. Her torso is flat on the sofa and her cheek is pressed against the leather as she shifts her weight, getting comfortable.

Her legs are resting on the side of the couch, and I'm just giving her time to situate herself and find a position she likes. Her wiggling in my lap doesn't help how hard I am, but I can be patient.

"Are you comfortable, baby?"

I swat her ass playfully. She tilts her head to the left, her right cheek pressing against the leather as she smiles at me.

"Yes, Daddy."

Her hands are pressed against the cool leather, and I'm slowly sliding up her dark red dress. I knew she would look fantastic in it.

"Do you need me to hold your hands or are you going to be a good girl?"

"I can be good."

"I know you can, you're such a good girl for daddy. You told them who you belonged to, didn't you?" She nods her head and licks her lips. "Do you want everyone here to watch me spank you, show them that you're mine, and only I can give you what you need, kitten?"

"Please."

I'm rubbing the back of her thighs and watching as her high heel-covered feet slightly twitch with each touch. My fingertips drag along her soft skin as I finally peel the material over the curve of her ass. She's wearing a black lacy thong and I hook my finger under the waistband and drag it past her ass and down her legs. I pocket the lingerie and continue my gentle touches of her skin.

I take a moment to look up and notice multiple sets of eyes on us, including Carmen and Leo. I'm not sure what possessive part of me Jessa has woken up, but I feel the need to show them that I don't share, and that I won't be shared anymore.

"You'll tell me if it's too much?" I check in with Jessa, her big brown eyes still on me as she licks her lips and nods. I swat her playfully again, and she smiles.

"Yes, Daddy."

"Ten for breaking a rule, and then we can get your good girl spanks."

"Okay."

"Do you like counting?" I ask her, and she shakes her head no. "Okay, one." I rear my hand back and it meets her right ass cheek with an audible smack. Her flesh pinkens and apparently the sound was loud enough to garner more attention from the crowd. I can't help the smirk that takes over my face.

Part of me feels guilty for liking this so much. I shouldn't like hitting Jessa for gratification, let alone in front of others. When I look down at her face, she gives me a small smile and nod, letting me know we're good and she's enjoying herself. I'm not sure she could possibly be enjoying herself as much as I am.

I get the view of her perfect ass and every motherfucker in this room wishing they were me, or her.

My next strike is in the same spot I already pinked. Her ass jolts up slightly, and her nails scratch at the lounge below her, begging for purchase. Her mouth is parted into a pretty 'O' shape, and she's moaning.

I want to test her limits and see how far she wants me to take it. My hand connects with the same spot so hard her ass bounces, and the previously pink spot is now turning a darker shade, nearing red.

She whimpers but nods her head. "Thank you, Daddy," she says, and I can't help but grind my hard cock against her stomach.

"Such a good girl." She moans at the praise, and I have to shake out my hand. The last slap made me ball my hand into a fist and then release it. When I see people looking at me, particularly Leo, it looks like they think my hand just hurts from how hard I spanked her.

I hate to admit that insecurity, especially since I'm the

one in charge right now, but Jessa needs me to take care of her and control this situation. My hand cannot become a problem —not here.

I knead her tender flesh for a moment, giving my hand a break. She's pushing her plush ass into my hands, begging for more, and as much as I want to play with her pussy and see how wet she is, I told her the consequences, no matter how adorable and well-founded her rule breaking was.

My left hand is braced in between her shoulder blades as I smack her other cheek, making it equally pink. She gasps and whines, but it's always followed by a noise of pleasure. I'm on her eighth smack when the pain in my hand starts to really bother me. I ball my fist on top of her ass and open and close it .

Without speaking, Jessa pops herself up and straddles my lap. Her eyes are glassy and she strokes my face.

"Are you okay? Do you need to stop?" I ask her.

"Umm... no, my hip was hurting. Can I turn the other way? Please," she says, searching my eyes. I realize she must have known my hand was hurting and this is her way of giving me an out without me having to be the one to stop the scene.

"Get comfortable, baby. Two more then Daddy is going to make it feel better."

She readjusts herself so it's my left hand smacking her perfectly pink and pert ass. The two last hits are sharp and concise. I may be more impatient than she's feeling right now. Fuck, do I want to reward her and make her feel so good.

She's slightly shaking after my palm hits her ass for the tenth time, and she's panting when I slide my hand over her tender flesh and dip inside of her dripping pussy. One of her hands is clutching at my thigh as I toy with her—enjoying the way her cunt is sucking my fingers inside of her so audibly I know anyone within ten feet can certainly hear it.

"So wet after getting spanked, aren't you? Such a messy fucking girl for your daddy."

She doesn't respond and just whimpers, so I smack her ass cheek even though my right hand hurts. She gasps and moans louder.

"Yes. Yes," she says loudly, not giving a single fuck that anyone is watching her become a begging and whimpering mess.

"Do you like having all of these people watching your greedy cunt taking my fingers?"

'Yes." Her voice is quieter this time. I increase my pace and start fucking her harder. The idea of her gushing all over my dress pants has me nearly coming as I shift myself so I can get the right angle as I finger fuck her.

"You can come and when you do, you better make a mess. I won't stop until you've squirted all over me."

"I don't know if I can," she pants. She only did it that first time I fingered her at her cottage, but I know I can make her do it again.

"Yes you can, and you will. Be a good girl and drench Daddy's pants."

"What if I can't?" she asks between pants.

"Then I guess we'll be here all night, baby." Her mouth parts, and I fuck her even harder with my hand. Wanting to make her feel so good she doesn't even have a moment to overthink this, I grip her ass tightly while my other hand toys with her pussy. Wet suctioning noises from my fingers going in and out of her spur me to go harder.

It's then that I feel a gush of fluid drip down my wrist and Jessa's back arches as she moans loudly and her thighs start to shake. Her grip on my thigh is near bruising as I continue fucking her, ringing out every drop of her sweet cunt that I can manage.

I can feel wetness pooling on my pants, and I feel satisfied as she shakes over my lap. Multiple club goers are watching, most of them with an amused or entertained expression. I reluctantly slide my wet fingers out of her and pat her ass lightly. She winces and then sighs.

"Come here, baby."

I have to help her spread her thighs, and she grimaces when she sits on my thighs.

"My poor baby," I say, and she groans as she leans forward, her lips against my throat as she breathes. "You did so good. Fuck, you're perfect." I kiss the side of her head, and she grabs my suit jacket and grinds her wet pussy against my trousers. Thank god I packed us both a change of clothes to leave in.

Her hands are all over my jaw and hair as she moves on my lap, stopping to wince every time she rubs a sore spot against my thigh. "Can I make you feel good?"

"I enjoyed myself thoroughly. Having everyone here see how beautifully my girl comes around my fingers and how much she likes it when I smack her sweet little ass."

She moans and leans forward, taking my lips against hers.

"I need you to come inside of me. I want them to see how I'm yours," she says, like it wasn't clear enough when everyone was staring at us as I spanked her and made her come.

"Then take Daddy's cock out," I say, and she licks her lips

and nods. She unfastens my belt quickly before undoing the top button and sliding down the zipper.

Her hands are confident as she tugs my boxers down, one of her hands stroking my length as the other fondles my balls and rubs my perineum with her fingers.

"Next time we come, I'm going to worship your cock for hours, but I can't wait tonight." I swallow, loving that idea, but needing her just as much as she needs me. She doesn't ask permission, just lines her dripping cunt up with the head of my cock. Wetting the length with her obscene release before she slinks down on the shaft, moaning as she takes me inch by inch.

I grip her ass, and she winces, but it's followed by a moan, so I keep my grip tight as I help her glide up and down my cock. I briefly look over her shoulder to see the sets of eyes on us. There are still multiple, while others are engaging in their own activities. Jessa is in her own world as she rides me, her pace erratic and wild as her dark hair fans her face. Something about giving her so much pleasure that she doesn't care about her surroundings makes my chest swell. That we can have this cosmic effect on each other is something I didn't know existed. It hits me right then that we could be everything, the perfect combination of affection, friendship, and desire.

My hands leave her ass to tug down the top of her dress, exposing her breast to me. I wrap an arm around her back as I bring one to my mouth, sucking on the tender skin and lavishing her nipples with my tongue. Her nails scratch my scalp as she rides me, her noise of pleasure evident and urgent.

She's losing stamina, so I have to grip her ass again so that

I can thrust up into her, fucking her from below. She grips my face and brings my mouth back to her chest, which I take as instruction to continue what I was doing before, and I do, sucking hard on her nipple as I fuck into her.

Her tight pussy clenching around me as she meets her second release of the night. Her face burrowing against my neck and shoulder as I fuck her relentlessly from below.

"Please come inside me," she whispers and that's what sends me over the edge as I spill deep inside of her. I hold her tightly against me as I make a feral noise against her chest. Just as tight as I'm holding on to her, she continues holding on to me. Her nails scratch my scalp and make me rub my face against her chest even more.

I'm ready to pull out when she stops me.

"I need them to see it dripping out of me," she says, and if I hadn't just had an erection for the longest time, I think I would already be hard again.

I lean forward and kiss her as I palm her ass and lift her up, spreading her cheeks apart as I feel my warm cum drip from her pussy back onto my cock.

"I think everyone knows you're mine now, kitten."

"I don't think they do," she responds with an arch of her brow. Her brown eyes are half-lidded and seductive, one of her tits half out, and her dress is ajar as she slides off my lap, avoiding my cock.

My eyes widen as her hands slide up and down my thighs before she leans forward and begins to lick my release and her own off my half hard cock. Her tongue leisurely swipes up my cum. She shows me it on her tongue before swallowing and taking another lick.

"Jesus Christ," I can't help but mutter as I wrap some of

her long brown hair in my fist. She just continues cleaning my cock as she blinks up at me. I can't help but smile at her as I give her the praise she's clearly asking for. "You're such a good, dirty girl for daddy, aren't you?" She nods, licking the underside of my cock one more time, making me shiver before using my thighs to help her stand up and lean forward and kiss me.

I kiss her eagerly, tasting the mix of us on her tongue as she parts from me with a mischievous smile. "Now I think they understand I'm yours." I can't help but laugh as I adjust her dress and cover her pink ass.

"Let's get you home." I stand and we head to reception to collect our bags and phones so we can change before leaving. I didn't know how tonight was going to go, if coming to Avalon was going to be the thing that broke this fragile beginning, but all I can think is it's made it stronger, and I can't help how intense my feelings are getting for this beautiful and adventurous woman.

Jessa

Whiskey Joe's

IT FEELS like I'm living my life outside of my own body, like this couldn't possibly be *me* living this idyllic life. A house by the ocean, a boyfriend who's into all the things I'm into, and a completely nonjudgmental best friend. Penny is turning out to be the best friend I always longed for. My mom was constantly moving us around, even if it was only twenty minutes away, I always wound up going to a different school. My mom definitely wasn't driving me a half-hour to see my old friends, either. It became easier to just not open my heart up to the disappointment of losing friends, so by the time I hit high school I had learned to protect myself. I had friends, but I always kept them at arm's length.

When I got to college is when I really started to make connections and friends, but then I met Sean and all of that got thrown away. He told me that I was his, and he didn't like sharing me with others. At first, I liked that. I liked that he wanted me for himself, but now as I reflect back on the relationship, it wasn't a loving type of control. It was toxic.

If someone really loves you, they would want you to be happy, not just for you to make them happy. I appreciate

Sean teaching me about some of the lifestyle, but I'm even more thankful that I'm able to learn what a healthy dynamic looks like with Aiden. I know I'm still young and have a lot of growing to do, and it's only become clear to me recently that Sean used my immaturity and age to his advantage.

I don't want to be used again, I'm fully ready to live my life for me, and it seems like everything I could have dreamed of is happening. But my life has had a lot of disappointments, and I keep fearing that the other shoe is going to drop. Maybe I'll have to move away again like I had to when I was a child. Even though logically I know I'm an adult and I make those choices, I still worry that all the good in my life is going to come crashing down.

Penny nudges my shoulder, and I stop all the negative thoughts and overthinking. She gives me a kind smile, and I return it. We're out at this beachfront bar called Whiskey Joe's. It's closer to my cottage, and Aiden was adamant on driving us. I'm supposed to call him when we're ready to go home. The bar is cute, and we're sitting at tables in the sand that are thankfully covered by umbrellas. A local band is playing cover band music, and it's nice to go out with a friend and have no obligation to be anything other than myself.

We order a few appetizers to share, and I'm thankful I convinced her that we in fact did not need gator bites. I shiver thinking about seeing the item on the menu again.

Penny takes a sip of her margarita and is swaying to the music when she looks back at me. "How are things with Aiden going?"

"Really good," I say. How much are you supposed to indulge your best friends?

"I need more than that." I decide to give her just enough to go off of, but to keep some of our relationship private.

"He's so sweet, thoughtful, and just... sexy."

She laughs and nods her head, and I give her an odd look. "I'm his adopted cousin, first off. And second of all, just because I'm his cousin doesn't mean that I can't agree that he's objectively good looking. Fuck, the entire Carlson family is gorgeous. Have you met anyone else yet?"

"No, not yet, but he did invite me to The Bahamas next month." I decide to leave the part about accidentally meeting his brother at Avalon out, because explaining that seems more complicated than anything.

Her smile turns feral as she takes another sip of her drink. "Maggie is going to lose her fucking mind," she says behind her straw.

"Who's Maggie?"

"His mom. Aiden is her only son who hasn't brought a girl for Labor Day before."

I swallow, feeling the pressure of her statement. "All the other brothers have?"

"Unfortunately," she says, taking another sip.

"The family didn't like their girlfriends?" Am I walking into the lion's den coming on this trip? Aiden doesn't seem like he's someone who comes from a judgmental or rude family, but I could be reading it wrong.

She waves her hand. "No, nothing like that. I'm just being petty."

I smirk at her. "You, a petty streak?"

She arches an eyebrow at me. "Do you want to talk shit about Tabitha?" she says, and I laugh and, well, talking about her might feel nice. Penny smirks and tells me about the time

Tabitha accidentally ordered women's cut jerseys for a male team, and how she caught her making out with Zach by the dumpsters behind the office.

I should probably feel bad talking about Tabitha, but it feels nice having someone who understands.

Maybe mutual hate for people is where true friendship thrives.

We're both holding our drinks and swaying to a cover version of *You Can Have Whatever You Like*, when my phone vibrates in my purse. I quickly see Aiden's name, which I have adorned with a pink heart, like I'm fifteen.

"Hey," I say, hoping he can hear me over the noise.

"Hey, baby. When do you think you and Penny will be ready to be picked up?"

"Not sure," I say, watching Penny sway to the music.

"It's just I had to pick Linc up from the bar, and I'm deciding if I should take him home or come and get you two first."

"Let me ask." I touch Penny's shoulder, and she doesn't pay attention to me, so I nearly have to shake her. "Penny, Aiden is trying to decide whether to drop Lincoln off first or come and get us."

She blinks at me a few times. "He's with Lincoln?" I nod, and she blinks a few times more. "Tell him to pick us up first."

"Did you hear that?"

"Yeah, I'll come and get you guys first.

"I'm not done drinking, asshole," I hear through the phone, clearly Lincoln speaking to Aiden.

"Shut the fuck up," Aiden says back to his brother and then sighs over the phone. "Sorry, I'll be there in fifteen."

"Okay. See you soon."

When I put my phone away and look up at Penny she's biting her nail slightly. "Everything good, Pen?"

"Yeah, maybe too many margaritas?" She has been pounding them back. I've had two and I'm feeling a little buzzed. I can't imagine what she feels like after five.

"Let's get some water and go sit till Aiden gets here."

I grab us two waters, and we sit down and look at the bay while we wait. I really wish a breeze would at least come through. I feel like I'm a sweaty fucking mess. I'm not sure I'll ever get used to this brutal weather.

Penny and I finish both of our waters as I see Aiden and another dark haired man stumble behind him.

"Oh, fuck," Penny mumbles.

"You've got to be fucking kidding me," I hear the man behind Aiden mumble, who I've met at Avalon—awkward.

"What is your problem, Lincoln?" Aiden asks as they walk to our table. Aiden gives me a tight smile, and his brother sits down next to Penny.

"Water?" Lincoln asks Penny, and she gives him a look, they clearly have their own language as he responds. "Good."

Aiden gives his brother a strange look before turning his gaze on me. He kisses the side of my face and Lincoln stares at me. Not in a judgmental way, just like he's trying to put the pieces together.

"Jessa, you've met my brother," Aiden says in an irritated tone, and I can't decide if he's annoyed with his brother at this moment or because he approached me at Avalon.

"Hey," he says, tilting his head, and Penny makes a noise in the back of her throat. Lincoln looks over at her. "What?" he asks her and she glares at him.

"You can be a little nicer to Aiden's girlfriend, considering he hasn't had one in forever."

Lincoln laughs at his brother's expense and shakes his head. Aiden sits down next to me and places a reassuring hand on my thigh.

"How much have you had to drink?" Lincoln asks Penny, like he hasn't been drinking a shit ton from the way he stumbled out of here.

"A few rounds, but one of them was free?"

"What?" I ask, and Penny looks at me and shrugs.

"This older dude wanted to buy us a round. I might not be the brightest, but I don't turn down free drinks."

Lincoln glares at his cousin, and Aiden shakes his head back and forth, clearly irritated by the entirety of this situation.

"Can I please drive you two degenerates home now?" he says, speaking to Penny and Lincoln. I'm glad that I'm not one of the degenerates he's irritated with.

"I need to eat something," Lincoln complains. He looks a lot like Aiden, but he's a little shorter, younger, and his hair is just as long but in a crazy way, like he's constantly running his hands through it. Unlike Aidens, his eyes are more blue than green, and he also just seems to be a little more on the grumpy side, whereas Aiden is more optimistic and upbeat.

"I swear, if you fucking throw up in my car," Aiden warns him.

Lincoln rolls his eyes but picks up the menu. He orders two pizzas, and I can't help but feel uncomfortable. I'm not sure what the tension is between these three, but it's thick. I put my elbow on the table and accidentally knocked my phone down into the sand. I lean forward and pick it up, and when I look forward, I notice that Lincoln's hand just so happens to be rubbing back and forth on Penny's thigh.

When I pop back up and blink at my friend, her eyes are wide, and she gives me a curt shake of her head. Well, that's fucking interesting.

"Aiden?" I say, looking over at him.

"Yeah, baby?"

"Do you want to dance with me?"

"Sure," he says, holding out his hand, and I give Penny a concerned glance as we leave the two of them at the table. Is he really the guy she was crying about over lunch that one day? She mentioned that they couldn't be together. Is it because they're legally cousins? It's too complicated for me to even wrap my head around. Instead, I wrap my arms around Aiden's neck as we sway to the acoustic guitar playing at the venue.

"Your brother seems..." I can't think of an adjective, and I regret speaking.

"Like a drunk asshole."

I feel heat creep up my cheeks and rest my forehead on his chest.

"I hope I didn't ruin your night with Penny. I can drop you both off at the cottage if you want and then go take Lincoln home."

"No, I want to go home with you."

"Oh yeah?" I nod my head, and he leans forward and kisses me softly. "I need you in my bed tonight. I have a conference in Atlanta next week. I want as much time as we can have before I leave."

I wonder how I'm going to cope with him not in the office, but I'm sure I'll survive.

"Then it's settled, we'll drop the children off and go home." I just sway against his body, not a care in the world. When I glance to my left, there's a man leaving the bar, and I swear he looks familiar, but he's too far away. I hold Aiden closer. My heart breaks for Penny with how complicated her situation must be, and my only concern right now is Aiden going on a business trip.

"Sounds good. At least we still have tomorrow," I say, playing with the ends of his hair.

"Do you have enough stuff at my place?"

I nod and lean closer to him, his arms wrapping around me. All I can smell is his cologne. I inhale deeply and exhale; everything is going to be fine.

Jessa

Butt Plugs and Wishlists

DROPPING off Lincoln and Penny was tense the other night, and I'm not sure if I should ask her about their situation or not. I'm leaning toward just waiting until she brings it up to me.

I'm naked on Aiden's bed, my stomach pressed against his soft sheets as he comes out of the bathroom, a cocky smirk on his lips. He falls hard on the bed and bounces before leaning in and biting my ass cheek.

"I want to fuck this ass," he says. I swallow, and my face must show my hesitancy. "Are you not okay with that?" he asks. Not in a judgmental or condescending way, he's just trying to gauge my limits.

"I'm not against it, I just... I don't know. I didn't enjoy it before."

He's wearing a towel wrapped around his hips. My hair is still wet, and I need to dry it before we go to work. My car is at home, so I wonder if anyone at the office will notice. I shake my head, coming back to the current conversation.

"What didn't you like about it?"

"It never felt good to me. It stung more than anything."

"Were you prepped beforehand?"

My eyebrows furrow as I answer him. "I mean a finger or two before."

He rubs his hand down my naked back. "I really fucking hate your ex, you know that?" I shrug, and he sighs. "We would take it slow, if you're willing to try?"

Honestly, Aiden Carlson can have whatever he wants, and if he wants my ass, then it's his.

"Okay," I say softly.

"Today?" he asks, and I blink at him.

"Were you that sure I was going to say yes?"

He shrugs his shoulders and stands up, his towel falling. He walks over to the side of the bed where he opens a black velvet bag. "I bought these last week and had everything sanitized." He flips the bag and a plethora of toys spills out, including a very heavy looking silver butt plug with a bulbed ending.

"We have to go to work."

He smiles at me. "I want you to wear it to work."

"You want me to wear a butt plug today at the office?"

He nods his head, and I know if I tell Aiden no, he'll be fine, but he doesn't ask for anything. He's been slowly fulfilling all my fantasies. If this is his, then I can do this. "Okay," I say breathlessly.

He grabs my hips, putting my ass high in the air and I'm worried he's going to just slide it right in there, but I should know better.

Instead Aiden starts eating my pussy from behind. His face completely pushed against my ass as he devours me. His tongue is lavishing my pussy like he's starving and his hands are rough against my ass. He slaps the flesh of my ass, before diving back in.

My face is pressed against the plush mattress of his bed, and I can't help the begging leaving my lips.

"Please. Please."

He doesn't answer because he's completely occupied, and when his tongue leaves my pussy and touches me where he wants to fuck me so bad, I can't help the moan that leaves me. Why is him wanting to lick and kiss there so fucking hot, like no part of me is off limits, and if he's willing to do that for me, I know he would take care of me during the act.

His tongue feels amazing. I'm not close to coming, but I don't want him to stop, and I tell him that. Unfortunately, he does stop, and I make a whining noise, which he laughs at before moving.

The bed shifts, and I can feel his thighs press behind mine. The tip of his cock brushing against my clit. I know he isn't going to do anything I don't like, but I must stiffen because Aiden rubs my back slightly.

"I want you full of my cum and wearing a butt plug all day," he says, pushing inside of my pussy and making my back arch. "All day you're going to be thinking about how badly I want to be inside of you and do this again." His thrusts are hard, and his grip on my ass is tight as he fucks me.

"Spank me," I beg, and he doesn't even hesitate as his palm meets my flesh. My pussy clenches around his dick when he does it, and he moans his approval. Doing it again and turning me into a whimpering mess beneath him.

"Look at you taking Daddy's cock on all fours. You should see this ass," he says, smacking it even harder. My back bows, and I let out a cry of pleasure. A clicking of a cap opening jolts my attention, and the cool liquid drips down my ass. Aiden just rubs my hole with the pad of his thumb. He doesn't penetrate me there, but I'm nearly about to beg him to with the way it feels. His other hand leaves my ass as he grabs something else from the velvet bag.

The small purple vibrator is about the size of a double A battery, and he hands it to me, turning it on by pushing the end.

"Play with your clit." I take the vibrator, adding the buzzing toy to my clit. I feel like I'm about to combust. The stimulation of his cock stretching me, his thumb rubbing my hole, and now this unreal feeling on my clit, I won't last, and Aiden knows it. "That's it, milk Daddy's cock." His strokes are long and hard and his thumb is only lightly entering me, and it feels so fucking good.

My thighs are nearly giving out, and that's when his thumb goes inside me. The feeling is better than any anal play I've done before. It's what makes me come. I'm moaning and shivering, and I'm ready to feel Aiden come inside of me. Instead, he pulls out. I can briefly hear the way he fists his cock. The warmth of his cum hits my ass, and I groan.

"Fuck." He groans behind me. And I'm not sure what I expect next, but him spreading my cheeks with one hand, and pushing his cum inside of my asshole wasn't it. It feels good, just his thumb. I know I can take more, and I'm relaxed and calm as he pushes his release inside of me.

There's another click of the lube bottle, and I feel the cold press of the butt plug against my ass. It's shaped differently than what I've seen before. Less pine tree and more like a lopsided egg that gets skinnier.

Aiden takes his time, just pressing in softly and then

pushing back out. "You should see how goddamn good your ass looks. Fuck." He bites my cheek and places a kiss on the flesh before he finally pushes the metal inside me. It doesn't hurt. If anything it feels good if not different. He tugs on the handle and pushes it back inside and groans.

"Are you going to wear this all day, baby? My cum and plug in your ass? I don't know how I'm going to be able to get anything done." He strokes my ass, and when I look back, he can't look at anything but his handy work. He kisses my ass one more time, and I sigh. Aiden's eyes meet mine, and he smiles. "How does it feel?"

"Good, better than I thought."

He kisses my ass again. The man is obsessed, and I love it. "Let me get you cleaned up and then we'll go to work." I nod, and it should be degrading to be face down ass up with your man's cum plugged in your ass, but all I feel is cherished and like I've been completely claimed.

≈ ≈ ≈

I thought I could handle this, that maybe after a while I wouldn't notice the butt plug.

Wrong... so fucking wrong.

Every shift in my seat, every walk to the copier, all I feel is this metal plug hitting me in the right spot. Why did I tell him I was unsure about anal? All I want him to do now is take it out and claim that hole for himself. Well, maybe...

I'm walking back to my desk from the copier, and I look into his office to see him smirking and gripping his chin as he stares at me.

He watches as I sit, and my mouth parts as I adjust to the movement.

It's at this moment I'm thankful I'm fucking my boss. Any other boss would be concerned with my productivity today, but one can simply not update our website when your boyfriend's cum and butt plug is up your ass.

I shift again in the seat, and my phone vibrates at my desk.

> Aiden: My dick is hard looking at you wiggling in your chair.

>> Do something about it.

Maybe I'm begging. Shoot, I will beg. It's past lunch time. How much longer am I supposed to suffer?

> Aiden: You keep it in all day and I'll go down on you until you can't feel your face.

>> That's a bold promise.

> Aiden: One I really want to keep, so be a good girl.

>> Only for you, Daddy.

> Aiden: That's fucking right.

I'm smiling like a fucking idiot when Tabitha comes up to my cubicle. She arches an eyebrow at me before she starts speaking.

"My client sent a jpeg and apparently it looks shit when printed. Can you fix it?"

No please or kind words, but I didn't expect any.

"Can you send it over so I can take a look?"

"I need it quickly," she replies.

"I'll take a look and let you know what I can do. I'm not sure I have time today."

"You have time to text whoever has you smiling like an idiot," she says. It's not playful. If Penny had said something similar, I wouldn't have felt like this. God, I'm so sick and tired of taking the highroad. But starting waves after my issues with Zach and the relationship I'm hiding isn't what I need right now.

"Well, the sooner you get away from my desk the sooner I can look at it." She narrows her eyes at me but walks away to send the email. I look into Aiden's office, and he gives me a look that says he's proud of me.

I squirm in my seat and give him a little show, knowing damn fucking well I'm getting my reward tonight.

I fix Tabitha's jpeg, which only took about five minutes, and I'm seriously considering calling it a day, driving to Aiden's house, breaking in, and lying down on his bed like the feast he promised. It's getting to be too much, I need this thing out.

I can't take it anymore.

He doesn't answer, and I look into his office. He stands from his desk and walks to the door, waving a hand for me to come in. There are still people here; Sharon, Tabitha, Huck, and Penny for sure are still here. I look around the hallway and follow him into his office. He shuts and locks the door behind him. I swallow thickly and my heart races in my chest. Are we really about to do something in the office while other employees are here? It rachets up my libido in a deliciously fucked up way that I can't deny.

"Bend over the desk," he says, looking me up and down like he wants to devour me whole. The dynamic that Aiden and I have works because he doesn't like back talk. He likes devotion, and obedience, and I like pleasing him, so I do as he says. Rounding the desk to the portion where he sits, I bend over, pressing my chest to the cool wood counter.

Aiden follows me and sits in his office chair, scooting it up until I can feel the hard press of his thighs on the outside of mine. His hands roam my thighs leisurely, like we have all the time in the world, and like there aren't people outside of his office door.

"Are you going to be able to be quiet?" he asks, and I nod my head. A harsh smack lands across my ass, and I bite the inside of my cheek to keep quiet.

"Yes, Daddy," I say in a hushed tone, and he rubs my dress-covered cheek.

"You've been so good today, I think you deserve your reward."

I sure fucking do.

He hikes my dress up, flipping it over my back. I'm not sure what I expect him to do next, but I've learned to trust the process when it comes to Aiden. He toys with the sides of my underwear, and I'm so close to begging, but I stay quiet. I think not opening my mouth is the best way to handle this. While I'm turned on by fucking in the middle of the day in his office, I would also be mortified if anyone saw what we were doing. Why does that make it even better?

His fingers rub the skin under my panties until his

knuckle bumps against the end of the plug, making my grip tighten on the edge of the desk.

Aiden tugs on the end of the bulb before pressing back in. I keep my mouth shut, but a low moan vibrates in my throat.

"Mmm, don't know if I can trust you to be quiet, kitten," he says before he grabs the waistband of my panties and rolls them down my legs. The relief is nearly instant. He's not changing his mind if he's taking my panties off. I help him by stepping out of the lace, and he rises from his chair. His hard cock grinds against my ass, pushing my pelvis against the edge of the table.

A firm hand glides down my spine before stroking my face, and then I see my balled up panties in his fist. "Open," he says, and I swallow thickly.

If I wasn't already wet before, I'm dripping now. I'm not sure what it says about me that this would turn me on. My boss stuffing my panties in my mouth to keep me quiet while he makes me come in the light of day at our office.

I open my lips dutifully, and his fingers graze my tongue before tenderly putting the material in my mouth. He groans behind me, and grips one of my ass cheeks harshly before grinding against me again.

"You're such a good fucking girl for your daddy, you definitely deserve a reward."

Needing to be quiet, as well as having my panties in my mouth, I just nod my head and place my warm cheek against the cool wood of the desk. Aiden's chair squeaks as he sits back down and grabs my thighs. He toys with the end of the butt plug one more time before gently pulling it out. I bite down on the fabric to hold back a moan. The metal clinks against his desk top, and then he's on me as he eats my pussy from the comfort of his desk chair.

He moves quickly, I'm sure knowing the longer we stay in here together, the higher the chances are of getting caught. My heart beats against the table as he devours me, his lips wrapping around my clit in such a fervent way that if he doesn't make me come, he might die.

Aiden's tongue is magic, but what truly sends me over the edge, what makes me come so hard that my thighs shake, is when his phone rings to his office and it hits me like a ton of bricks—the CEO of Kemper's Sports Supply has his face pressed against my ass and pussy. I can feel myself wetting his face as I attempt to not make a single sound.

My panties muffle my breathing noises as he continues eating me out. It's only when I'm nearly trying to crawl over his desk to stop the sensation that he lets me go.

Aiden helps me sit up on his desk, and he gingerly takes the panties out of my mouth and places them in his pocket. He leans forward and kisses me, my taste plastered on his tongue and chin.

"Feel better?"

I nod my head, and Aiden helps me fix my hair and get me presentable enough to go back to my desk.

"What about you?" I ask breathlessly, and feel like a greedy bitch for having had that be just about me.

"There's no way I'd be able to keep quiet fucking that sweet pussy," he says with a smirk, and I lightly smack his chest.

"Maybe I should stuff my panties in your mouth and see how you do," I say, and he arches a brow at me.

"How about you come over tonight and ride my cock the way you want," he says, and I smile.

"Don't you leave for Atlanta early tomorrow?"

He leans in and kisses my jaw. "Yes, so I want every last second with you."

"I can drive home when you leave," I say, and he shakes his head.

"No, you can stay the night and come right to work. I'll give you a key."

I blink up at him a few times. He just ate me out while he sat in his office chair and now he's trusting me with a key to his house. I'm not sure that I deserve this treatment, but I'm going to take it anyway, so I give him one more kiss before I go and complete the rest of my work for the day.

I'm not exactly sure when I became so codependent on Aiden, though it's part of our relationship. I hate being at the cottage right now. Well, I'm hating being alone at the cottage right now. Today at the office sucked without Aiden. It's clear that people are on their best behavior at the office when he's around. I've gotta make sure that I talk to Aiden more about finding something else.

I grab a fork out of the top drawer so I can eat the Chinese food I picked up on my way home, when I see the back window facing the beach open. I could have sworn I shut that yesterday. There's a storm coming tonight, and it's fucking hot, so I walk over and shut the window and lock the hatch, shaking my head as I take my food into the living room.

I put on one of my favorite shows and have my phone up so I
can buy some items before our trip in two weeks.

> Aiden: *picture of him lying in his hotel bed,
> looking relaxed and sleepy*

> Aren't you cute?

> Aiden: This is true, what are you up to?

> Just eating, doing some shopping for our
> trip.

> Aiden: Send me the links of what you're
> looking at.

I shake my head, but send him about ten links at once. He
doesn't answer for twenty minutes. I just keep eating my food
and watching my show until my phone buzzes.

> Aiden: I got everything and then some, will
> be at my place when I get back.

> Thank you, Daddy.

> Aiden: Anything for my girl.

I'm feeling lonely, but having Aiden spoil me and
knowing that he'll be home in a few days brings me enough
comfort to get some sleep.

Jessa

Cracked Trauma Eggs

APPARENTLY THE BEST way to get over your nerves about going on vacation with your boyfriend's family is to go to a sex club poker game. Aiden said some of the ladies play, and if I wanted to, I could as well, but the idea of sitting on his lap and squirming in anticipation all night seemed a lot more my speed.

The dress that Aiden picked out for me is blush pink and adorable. It's a silky material, and while I'm covered, it's still sexy and gives him plenty of room to slide his hand up the skirt of the dress.

I've been hiding it pretty well, but I continue to worry about the other shoe dropping—that Aiden is going to do something I don't like and whether I'll be able to speak up. I stayed silent far too many times with Sean. I even hated his pet name for me, and I just never said anything. I cringed in silence. It makes my stomach hurt, and it makes me feel like the way he treated me was my fault because I never stood up for myself and told him that I didn't like something.

Like when he would go too far with spankings, I would just push through and bear it. And when he wasn't keen on aftercare, I would just go in the shower and silently cry while the warm water splattered against my body.

I feel like I've given Aiden this impression that I'm not scared to ask for what I want. It's truly hard for me, but I know I have to do it. If I go quiet again, I could find myself so lonely and hurt even when in a relationship, and I don't want that again. I also feel guilty for putting so much pressure on my relationship with Aiden. Everything he's shown me so far makes me feel like an asshole for having doubts.

I push this aside as I do my hair, Aiden requests it down. My hair isn't super curly, but when I use a few products and my diffuser it has a strong bounce to it. My heart squeezes in my chest. Sean always requested that my hair was bone straight or in a braid down my back.

I've got to stop comparing them, even though Aiden wins at every turn, it's just not fair to him that I have this scoreboard in my head.

My makeup is light, well, to the human eye. Meanwhile I spent forty-five minutes trying to achieve this look. But I'm feeling beautiful, and I refuse to let negative thinking get in my way tonight.

I'm going to need Aiden to spank me. I need to get out of my head. There's no better way to do that than letting your daddy take complete control for the night.

The door clicks, and Aiden steps behind me, his smile reflecting in the mirror as he grabs my waist and kisses the top of my head. I thoroughly enjoy how much taller he is than me. It makes me feel safe and cherished when he looks down at me like he is now. He looks so damn good, I'm about to cancel and tell him we should just stay home and play.

I love when Aiden is casual at a baseball game, and his

business casual clothes at work, but Aiden Carlson in a suit is just a complete panty dropper. He looks like a boss, which he is, but in all aspects, his expensive pressed suit demands compliance, and I plan on giving it to him.

"You ready to go?" he asks, placing another kiss to the top of my head before I nod. His brows furrow, and his fingers stroke down my arm, leaving a trail of goosebumps in his wake. "Everything okay?"

I spin around and grab his lapels. He immediately leans down to give me the kiss I need. "Everything is perfect."

"You look beautiful, baby." I smile at him and flatten his lapels back down and take some extra time to feel the expanse of his chest. Aiden isn't ripped, but his body is solid. He takes care of himself, and it shows. I love everything about his body, and I think that I need to tell him that more.

"Thank you for the dress. You look pretty damn good yourself."

"I'm starting to debate how bad I want to play in this game," he says as his hand travels south to squeeze my ass. I can't decide what would be better, being a needy, wet, begging mess sitting on his lap in front of others, or getting my gratification right away.

I chew on my lip while I contemplate. "I think I'd like to watch you play poker, maybe you can explain it to me."

He nods his head, letting go of my ass as we head to his garage to leave for the night. When we pull out of his house, I feel a moment of unease. I look around and don't see anything on the sidewalk or outside of his house. I chalk it up to nerves, and when Aiden squeezes my thigh, his watch chilling my skin, the feeling goes away immediately.

✻ ✻ ✻

I know I've made the right choice as I sit on Aiden's lap—the soft material of his pants pressed against my thighs is nearly as comforting as his hand possessively gripping my hip. I already knew that I liked being shown off this way by a partner, but with Aiden it feels more reverent. I feel completely cherished. Maybe it makes me a show-off or someone who needs validation from others, but the way Aiden only pays attention to me and his cards means I don't give a fuck.

Everyone at this table has no doubts who Aiden is with and that no one can have either of us. I guess that's truly a new facet of myself that I've learned. I like others being jealous of what I have.

Aiden is the most attractive man here. I'm sure someone will say that it's subjective, but they would be wrong. He's the most handsome, confident, and sexy man at Avalon tonight, and I like that everyone here knows that he doesn't share and has no other interest beyond me.

Maybe I'm a bigger princess than I realized. *Oh fucking well.*

I shift on Aiden's lap, begging for a little more attention, and he immediately gives it to me by placing a chaste kiss against my collarbone. He only has one hand since his other needs to be free to play the game, but the other one roams my body. Squeezing my hip, rolling my dress up slightly higher, and rubbing my back.

Leo is at our table, but his wife isn't on his lap, or anywhere to be seen, which I find extremely odd. But I know the rules, and I'd much prefer good girl spanks over punishment ones tonight. The difference between the two is usually when I get to come, and well, waiting around at this damn poker table is about as much waiting as I can take. There are four other men at the table, two of which have beautiful women on their laps.

If we were comparing though, none of them seems as genuinely attentive as Aiden, but that's none of my business. I'm not sure when I became such a possessive bitch, but having a man like Aiden will do that to you. I rub the back of his neck and toy with his hair as he plays.

"What do you say we make this more interesting?" Leo says, and I have to actively force myself to not look at him. The man gives off weird vibes. I'm not sure if he has an attraction toward Aiden or me, but I don't like it.

"Like you have anything we want?" one of the older men says—he must be nearly sixty, but in decent shape. The woman on his lap is easily my age. She looks happy enough to be here, so as long as she's getting what she wants out of this arrangement, I'm happy for her.

"Times getting a little rough?" Aiden says to Leo, and I have to turn my face to hide my smirk. Aiden grips my ass like a man marking what's his, and I squirm a little bit as Leo responds.

"You used to be so fun, Aiden." Aiden's hand grips me harder, and he puts his cards down to glare at the man across the table from me.

"What is this about, Leo? Are you upset that your wife isn't coming anymore because I'm not the one fucking her, or is there something else?"

I don't like Aiden talking about his previous arrangement with this couple, and he must sense it as he doubles down on his statement.

"I just don't understand why our arrangement had to change. I could have done the same for you with your little girl," Leo says, holding a hand in my direction. I swallow thickly at the term he just used, and my heart is racing in my chest. I didn't think it would hit me this hard, being called that. But I hate it. I feel sick and part of me just wants to run away.

I can hear Sean calling me that in a demeaning way. He always called me that as a way to put me down a peg, and even though I hated it, I never said anything. I doubt he would have stopped if I told him anyway. It was more for complete control and ownership to him, not a dominant affectionate relationship.

All my excitement from earlier feels squashed. I just want to go home and sleep. How can two little words make so much insecurity bubble up inside of me? Aiden must sense this written on my face as he glares over at Leo, wrapping both his arms around me in a protective hold.

"Part of being at this club is respecting boundaries. I placed one. I'm only with Jessa from here on out. So stop being a little bitch and find someone else to cuck your ass."

There's a noticeable silence filled with shocked glances toward Aiden and me. The comeback came so quickly for Aiden, and I can't help but be attracted to him even more.

"I don't even see what the fuss is about," Leo says, waving his hand at me again. I swallow.

"Hop up, baby," he says softly in my ear, which I do. Aiden directs me to sit in his chair and a few of the girls look at me with wide eyes as he walks around the table.

He straightens out his lapels as he places a hand on the poker table to lean in and get in Leo's face. The man swallows thickly as he looks up at Aiden, who grins maniacally as he gets in his face and speaks loud enough for everyone at the table to hear.

"I know your feelings are hurt, aren't they, you little cuck?" Leo's face is red but he doesn't speak as Aiden puts a finger in his face. "I'm going to tell you this once: she doesn't exist to you. Don't even fucking look at her, speak to her, or even think about her. You bring up my girl again and we're going to have some real fucking problems. Problems bigger than your wife not getting off 'cause her husband is a pathetic, weak, little man. You got me?"

Multiple women shift on their partner's lap, and I don't blame them. I'm so wet from this encounter I'm clenching my thighs together.

"You're excused. Cash out," Aiden says to him before rounding the table and taking my hand, helping me stand before sitting back down and placing me back on his crotch. Leo doesn't say anything back, and I'm not sure if he hated or loved Aiden telling him off. I've never been a part of a dynamic like that, but part of being cuckolded is being degraded.

Aiden moves my hair to fall down my back and kisses my exposed shoulder before looking around the table.

"Does anyone else have a problem?" he says and there's a shaking of heads. If anything, it's a look of respect from multiple men around the table.

He leans in against me so he's only speaking to me. "Are you okay, do you want to leave?"

I shake my head no. I'm still feeling a little exposed from my reaction to Leo's words, but I'm equally as turned on by Aiden's. There's a lot going on inside of me right now.

"What was it specifically that made you tense up?" Aiden says softly. To the others at the table, it probably looks like he's just whispering nasty things to me, but I find a lot of their attention is directed elsewhere. Partly because Aiden just laid down the law, and half of the men have pretty women on their laps to occupy their time anyway.

I take a deep breath. "Little girl. I don't like that term at all. Sean used to call me it in an insulting way, and it just brought up some less than great feelings." He nods and brings his lips to mine and grabs my chin so I'm forced to look him in the eyes.

"You tell Daddy when something bothers you, always." It's not a question, it's a rule, and I like rules. I nod my head and his grip on my chin brings his lips back to mine. "Do you want to go home?" he asks, looking over my face, trying to read my feelings.

I blink a few times, knowing that Sean would have been pissed if I asked to leave after we got all dressed up to go to an event like this. But if I'm being honest, my head is all over the place, and the idea of having everyone at this club see me that vulnerable feels like too much.

"I don't want you to have to miss your game," I say, and he scoffs.

"Fuck the game. What do you need?" His green eyes are soft, and it's at this moment that I think the comparisons in my head can stop, even if most of them are in Aiden's favor, I'm so tired of second guessing myself because I'm jaded from Sean. I'm ready to completely give myself to Aiden and that means letting the past go.

"Can we go home?"

He squeezes my hips roughly and leans into my ear. "Good girl telling Daddy what you need."

Who would have thought the moment I knew I was absolutely in love with this man would be sitting on his lap at a sex club? I wrap my arms around his neck and rest my face against his chest, not wanting him to read my face right now. He holds me tightly, until I let go and leans in to give me a smile and a kiss before excusing us from the table.

He shows me what a good girl I am in private, and at this moment I wouldn't want it any other way. I feel safe and truly cherished for the first time in my life, and the thought of meeting his family now has me even more nervous, because I'm never letting this man go.

Aiden

Again, Why Couldn't I Be An Only Child?

I DIDN'T WANT to scare the shit out of Jessa and take the chartered plane with my family. I am hoping things go well enough to fly back with them.

So for now, we're getting on a commercial flight that stops in Miami before flying to North Eleuthera. At least it's just one stop. God, I sound like a spoiled shit.

I'm grateful that Jessa is openly accepting of gifts and presents. If anything, it makes her extremely happy, and I just can't help myself. When I hand her the new, and very pink, noise canceling headphones I got her for the flight, she just thanks me and showers me with kisses.

"Are you still feeling nervous?"

She shrugs her shoulders. "Yeah, a little. I mean, I know it doesn't feel like it, but this is still new, and I want your family to like me."

"They will, I promise."

"Lincoln didn't seem to like me."

I shake my head and make a note to punch my brother in the arm when we get to the house. "Linc is just a fucking asshole and he had been drinking, it had nothing to do with you."

She nods, and I take her hand in mine. "They're going to love you."

Her gaze meets mine, and I know the word is thick between the both of us, but we don't say anything. It feels like we've been on cloud nine lately, and I don't want to say anything that shifts that balance. I feel like Jessa was made for me, and I'm excited for my family to meet her, but I know that this is going to be the moment that things get real for everyone. I've never brought a girl on vacation with my family before.

The plane ride is longer than I would like, but it is what it is. We're finally in the tropical paradise I've grown accustomed to. The car picking us up from the airport is on time and Jessa looks at our surroundings through the window the entire drive.

I honestly considered renting our own place for the trip, but I knew it would hurt my mom's feelings. While the vacation home is large, it only has two master bedrooms. The thought of sharing a queen bed with Jessa while one of my brothers or cousin is in the same room feels kind of gross. But I'm sure we can all be adults, and I can keep my hands to myself—for the most part.

"Can I have a rundown of your family again?" Jessa asks, I knead her thigh in her cute little sundress and give her a soft smile.

"I'm the oldest. Linc is three years younger than me. The twins are Gavin and Benjamin, he usually goes by Ben. They both just turned thirty and are something else." I shrug and she smiles, not sure how to explain my brothers who seem to not have a care in the world. "My parents are Maggie and Jeff, my aunt is my mother's sister, Holly and her husband Tim."

"Penny's parents?"

"Yes, they adopted her when she was three. She's a year younger than the twins and their only child."

"Is there anything I shouldn't bring up or talk about, any touchy subjects?"

"Not really, my family is just a little chaotic at times. If you ever need a break, just tell me and I'll get you out of there." She nods and rests her head on my shoulder. "I promise you have nothing to worry about."

She sighs and leans to kiss my jaw. "I know you wouldn't put me in a bad position." I can't help myself when I grip her chin and kiss her far more passionately than I should with a stranger driving the car. When we break apart, she gives me the smile I've become addicted to, the one she gives when I've pleased her.

I'm not sure how I've earned her trust, but I'm sure as fuck not going to break it. When we pull up to the house, her jaw drops.

"Holy fucking shit. Your parents have fuck you money."

I clear my throat but don't reply as the driver opens the door and I hold out my hand for her to get out of the car. We're assaulted by the humidity, and I get our luggage as we walk to the front door. Jessa is just taking it all in as I open the front door. It seems like luck is on our side and everyone is outside. I'm about to show Jessa around the house before we meet my family.

She looks shell shocked by the house and doesn't even bat an eye at the room we will be staying in with multiple beds.

"Looks like the twins will be in here with us," I say, feeling a little insecure about the whole thing.

"This place is beautiful," she says, looking around as we walk through the upstairs, and I show her each room. The kitchen is massive with a large table that seats twelve and connects with the living room that has a ridiculous sized sectional and massive TV.

"You ready?" I ask her, and she swallows and nods her head. I take her smaller hand in mine and slide the glass door connected to the living room open. The breeze from the ocean hits us right away, and I see my family on the lower deck. We walk down, and we're greeted with smiles all around.

"You made it!" Penny says, wrapping her arms around Jessa and giving her a tight hug.

My family acts like I'm a goddamn ghost as they all introduce themselves one by one. Jessa seems a little overwhelmed but takes it in stride, shaking hands and giving them a true smile. I give my mom a stern look that says now is not the time for an interrogation, and she rolls her eyes at me.

"Why don't we all get ready for dinner? Xavier will be plating everything outside in the next half hour."

Jessa blinks at me a few times, and I hold her closer. I can't help but notice multiple pairs of eyes tracking the motion.

Jesus fucking Christ.

I don't think I prepared Jessa enough, or myself, for how bewildered my family would be seeing me so affectionate with someone.

Everyone is scattering to go get showered or changed. They have been here for hours, and we just got here.

"Is what I'm wearing okay?" Jessa whispers. When I look around and none of my family is around, I cup her face, lean down, and give her a kiss.

"You look perfect." She looks nervous as fuck, and I stroke my thumbs against her face in a soothing motion. "Are you okay?"

"Everyone seems nice, but..." I tilt my head for her to continue, and she sighs. "Are they going to think I'm good enough for you?" It's almost like she slapped me when I physically recoil from that insecure thought. Jessa has her moments of being passive, or unconfident with others. But the more we've gotten to know each other I've seen her for the beautifully confident woman she is, and to know she's feeling this way hurts me.

I lean forward, kissing her head. "I don't want to hear you say that kind of shit again. I don't care that we're on vacation with my family. I will find somewhere to spank your pretty little ass and remind you who you belong to. If you need a reminder of how good you are for me, just let me know, kitten."

She swallows, and her pupils dilate as she looks at me. "This is just a lot."

"I think I should have done a better job preparing you, that's on me. But I never want to hear you say anything about being good enough for me. You're fucking everything."

She blinks up at me a few times, before fisting my shirt and dragging me down to give her a kiss.

"I'll be good, Daddy," she says, before her perfect, in need of a spanking, mischievous ass walks back into the house.

This is going to be a long weekend.

❊ ❊ ❊

Dinner is going as normal as it could be and I'm so thankful it isn't the inquisition toward Jessa and me. I'm wondering who enforced that, my guess is Penny and my mom.

"Bonfire tonight," Gavin declares. There are a bunch of nods of agreement.

"We're going to go to Ronnie's tonight," my dad says, and I can't decide if that was planned or if they think having a smaller group will help make everything more comfortable for Jessa.

"We're still going fishing tomorrow?" Lincoln asks, and my dad and Tim both nod in agreement. I lean over to whisper to Jessa.

"You can come fishing or stay here." She's about to answer, when Penny leans in from the other side.

"Fishing fucking sucks. We're doing a beach day and shopping."

She smiles at Penny before gripping my hand under the table. "The beach and shopping sounds nice."

"Only if you're sure." I notice my mom staring at us with a serene look on her face.

"So, Jessa, are you enjoying working at Kemper's?" my mom asks.

"I like working with Penny and Aiden. I don't think it's what I want to do forever, but it's been nice learning new things."

News to me. I guess I haven't asked how fulfilled she is in her position, and I make a mental note to ask her more about that later.

"How long have you been vacationing here?" Jessa asks, my mom smiles and tilts her head.

"It feels like forever. Since the twins were born, for sure. We try to come a few times a year and rent it out the rest of the year."

"It's beautiful," Jessa says, her hand in mine under the table.

"Thank you, Jessa. We're so happy to have you here." My mom smiles at Jessa, and I hope she can see how sincere she's being. Now I just have to figure out how to make sure my brothers don't say anything fucking stupid tonight.

The bonfire is in a hole in the sand, Gavin has music going, and Ben and Linc carry out a cooler of drinks. We're one chair short, and I immediately pop down in one and drag Jessa to my lap. She stills, and I tap her thigh and lean in to whisper in her ear.

"It's fine, relax." Her body shifts against my lap a little closer, and I wrap my arms around her. Linc hands us two beers, and I know Jessa will sip it but not drink the whole thing.

"Who would have thought that big bro would bring a girl on vacation. I thought you were going to become a cat lady, Aiden," Ben jokes, and I roll my eyes.

"True, I thought his social security would be on auto-pay to Avalon," Linc says. He's been a real fucking dick lately, and I wish I knew why.

I narrow my eyes at him, but Jessa speaks up.

"It will be, except it will be a couples membership." Ben

and Gavin start cackling and Linc gives Jessa a nod of approval with her comeback. It seems like my sweet Jessa has a hard time standing up for herself, but when it comes to me, my little kitten seems to have claws.

"Can we talk about something else besides Avalon?" Penny says, directing it toward Lincoln, who gives her a shrug of his shoulders. "It's so nice to have another girl, don't you fuckers ruin this for me," Penny says, pointing at each one of my brothers. The twins hold up their hands in mock surrender, and she glares at them a little before turning and smiling at Jessa.

"So, what did our precious brother have to do to nab you? It surely wasn't his ugly mug," Gavin says, and I take a deep breath before Jessa shakes her head. Clearly catching on that my brothers are a bunch of dickheads and this is how we show our love.

"I did have to look past his face, you're right." My twin brothers and Penny laugh as she leans closer to me. "But if I had to pinpoint a moment, it was probably when he took a splinter out of my finger and kissed it."

Penny makes an aww sound while my brothers act like they're gagging. "Disgusting," Gavin says.

"One day you two will eventually stop acting like children."

"We're planning on being single forever," Ben says for the both of them, and Gavin nods in agreement.

"Single by choice or because no one wants to date you assholes?" Penny asks, and I feel Jessa's back shake from a small laugh.

"We can't all date a bunch of winners like you, Penny,"

Gavin says, and Penny glares at my brothers. To no surprise Lincoln steps in for her.

"Will you two shut the fuck up, already?" he says, glaring at my brothers. Jessa stills slightly in my lap, but then relaxes again.

"What about you, Lincoln, hmm? You can't seem to hold down a girlfriend either," Ben says, always wanting to get under Linc's skin. He always lets them; it's a never ending cycle.

"I'm going to head in for the night," Penny says, not waiting to hear Lincoln's answer and giving Jessa a small wave before walking back in the house.

"Yeah, I'm done too. Make sure you put the fire out," he says to Gavin and Ben.

Ben rolls his eyes and looks at his twin. "Beach walk?" he says, holding out a joint and lighting it. He holds it up toward Jessa and me, and I shake my head with a sigh.

"Still a straight-laced asshole," Gavin says.

"Will you two just fuck off," I say, and Jessa laughs. Both of my brothers give her a salute as they walk down the beach and share a joint.

I spin Jessa in my arms, her legs around my thighs in the large beach chair.

"Thank you for coming with me. I know my family is a lot. But it means a lot to me and them that you came."

Her dark hair blows in the night air, and I can't help but think about how beautiful she looks right now.

"Your family is fun so far. I've never seen so much ball-busting before, but it seems like the way your brothers express themselves."

I shrug my shoulders. She leans against my chest, and my arms wrap around her.

"Are you sure you're okay hanging out with the girls tomorrow?"

She nods against my chest. "Yeah, it will be great. I'll have Penny. It will be fine."

"We'll have the afternoon and then the day after I can show you the island."

She perks up, sitting up and gripping my shoulders as she smiles. "I'd love that."

All I want to say back is how much I love her, but I hold it back and kiss her instead.

Jessa

Motherly Hugs

IT TOOK me a while to fall asleep last night. Thankfully Gavin and Ben went to sleep quickly. But it was still a little awkward sharing a bed with Aiden and having them in the same room. I'm more than willing to let strangers watch Aiden and me do very naughty things, but the idea of his brothers seeing us cuddled together in the morning just makes me feel strange.

I'm woken up at what feels like the crack of dawn by Aiden kissing my face.

"Baby, I've got to go. Have fun with the girls today."

I barely open my eyes as I kiss him, completely ready to go back to sleep. "Be safe," I say groggily. He laughs and kisses my face again.

"I put some money in your purse. Get lots of pretty things, okay?"

"Okay, Daddy." I hear a whistle from the top bunk where Gavin is sleeping, and I groan. "Fuck."

"Gavin, I swear to God, I'll throw you off the fucking boat today if you bring this up."

"Okay... Daddy," Gavin says. I hear the tossing of pillows

and curses as I burrow myself deeper into the bed, wishing I could be suffocated by the sheets. There's a bunch of movement in the room as the blankets are ripped off of me and Aiden is kissing my face again.

"Don't worry about that asshole. I'll see you later tonight."

"Okay." He kisses me one more time, and there's nothing quite like the mortifying moment of your boyfriend's brother hearing you call him daddy to prevent you from falling back to sleep.

I lie in bed for a ridiculously long time before giving up and showering and getting ready for the day. I've never met anyone's mom before, and I'm nervous to be spending one-on-one time with her, but she's been warm so far, and I need her to know how much I care about Aiden.

I go with a green sundress and put my hair up in a long pony tail with how fucking hot it is here. Sunblock is a must, and I put it on before heading up to the kitchen. Maggie and Holly are both drinking coffee and eating breakfast when I take a seat.

"Morning," Maggie says with a smile.

"Morning," I reply, grabbing a pastry and some bacon and sitting down in my seat.

"Where in the world is my daughter? I'm going to go find her," Holly says, leaving me alone at the table with Maggie.

"It's so nice to see my son happy with someone.I always worried he would get in his own way when finding someone. But it's clear you make him so happy, which means I'm happy," she says softly and in such a motherly tone.

"He makes me really happy too. You raised an amazing son."

"Now I just have to worry about the other three." She lets out a puff of breath and I can imagine her frustration. Gavin and Benjamin seem like they're in no rush to grow up. And what I know about Lincoln, well he's in love with someone he shouldn't be. Surprisingly, no one else in this family has picked up on that tidbit. I'm not sure if Penny was a little too drunk that night at Whiskey Joe's, but she hasn't brought it up either. So, my lips are sealed on the Lincoln and Penny front. My only job right now is to make Aiden happy and survive this weekend without his family hating me.

Penny and Holly come back into the room, and we finish breakfast, Penny clearly didn't sleep a ton last night. Using my deductive reasoning, I can guess it's because she and Lincoln are sharing a room, which no one in this family seems to think is strange.

Aiden put a ridiculous amount of cash in my purse this morning, and I plan on buying us both something with it. We start off at a few clothing shops. I get myself a floppy hat and a new pair of flip flops. Holly and Maggie act like money isn't real and spend to their heart's content. Penny only grabs a few things like I do.

The next stop is the jewelry store, and I find a few things I'm definitely not leaving behind. There's a necklace with a baseball bat and it just seems too symbolic and cute. I can't help purchasing it.

Maggie is next to me when I'm checking out. "Aiden will love that," she says.

"I think so too." She has this crystal bunny in her hand, and I have to hold back my emotions as I look at it.

"Everything okay, honey?"

I shake my head. "My mom just used to call me bunny."

"She isn't with us anymore?"

"No, it's been a few years now."

"And Collin was your father?"

"My biological father," I say sadly.

"That's got to be a lot to go through," she says softly. "Would you be okay with me gifting this to you?" she asks, holding the bunny, and I have to try so hard to hold back the tears that want to stream down my face. I just nod instead. She offered, and it's clear the woman isn't hard for cash, plus it's just a sweet gesture. Maggie puts the bunny on the counter to pay, and when I look into her green eyes that are so much like Aiden's, all I feel is comfort. "Can I hug you?" she asks, and I nod my head again.

Maggie wraps her arms around me, and she smells like coconut and honey. Her hug is so motherly and soft that I just let myself melt against her. I'm not sure what I feel at that moment; it's a combination of things. I feel loved, sadness, and hope all at once. Maggie rubs my back softly before we part.

She hands me the case that the bunny is in, and I hold it tightly. "I obviously don't know anything about your mother, but I can't help but feel that if she were here, she would be proud."

"Thank you, Maggie."

"Anytime, honey."

I somehow manage to hold it together the rest of the day,

dissociating and not thinking too much about how I felt when Maggie hugged me.

It's a totally different story when we get back to the beach house. I tell everyone I'm just going to check out the beach for a minute. Penny almost insists on coming, but I think the look on my face speaks volumes that I need a minute alone.

I grab a towel, take it outside with me, and lay it down before taking a seat. The beach is gorgeous and the white noise of the waves is serene as I finally let myself break.

Something I haven't afforded myself in a long time. I always knew grief was something you carry with you until you die and pass that grief onto others. A few weeks ago, I thought my grief would end with me, that no one would be sad if I died. But being here, the way Aiden's mom held me, the way that Aiden treats me, I know that isn't true anymore.

But it doesn't change this lingering feeling of being left behind. The tears stream down my face as I think about the way my mom would hug me, and how Collin never even had the chance to give me that parental comfort. I know Aiden thinks his family is a lot, but there isn't much I wouldn't trade to have what he has.

A presence next to me startles me, and I start wiping my tears when I see Aiden's horrified face.

"Oh my fucking God, what happened?" I sniffle and shake my head as he joins me on the towel. "Which one of my family members do I need to yell at?"

"None," I say softly.

"What happened?" he asks, wrapping an arm around me and holding me at the waist.

"Nothing."

"Baby, you're crying, that's not nothing."

"I was just thinking about my parents."

"Do you want to talk more about it?" he says, and usually I would say no, not wanting to burden someone else with my feelings. But I know I can be vulnerable with Aiden, that he will be that support I haven't had and so desperately need.

I sigh and rest my head against his shoulder. "Your mom hugged me today and bought me a bunny."

I don't have to see his face to know he's confused. "A bunny? Like an animal?"

A small laugh escapes me. "No, it was a crystal bunny. It's what my mom called me. I know I've told you a little about her. She had her problems, her own monsters that eventually took her. But I loved her, and there were times when she was so shiny and bright. In those moments, I was the center of her world. Most of the other times she was just more absent. She wasn't mean or abusive. She would just disappear. But when she was present, even if she was high on something, she was so fun and told me how much she loved me."

"Of course she did," he says softly, and I rub under my eyes.

"I think when she first died I was so angry, you know? That I wasn't enough for her to sober up. That she left me and that she never tried harder. And in the past couple of years, I've just avoided truly thinking about her. Even with her problems, I still wish she was here. I'm just so sick of being mad at my parents." A bout of fresh tears pour down my face, and I feel so fucking stupid for crying in paradise. Aiden scoops me up in his arms, placing me on his lap.

"Hey," he says, using his thumbs to wipe away my tears. "You can feel however you need to, baby. I got you."

That just makes me cry harder as I wrap my arms around him and hold on for dear life.

"I don't want to be mad anymore. I want to love and grieve them for who they were," I say, and Aiden holds me tighter.

"Okay, just tell me how I can help."

I look up at him. I'm sure I look a mess. But the way he looks at me is like I'm precious, it's the only thing I've ever wanted. I stroke his face. "Just being you, that's all I need."

His lips meet mine, my tears transferring to his cheeks, and I think it's the first time I've truly been seen in my entire life.

Aiden

Kissing In The Rain

THE LONG WEEKEND appears to be bringing out more for Jessa than I anticipated, but it seems like something she needed. At least my family has been extremely welcoming and loves her, which isn't a surprise to me at all. I'm just happy we have the whole day together. I'm definitely feeling guilty for leaving her with my mom yesterday. Even if she did need to let those feelings out, I never want to see her crying sad tears.

The first part of the day is with my siblings and Penny, going jet skiing. Gavin was in charge of booking this and of course he fucked it up.

"We only have three available for today. We could get some paddleboards out," the owner says, and Gavin shakes his head.

"Penny can share with Linc, and Ben and I will take turns," Gavin says and no one else seems to have any problems with this arrangement. I thought Linc might complain, but the grumpy bastard just zips up his life jacket and hops onto his jet ski before holding out a hand for Penny to hop on the back.

I spin around and look at Jessa, who looks insanely fucking good in her black bikini and sunglasses right now. She puts the pink life jacket on, I zip it for her, and she gives me a smile before we get on our own jet ski. Her grip is tight on my waist as I start the engine and we start riding over the water. She laughs, and I can't help but smile at the sound, and it makes me get more creative with our movements and how fast we're going. At a certain point, I lull the engine and have to turn slightly to speak with her.

"Do you want to drive?"

"Hell yeah," she says, and I wonder how the fuck we're going to maneuver this. Jessa just uses my body to hold herself steady as she climbs over me. I have to scoot back and give her room. I loathe the lifejackets and the way they separate us. She takes me by surprise, and the jet ski lurches forward as she hits the throttle. I have to grip her hips and life jacket so my ass doesn't go flying off.

If I thought her laughter and excitement was palpable when she was just riding, letting her drive brings out another side of her. She's acting like she's a trained professional or in a stunt movie as she goes fast as fuck, doing circles.

She even makes a sharp turn and sprays Gavin and Ben on their jet ski—which has me laughing hysterically—and turns into a dangerous high speed water tag.

Once our time is up, we bring the jet ski in and everyone seems to have a permanent smile on their face, minus Lincoln.

"We'll see you guys back at the house," I say, waving my brothers and Penny off and taking Jessa's hand in mine. She throws on her dress over her bikini, and I grab my shirt as we walk over to the restaurant for lunch.

"That was so fun. We should do it again."

"Okay, Evil Knievel."

"I wasn't going that fast," she says, and I laugh.

"If you say so."

"Well, I do say so. I'm starving. Where are we eating?" I lift my hand, and we walk into the dive bar. One of the things I like about Jessa is how willing she is to accept gifts, but how content she is just being with me no matter where we are.

I put our orders in and we sip our drinks on the outdoor patio. "What are we doing this afternoon?" she says.

"Thought we could go for a walk, spend some time at the beach."

"Sounds good to me," she says with a smile, but she fidgets with the pineapple piece in her cocktail. "I'm not taking you away from spending time with your family, am I?"

I shake my head. "We will see them this afternoon, and we just went jet skiing with my brothers. You're not hoarding me. If anything, I'm just making sure you get them in doses so you don't realize how insane they all are and decide to leave."

"I like your family a lot," she says with a shrug. "I've never been around a family who jokes like yours or has this much money." She grimaces but continues. "But I like it. I feel welcomed, and it would take a lot more than your family being difficult that would make me run for the hills."

"What would be a deal breaker for you?" I ask. Her big brown eyes blink at me, and I try to not let any insecurity seep through my expression.

She smiles at me sincerely. "Unless you have a secret wife or are against a woman's right to choose, then I think we're pretty solid."

"Good," I say, hiding my relief. I'm not sure why I still

can't grapple with the thought that I deserve Jessa. Maybe there's some residual guilt with her being Collin's daughter or that we're still keeping this a secret at the office. But I need to let these things go. It's obvious she's as dedicated as I am in this relationship, and I can't self-sabotage this.

We eat our food, and I take her hand in mine as we walk down the beach. The clouds start to look a little ominous, but we keep walking. Her hand feels so right in mine, and it's just so easy to hold a conversation or stay completely silent.

When I see how much bluer the sky is in the direction we came from, I go to spin us so we can walk back when the flood gates open. Rain is just pelting down on us. We look at each other and just start laughing as we attempt to run in the sand. Small droplets of water splatter on the hot material, cooling it down.

It takes us a while until we reach a spot with a few palm trees. We're both soaking wet as we catch our breath and there's this moment. Between a light laugh and trying to breathe when we both just look at each other.

It's then that I know I'm completely fucking in love with this woman.

I'm not sure what I look like, but I can just tell she's thinking the same thing as me. I don't care that we're still getting drenched despite being by the trees, I take her face in my hands and kiss her hard. Hoping that my feelings for her are clear in the kiss. She's slightly shaking, and I don't know if it's because she's cold or maybe she's just as overwhelmed as me.

"Aiden?" she says softly between our kisses.

"I love you," I tell her, pulling back slightly, still holding her face and reading her expression. Her face softens, and her eyes look watery as she smiles up at me.

"I love you too."

My mouth is back on her in a second. I've never felt this much need to devour someone in my life. It's like I can't get as physically close to Jessa as I need to. I want every part of her body touching me, and I never want this feeling to end.

I don't give a shit that I'm drenched and cold; my adrenaline and thrashing heart beat keep me warm enough as I take my hand away from her face to grip her ass.

I'm not even sure when we started moving, but her back is pressed against the trunk of a palm tree, and I'm suddenly gripping her thighs and wrapping her legs around me. The tree and my hands hold her in place while I grind my cock against her covered pussy.

"Take my cock out and push your bikini to the side," I say. It takes a moment for her mind to catch up with what I said. As I hold her up, I watch as she uses her hand to dip into my swim shorts and pull my cock out of the top.

She pushes her back harder against the tree as she pulls her bottoms to the side and lifts her dress just enough to give me access.

I thrust into her, and the back of her head thuds against the bark of the tree. The only sounds besides her whimpers are the crashing of the waves and the rain beating against us and the surrounding area.

There's no finesse to how I'm fucking her. It's just a complete urgency and need to claim her completely as mine. She needs it just as badly as me when she wraps her arms around my shoulders and brings me closer.

I thrust into her hard, and she moans deeply. "Fuck, I'm going to come." I haven't finished this early in a very long time, but the high emotion, being outside, and how fucking good she feels is too much to take.

"Please come inside of me," she says.

I groan, and my face is right next to hers, placing frantic kisses over every inch I can reach. "Play with that pretty pussy for Daddy. I need you to come first."

She makes a noise but slides one hand from my neck down her front and between our two pelvises where she plays with her clit.

"I'm going to need you to do that for me at home next time so I can watch," I tell her, and her head tilts back, giving me access to her neck, which I kiss and suck as I fuck her. Not until I feel her clenching around me and her thighs are shaking under my hands, do I finally stop holding back and really fuck her through her orgasm and reach my own.

I take her mouth in mine as I fill her with my cum and continue holding her in my arms. We both stare at each other, my wet cock inside of her and the rain pouring around us. She pushes my wet hair back off of my face and smiles at me.

"I love you," she says softly, like she'll never get tired of telling me that. I can't help but feel the same way.

"I love you too." We kiss again before I put her down gently, making me slide out of her. With a ridiculous amount of masculine pride, I adjust her bottoms and dress, knowing I'll be dripping out of her this afternoon. She rolls her eyes, knowing where my mind is going, but doesn't say anything as I tuck my dick away and we stare at the rainy beach. When there's a pop of thunder, we both jump and that's my sign we need to get the fuck out of here.

I call my dad and have him meet us at the closest public road. Jessa and I look like drowned rats when he finally meets us, but despite being cold as hell, I've never had a bigger smile on my face, and it's clear that my dad notices.

It's our last day on the island before we go home tomorrow morning, and I wish we could just stay here. There's no office drama, no one trying to hurt Jessa, no bullshit to deal with. But it's real life. I'll have to talk to her about telling the office, because there's no way either of us can keep this a secret much longer.

It was easier when we were just seeing where this was going, but it's clear that we both know where we stand now, and it seems like the appropriate time to make our relationship status clear. Once everyone knows I'm her boyfriend, there's no holding myself back when it comes to Zach or Tabitha.

Jessa is still sleeping, and I'm out on the porch drinking a coffee when my dad joins me.

"It's good to see you so happy, Son."

"Thanks, Dad."

"Your mom says she has a lot that she's working through right now. You're up for that challenge?"

I furrow my eyebrows and look at my dad, trying to see if he disapproves or if he doubts that I can give Jessa everything she needs. "Yeah, I'm there for what she needs."

My dad smiles. "You deserve this happiness. You've always been so hard on yourself. Never thinking you deserved your accomplishments, even when you did great things. You're a good man. I'm proud to be your dad."

I blink at him and take a sip of my coffee before I ask him a question I never thought to ask him before. "How did you know mom was the one?"

"We made each other better. And I knew that if I lost her it would be the biggest mistake of my life." My dad clears his throat. "She's a bit younger than you. Do you think she's ready for that?"

"I don't think either of us are there, yet. But I think she could be the one."

"Then don't let her go and just keep doing what you're doing. Loving someone truly sometimes means you have to swallow your pride and let them take care of you too."

"My job is to take care of her," I say with confusion.

"Of course you should take care of her, but you need to make sure you don't let your pride get in the way and not accept when she wants to return the same care to you."

I'm not completely understanding my dad's words, but I nod anyway. There are many ways that Jessa makes me feel loved and cared for, but it's my job to make sure she's safe and wants for nothing.

"I have a feeling we'll be seeing her next year, just don't let yourself get in the way of your own happiness," he says, slapping me on the shoulder and heading off.

I stand there for a few moments, drinking my coffee and staring at the ocean. I think back to my last letter from Collin and how he wished for me to make sure his kids were okay. I'm not sure what I can do on the Zach front, and I'm sure this isn't what he had in mind for Jessa. But if he could see how happy I make her, how much I care for her, I can't help but think he would be supportive.

It's the last push I need mentally to get ready for the next step in our relationship. When we get home, we need to go public at the office. I want her in my bed every night, and I'm going to do what my dad said and not get in my own way.

I'm all fucking in.

Jessa

Exposed

GOING BACK to work on Tuesday is a complete buzz kill. I stayed at Aiden's last night, purely for convenience, and maybe I'm slightly addicted to waking up next to him. But, given the choice between staying in The Bahamas or coming back here, I would pick The Bahamas every single time.

We're an hour late because he somehow seduced me this morning, and we're clearly unable to have a quickie.

Aiden parks in the back of the building, and we kiss one more time before walking toward the office. Penny is out front ripping taped pictures, and I tilt my head at her.

"Fuck, I thought I'd be able to get them all down by the time you got here," she says, her cheeks pink as I walk closer and see the picture. It's a still shot of us kissing on the kiss cam at the Rays game.

"Okay, so everyone knows we kissed," I say in a calm but irritated tone.

Penny pales. "Zach is on a bit of a tirade inside."

"Who put these up?" Aiden asks, taking my hand, and Penny looks just as frustrated as him.

"I called our security company and asked for the footage."

"Thank you," Aiden says, and Penny keeps ripping them down as Aiden pulls me to the side. "I was tired of keeping it a secret anyway. Are you okay with everyone knowing?"

I sigh. "Yeah, I'm okay."

"I'm not going to let Zach or anyone else treat you differently because of this."

"I'm not sure if their treatment can get any worse." He folds his arms and takes a deep breath, looking up at the sky. "I've been thinking about finding another job." He looks down at me with a frown.

"What?"

"I mean, I love being with you all day, but I don't really enjoy what I do. I think I want to go back to doing freelance, or I was thinking about creating some apparel designs. I was worried you wouldn't like me leaving."

"Baby, I want you to be happy."

I shrug my shoulders. "I think I want to save some more money first because I don't know how quickly I'll be able to get business."

He arches an eyebrow at me and shakes his head. "You know I'll help you get up and running."

"I know, and I love you for it. But I think I need this to be something I achieve on my own, you know?" Usually, I would accept his gift with no hesitation, but the thought of being on my ass again because I let a man provide everything is terrifying. I hate thinking negatively, always thinking about how things could go wrong, but when life has proven to me over and over that it loves to fuck me over, I have to protect myself.

I also want to prove to myself that I can do it on my own terms.

"You could move in with me and sell the cottage," he says, and I stare at him. As much as I want that, I can't do this again. Be left on my ass if this fails. I never want to be that floundering mess of a girl ever again. I have faith in Aiden, and deep in my bones I know he's a good man. I can't see this going south, but didn't I think the same thing when I first started dating Sean?

I want to be able to completely hand over all my trust and dreams in Aiden's caring hands, but I can't help but feel afraid to do that. What we have now is amazing, and I know eventually it will lead to more, but I feel like I have something to prove to myself. That I want Aiden, not that I need him. I'm more than willing for him to be in control of most things, but I want it to be a choice, not because I can't take care of myself.

"Can we put a pin in that for later?" I ask him, and he sighs and nods his head.

"Let's go get this over with," he says as we walk into the office together. It feels like I have a red target on my head as every pair of eyes stares at us as we walk in. Heads popping up over gray cubicles. And then there's smug Zach as he leans against the doorframe of Aiden's office. I can feel the tension rolling off of these two, and I know that if it doesn't get defused soon, it's going to explode all over this office.

"Did you have a good time in The Bahamas?" Zach says, looking at Aiden, and I can tell that he doesn't really give a shit, he's just trying to get under Aiden's skin.

"Good. Excuse me," Aiden says, trying to walk past Zach and into his office.

"What did you do for the holiday weekend, Jessica?" I fucking hate being called Jessica and I've told him this so many times. It's become clear that no matter how hard I try, Zach and I will never be anything, and I've accepted it. If anything, I'm about ready to give him a piece of my mind. Now that everything's out in the open, what does it matter? He was never going to be kind or gracious to me, and I'm so sick of the high road.

I ignore him and sit at my desk. He leans against the thin cubicle wall with a smirk on his face. "So you couldn't just help yourself, huh? Couldn't just come here and take shares that don't belong to you? You decided that you needed to fuck the boss too."

I can hear Aiden getting out of his seat, and I'm already scrubbing my hand over my face. No job is worth this, I was already dreading coming into the office, and dealing with Zach is the last thing I want to do.

"Zach, that's enough. If you have a problem with our relationship you can bring it up with me," Aiden says. His tone is calm, but I can sense his anger bubbling up under the surface.

Zach spins on his heel to look at Aiden. "What a great way to treat your best friend by fucking his bastard daughter."

That's it.

Fuck the high road and fuck this douchebag I somehow share DNA with. I've never gotten physical with someone, but I shove him, which shocks him, his eyes widening as he looks at me.

"I get it, you're mad at your dad, at the world. But you're

not going to talk to him like that, and I'm not going to let you talk about me anymore either."

He rolls his eyes, and I glance at Aiden who looks like he's barely holding on.

"I'm mad that you're here. I want the office to go back to normal, back to when you didn't exist," Zach says.

Aiden takes a step behind me, and I can feel his body heat and I know that I need to settle this.

"Fine, then I quit."

"What?" Aiden says behind me. I know I told him I needed time to figure this out, but dealing with Zach and some of the other people in this office isn't fucking worth it. I know Aiden has my back, and I'll just have to get over my fears and my pride. I know I won't be out on my ass. I'll figure it out.

"Great, and you can transfer your shares," Zach says with a condescending look on his face.

"You mean when I sell my shares to Aiden, making him the majority shareholder. Fantastic idea." Zach glares at me, and I feel Aiden's hand on my hip.

"You... you can't do that."

"You have no one but yourself to blame, Zach. You've been nothing but a dick to me since the moment I got here. You talk about how Collin would feel about Aiden dating me, but just think of how disgusted he would be with how you've treated me. If anyone doesn't deserve a handout, it's your spiteful ass."

"This company is supposed to be mine. The fucking company is called Kemper's for Christ's sake."

"Zach, you should go home before you make things worse

for yourself," Aiden says, trying to be pragmatic and far kinder than he should be.

"The company was supposed to be mine," Zach says petulantly.

"If it weren't for me, there would be no Kemper's Sport Supply, so if you still want a job, and for me not to make your life a living Hell, please get the fuck out," Aiden says. I look around the office, and everyone tries to duck their head, like they aren't snooping. I don't blame them, obviously the drama is interesting, I just wish I wasn't at the center of it.

Zach looks at me and takes a deep breath. "Will you reconsider selling your shares?"

Aiden gives me a light squeeze, I guess telling me not to poke the bear. I roll my eyes and sigh. "I'll consider it." When truly I won't. I will only sell in a way that makes sure Aiden is still the majority shareholder because he deserves it and Zach made an enemy of the wrong girl. I'm so tired of being walked over by people who are supposed to be my family. I'm not letting it stand any longer.

Zach and Aiden share a look, and my half-brother leaves the building. Everyone sits down at their desk, and Aiden directs me into his office.

"You don't have to quit," he says.

"It felt good to, and being around him isn't worth it."

"You also don't have to sell your shares," he says, sitting at his desk, and I stand in front of him.

"It's kind of perfect though. This way I have the money to start up my own company and keep the cottage."

He scrubs his chin. "Are you sure about this, Jessa? I think you should think about it a little more."

"Which part?"

"Your shares. I don't think you realize what you're giving up there. Will you please let me have my lawyer go over your options with you. If it's about the cottage, you could rent it out or just let me give you the startup money you need."

"I'll think about it, and I'll talk to your lawyer."

"Okay, good." He rubs the back of his neck, and his hand squeezes into a fist as he rests it on his knee. "So you really quit?"

"I really quit," I say with a smile.

"Can we be your first client?" he says, and I nod. The design part of the job was fine, it was all the admin and bull-shit from the sales people.

"I'd love that," I say, leaning forward and kissing him on the lips.

"I like that you're protective of me, even if it's my job," he says, wrapping his hands on the back of my thighs and pulling me closer to him.

"You're just as much mine as I am yours."

He lets go of my legs. "I'll come to your place tonight?"

"Yes, we can talk more about the living situation tonight." I might not be willing to give up the cottage completely, but his idea of renting it out is smart. If I can make enough doing that, I might not even need to take on that much work. Maybe I could truly just do apparel designs, and I wouldn't even have to bother with finding new clients.

I haven't felt this hopeful in such a long time, like I have an actual direction. I know what I want to do, and who I want to be with. I'm ready for this new adventure with Aiden by my side and for all this bullshit that's been eating away at me: this job, Zach, and Sean, can finally be put to rest.

I kiss him one last time before going to my desk and

collecting my personal belongings. I have them all in a tote bag when I walk past reception. Penny has a solemn look on her face and I sigh as I stop and cross my arms over her desk.

"This doesn't change anything between us, you know?"

"I know, but now who am I supposed to get lunch with? Sharon?" She makes a face, and I laugh and shake my head. Sharon is sweet, but she does over share and can be a lot in large doses.

"Who knows, maybe this will take off and I could use some help."

"What exactly are you going to do now?"

"I think a mixture of freelance design and finally putting my designs on apparel. That's always been something I wanted to do, but just never moved forward on. I think it's time I start following my dreams, and working here with Zach breathing down my neck isn't it."

"But Aiden," she says softly, her blue eyes glancing over to where his office door is now closed.

"He understands, and we're going to be okay. More than okay, actually."

"No kidding. The family loved you by the way, if you didn't pick up on that. I've never seen Aiden this happy, and of course he wants you to follow your dreams, but who is he going to stare at all day?"

I laugh and wave her off. "I'll come by for lunch next week, okay?"

"Okay," she sighs, standing up and walking around her desk to wrap her arms around me to squeeze me tightly. "Don't be a stranger," she says, and I wonder if Penny is feeling as needy as I am about making sure this friendship sticks. Sometimes when you leave a job the people you leave behind disappear even though your identities used to be wrapped up in each other. Besides the fact that Penny is my boyfriend's cousin, there's no way I'm letting this friendship fall to the wayside just because I'm leaving the company. I hold her back and put as much reassurance in the hug as I can.

Jessa

Where Did You Get This?

I'M WORKING on my website when there's a clanging noise at the backdoor, which is odd. No one comes through that door unless I'm going to the beach. It's only four in the afternoon, so I know Aiden won't be here for another two hours or so.

I leave my laptop open on my bed as I open my bedroom door. When I see a man standing inside of the cottage looking around, I quietly shut my door and lock it. I grab my phone off the bed and as quietly as I can, I move into the bathroom, locking that door behind me.

The man wasn't facing me, and I couldn't see his face, so I don't know if they are just trying to rob me or if they want something else.

My hands are shaking as I call Aiden first.

"Hey baby, I left work early. Security sent the footage, but the guy was wearing a trenchcoat and a hat who put up the—"

"Aiden," I cut him off. My voice is shaky, and I'm on the verge of tears.

"What's wrong? What's going on?"

"Someone's in my house." That's when I hear the bedroom door being kicked down. "They just kicked down my bedroom door."

"Fuck. Try to be quiet and hide the best you can, I'm on my way and I'm going to call the police."

"Please don't hang up," I say quietly, tears now falling down my face.

"I'm coming as soon as I can. I'm calling them now. You're going to be okay, I'm ten minutes away. I'll be right there," he says, the line going dead. Logically, I know he has to call the police, that's who I should have called first.

I do as Aiden says, getting into the tub and hiding behind the shower curtain. I hide my phone under my bra and use my hands to cover my sobs and to control my breathing. Every part of me is shaking. I can hear the intruder walking around my room for a while, and I'm hoping that they retreat. But then I hear them open the closet and rummage around my clothes. It's then that it clicks that they're here for me. They aren't looking for things to steal, they know I'm home and the only reason they would be looking for me is to harm me.

My heart is racing in my chest and I feel like I'm on the verge of having a heart attack with how fast it's thumping away under my rib cage.

The intruder jiggles the bathroom door handle, quickly realizing that it's locked. He kicks it once, and I hold my mouth tightly shut so that I don't give myself away, though I'm fully aware that he is going to break down that door and there's nowhere for me to go. The window in here is so high and small there's no physical way for me to climb through it.

I wonder if I should have said more to Aiden, or if he will

be able to get here fast enough, or the police. I can't tell if we've been off the phone for one minute or ten. They hit the door one more time, the wood splinters and cracks, and what remains of the door smacks the opposite wall, making me jolt.

My hands stay firmly on my mouth as I try to breathe and pray that maybe he just won't check behind the curtain.

Suddenly the sharp slide of the curtain startles me, and I'm looking into familiar green eyes. And they aren't the ones I've fallen deeply in love with.

"You know Daddy hates it when you hide, sweetheart," Sean says, like this is completely fucking normal and not like he broke into my home and physically broke down two doors.

He looks over my face, and he doesn't seem disheartened by the tear stains tracking down my face or how absolutely terrified I feel.

"Sean, what are you doing here?"

"I'm here to bring you home," he says plainly. He seems different, still as arrogant as ever, but like he's on edge. The man I knew was always so sure about himself, at least in front of me. But as I look at him, he seems twitchy and irritable, and I know I can't be stupid in how I handle this. Maybe I can keep him talking and in the cottage, that's the most important thing. Aiden and help is on the way, I can't let him move me to another location.

"How did you know where I was living?" I ask, staying in the tub. He looks me up and down. His pupils are blown, and he grabs me by the arm and yanks me out of the safety of the tub.

"That man who answered the phone, it wasn't hard to find him and where he worked. Low and behold, he was your boss. You don't change, do you, sweetheart?" I don't fight, but

I don't make it easy for him to drag me into the bedroom either. His grip is tight on my arm, and I have to stop myself from wincing. "This little rebellion is over, you're coming home. Things have changed, but you still belong to me."

Sean might have been a controlling, selfish prick when we were together, but he wasn't delusional.

"Sean, we broke up." He yanks my arm again and bends down to get into my face.

"I decide if we're done. I'm the one in control, which you clearly have forgotten. Daddy's going to work on that. You just need more discipline. You need to understand your place, little girl."

The blood drains from my face, and I try to hold back my visceral response to the name. I bite the inside of my cheek to keep my mouth closed. "I don't want to go back to Virginia," I tell him.

"Perfect, because we're not going back there." I blink at him, he's grabbing some of my things and tossing them into an open suitcase. "Where did you get this?" he asks, holding up the dress that Aiden bought me. I shake my head, not answering, and that's when he shocks me by raising his palm and striking me across the face. I have to blink a few times, the vision in my right eye spotty as I let it sink in that he actually hit me. "Now you know how you're going to be punished for not listening to me. Did he buy it for you?"

He lifts his hand to hit me again, and I sputter as I answer. "Yes, he bought it." He tosses it on the floor.

"Ungrateful bitches don't get presents, you need to remember that."

"Sean, where is this all coming from?" I ask. I guess with his treatment of me, I didn't expect him to care about me leaving. I knew he was upset because of the frequent calls and texts, but this level of behavior is beyond anything I ever thought him capable of.

I see some movement from the backdoor, and I steady myself. Someone is here, they have to be, it has to have been enough time between when I spoke to Aiden for him or someone else to come for help.

"You're mine. I'm not sure what made that unclear. This is over when I say so. Be grateful I want you back and don't hurt you more for sleeping with another man."

So clearly, Sean is having a psychotic episode of some sort, and in an effort to not have him hurt me again, I just go along with his mumbling and nonsense.

"I think you'll like Michigan," he says, muttering under his breath and grabbing more of my things and tossing them into my luggage. He grabs the back of my neck roughly, making me whimper, and he smiles sadistically in my face. "Things are going to be so much better, sweetheart. You're going to be better trained, and it will be fine."

Fresh tears of fear trail down my cheeks when we hear something in the cottage. His hand grips my neck even tighter, and I tense up.

"Who the fuck else is here?" he asks.

I think quickly. "It's my cat."

"I haven't seen a fucking cat here." He looks around and doesn't see anything, and he's in my face. "We're leaving. You can have whatever is in this suitcase when I allow it. Act up and you lose privileges, upset me and you will be punished. Do you understand?"

I nod my head, and his fingers grip my jaw, denting the flesh of my face. "I said, do you understand?"

"Yes," I rasp out. His grip gets firmer, and he shakes my head.

"Yes, what?"

"Yes—"

I'm saved from saying what he wants as Aiden's fist connects with Sean's face. The crack of his knuckles against his jaw is jarring. Sean goes falling to the floor. He isn't a small man, but Aiden has a lot of muscle over him, not to mention general athletic ability. Aiden climbs on top of Sean and punches him repeatedly in the face.

Sean is gasping on the ground, trying to fight off Aiden with no luck. The backdoor flings open, startling me. Four police officers have their weapons drawn as they defuse the situation, getting Aiden off of Sean. Sean goes to reach for something behind his belt, and the dark metal is clear as day. His gun is barely visible when he's shot in the arm. I cover my ears from the intrusive bang and watch as he bleeds out on my bedroom floor.

Suddenly Aiden is in front of me, his hands bruised and shaking as he touches my face. My hearing is absolute shit, and I just stare at him as he gently takes my elbow and directs me outside. The hot salty air gives me enough room to breathe, and when I inhale, it's like I can't get enough air, and I'm heaving and hunched over.

Aiden drags me over to one of the beach chairs and squats in front of me, his hands tenderly touching me, seeing where I'm hurt.

It's then I catch a glance of his hand, my sobbing coming to a standstill as I take his hand in mine. It's trembling, and I can tell he's in pain.

"Your hand." I'm not sure how loud I say it, but his hand

is pushing my hair, and I wince as he touches the fresh bruise on my face.

"Did he hurt you anywhere else?" I shake my head, and my neck hurts from the motion. Aiden, of course, notices.

"They need to look at your hand." His knuckles are bleeding and broken open. He already has so much pain in his right hand, what if this made it worse? What if this is too much for Aiden? I already left the office and put him in an uncomfortable position where he works, and now I've literally endangered his life.

My past has come back to bite me in the ass in such a brutal way. Sean had a gun, he could have killed me or Aiden.

I know I didn't ask for this to happen, but the guilt feels so heavy in my chest, I can't help but cry again.

Aiden is far too gracious as he sits across from me and pulls me into his lap, rubbing my back and comforting me. I should be giving this to him too; he just saved my life. On top of the guilt there's also this warning feeling that I don't deserve this. It's like Sean came here because I was too happy. I don't deserve my own business or a man who treats me the way Aiden does. Maybe I deserve everything Sean said.

"You don't have to stay," I say to Aiden. This is too fucking much, there's no way he wants me and all this baggage.

"Did you hit your head?" he says softly, his poor fingers tangling in my hair and rubbing my scalp.

"No, this is just too much, Aiden. He could have killed you," I say between sobs. He doesn't push me away, call me names, or even scoff. He just pulls me closer to his chest.

"I'm not going anywhere, and this isn't your fault."

"Aiden," I sigh his name.

"I'm going to take care of everything, baby. That mother-fucker is going to jail and you're moving in with me." I pull away and blink up at him. He shakes his head, like he's got a retort for anything I argue with him. "There's no fucking way I can sleep or function not having you with me right now. After this bullshit? You're coming home with me where I can keep you safe."

"I don't deserve you," I say while I rub my face against his perfect chest.

"None of that either, just let me handle everything, okay?"

"Okay," I say quietly and just hold onto him. I do my best to ignore the sirens or people walking by the cottage. The police ask me to retell everything that happened. It's exhausting and so hard to bring up with Aiden right next to me. I can tell how angry he is when I talk about what Sean said to me and that he hit me. Though he knew that from the bruise on my cheek. But I think him knowing it was over a dress he bought me makes him feel even more furious about it.

I just want to crash in bed, but when I look at Aiden's abused hands, I force him to get looked at by the paramedics, they do the same to me. Taking photos of Aiden's hands as well as the bruises forming on my face. Since I have no other injuries and Aiden's hand just seems to be bleeding from where he struck Sean, they tell us we don't need to go to the hospital. I know I'm going to make him get this hand checked out this week. I will never forgive myself if he did further damage to his hand.

When we get back to his house, he takes Tylenol and makes me take two as well. I feel taken care of, and like I don't deserve Aiden at this moment. But I'm so thankful I have him as my rock right now. If I didn't, I'm afraid I might completely fall apart.

I try to sleep, and even though I'm surrounded by Aiden's scent and his body wrapped around mine, I can't help the lingering fear that Sean is just waiting for me to fall asleep so that he can come after me again. I know logically that he was arrested and he isn't going anywhere any time soon. But this terror doesn't leave me, and as hard as I try to sleep, I just find myself tossing and turning and startling at every sound I hear in the house.

Aiden

It's Daddy's Job

I GROAN as I stretch my arms and wake up. Sleep was hard to find, but I was so exhausted I somehow managed. But when I look over at Jessa, it's clear she hardly slept.

She blinks at me, her eyes red and puffy, and I gather her up and hold her against my chest. The situation alone, with her ex trying to abduct her when he had a deadly weapon, but how Jessa is processing scares me just as much.

"Are you going to the office?" she says quietly, and I stay calm and shake my head and kiss her hair.

"No, I'm staying here with you. I'm awake now, if you want to try and sleep?"

"I don't know if I can," she says, and I hold her closer.

"What do you need, baby?"

"You promise this isn't too much? That you're not going to leave because of this?"

"I'm not going anywhere, and I'm going to take care of you. Whatever you need, just tell me."

She sobs in my arms, and I wish I knew why. I mean, there are a multitude of reasons right now, but I just let her get the emotion out. Her tears drip on my bare chest as I hold her tightly.

"I never thought he would do something like that. I knew he was upset about me leaving, but I didn't think he was capable of hurting me that way. I didn't even know he had a gun."

"His actions aren't your fault, you know that, right?"

"Logically, yes. But this somehow feels like my fault. You hurt your hand more because of him. You put yourself in danger for me."

I cup her face, and wait till her sad and sleepy eyes meet mine. "And I'd do it all over again. I love you, you're mine, and I'm always going to keep you safe."

Her crying continues, and she lets me hold her and comfort her until her tears stop and she's finally sleeping in my arms. I hold her as she finally gets rest, and I get some comfort in knowing she feels safe enough with me to fall asleep. It's going to take a lot of work to handle this moving forward, but if anyone can do it, it's us.

Working from home is more pleasant than I'd like to admit—not having multiple people in and out of my office—and I spend all day with Jessa.

We both work in my office. I cleared off half of the space and ordered her a desk chair. It's companionable and while she's still struggling, she's out of bed, and she isn't crying. She's completely thrown herself into getting her company up and running.

While I'm happy that she's found a distraction, I want to make sure it's in a healthy way. I'm probably overstepping, but when we entered this relationship, we agreed what some of the dynamics would be. Learning what a psychopath Sean is, I'm even more cautious of what lines I'm crossing, but I say it anyway.

"I made you a virtual therapy appointment." She pauses her typing and looks up at me.

"I don't have health insurance. I left Kemper's, remember?" I want to scoff at her, but I don't.

"I'm taking care of it."

"Okay," she says, and I let out a relieved breath of air. "Did you think I was going to fight you on this?"

I shrug. "I mean, I was prepared."

"I think I need it, have needed it for a while now. Plus, I want to leave the house again." I nod and round the table and pet down her hair.

"We're moving at your pace, whatever you need."

She places her face against my stomach. I'm so fucking thankful she hasn't retreated from my touch. She seems to need it more than ever, and I'm more than eager to give it to her. Jessa grabs my right hand and kisses it softly. "How's your hand?"

"Still tender but better." She kisses it again. "Penny wants to know if she can come by today?"

Jessa smiles and nods her head. Wanting her friend over is another win in my book. I kiss the top of her head and text Penny to come by around lunch.

I leave the room and call the station.

"Sargent Paulson," he answers.

"It's Aiden Carlson, I'm checking in on Sean McPherson's case."

"He's not going anywhere. The judge is refusing bail. It will take a few months for his hearing, and you will both need to prepare yourselves to testify."

I groan, thinking about Jessa making progress with her therapist and with me, only be brought back down months later when she has to confront him.

"Does Jessa have to testify? I will. But does she need to?"

"She's the whole case. Without her testimony, there's a chance his sentence won't be as long. He did pull a deadly weapon on officers, but if you want the attempted kidnapping and aggravated assault to stick, then she needs to be there."

"Thank you," I say abruptly, feeling like they aren't doing enough and this isn't moving fast enough. I'll just have to figure out a way to get Jessa through this. Whatever I have to do, I'll make it happen.

It's been a month of hardly leaving the house, but she's doing better. She sees her therapist virtually twice a week, Penny visits at least twice a week, and Jessa has been going outside. She swims in the pool and is getting fresh air.

Today feels different though. I can't put my finger on it, but as I watch her smile on the pool float. It makes me feel brave in my own regard. I put on my swim shorts and sunglasses and join her outside.

Her smile is bright as she looks at me, and I jump in the pool, splashing her in the process. She laughs and is now soaking wet as I flip it over and send her into the water.

When she breaks through the water and is still smiling, my heart beat evens out as I look at her. She wraps her arms around my neck and we both float, staring at each other.

"How was therapy today?" I ask her, and she kisses my cheek.

"Really good. I think I'm ready," she says.

"Ready to leave the house?" I ask and she shakes her head.

"Ready to be with you again," she says, and I stare at her for a moment. Even though Sean didn't violate her in that way, she hasn't been in the right headspace, and I don't blame her at all. I see the fear she used to carry over her head beginning to vanish, and I'm so thankful, because I never thought it would stop tormenting her.

I push back her dark wet hair. "You're sure?"

She nods her head. "I miss being intimate with you so much," she says, pushing her body closer to mine. I spin her so that her back is against the pool wall as I touch her face and lean in and kiss her. She isn't timid during the kiss, and I don't doubt her. If she says she's ready, then she's ready.

I slide my hand under water and rub her pussy with the palm of my hand. "Does this needy pussy need me, baby?"

"So bad."

"Sit your sweet little ass on the edge of the pool."

Jessa is always eager to please, and it's one of the things I love most about her. Her arms in tandem with mine, I grip her waist and lift her body out of the pool so she sits at the pool's edge. Water cascading down her body like it's trying to touch every perfect inch of her skin.

"I missed eating your sweet cunt." I've purposely not gone back to her term of endearment for me. Though I've truly grown to love her calling me Daddy, I worry that after what happened it's been ruined for her. If it has, it's part of our dynamic that can go. Everything else: the way I dominate her in the bedroom, my affection and care for her. That will always be a part of our relationship.

Her hands are behind her, firmly holding her upright as I shift her bikini to the side and place a soft kiss to her pussy. The taste of the pool water invades my lips, and I slip my tongue inside of her, tasting her after what feels like forever. She moans and shifts her hips so it's easier for me to eat her out, and I hum my approval against her clit.

I hold her hips as I go down on her, loving every noise that escapes her, and needing her to know how much I enjoy this. How much I enjoy bringing her pleasure, that she's mine and always will be. Part of being my girl is that she never has to worry again. I'm going to take care of her every need, and she never needs to live in fear again.

She's going to come often, never have to worry about a single bill, and above all else, I'm never letting anyone touch her again.

Jessa comes with a shout, the sound ricocheting off the covered patio in the pool. It rings in my ears as I kiss her cunt one more time before standing at my full height in the pool. Jessa blinks at me and holds her hand out in a gesture for me to get out of the pool. Water drips off of me as I pull myself up over the edge and she directs me to sit on the outdoor furniture. I do immediately, my wet shorts losing the battle to my hard and aching cock.

She tugs at the top of my shorts, and it takes some effort, but we work together to get the offensive material down my legs. She tosses them with a wet plop to the floor before removing her bottoms and quickly straddling my lap. Her soft thighs bracket mine as she sinks down on my cock. Her hands tangle in my wet hair, and I can't help but just be in awe of this woman in my arms. That she's able to be vulnerable and soft with me, but also able to claim what she wants.

"Use me, baby. Take what you need."

She does just that as she rides me at a pace that works for her. Her clit grinding against my pelvis with each bounce.

"Are you going to come on my cock, kitten?"

"Yes, Daddy," she sighs out, and I grip her ass, unable to control myself at that word. I begin to fuck her from underneath and she collapses against my chest. I continue fucking her as she gushes around my cock and her pussy grips me tightly as she orgasms.

I'm not far behind, as I fill her with my cum. I don't think I've ever cum so much in my life as she settles down against my thighs, her breathing shallow as her wet body holds on to mine.

I stroke her back, and we sit there in silence, just enjoying a moment of normalcy in what has been an absolutely hectic life as of late.

Shockingly, she's the first one to speak. "Thank you for being everything I needed. I love you," she says before leaning in and kissing me softly.

"It's Daddy's job," I joke, and she laughs, and fuck does it feel good to hear her laugh again.

"You didn't miss that, did you?"

"I didn't know how you felt about it," I say honestly.

She cups my jaw and kisses me again. "All I know is that title never belonged to anyone else, and it never will again."

I'm still deep inside of her, and I almost feel like I could go again at her words. I pull her against me and kiss the side of her face.

"Good, and I love you too."

Jessa

Butt Plug Graduation

THERAPY IS LIFE, and that's really all I have to say about my experience. My therapist, Colleen, is more than I could have hoped for. I even see her in person now, that's right, I've graduated from being holed up in Aiden's house and I go places now. I'm not a huge fan of going anywhere alone, but I'm working on it.

Colleen says baby steps are the best ways to deal with a trauma like this, and that's exactly what I'm doing. Though I wouldn't call basically moving in with Aiden a baby step, Colleen approves of the move, and at this point, Colleen's word is gospel to me.

Aiden hired cleaners to clean up the cottage, and they are taking pictures so we can list it for rent. If I can't get a long term tenant, then we'll do vacation rentals. But it feels good to not go back there. I love Aiden's house, I guess our house, but I'll get there eventually.

I was so worried that I would be afraid forever and push Aiden away, but he hasn't let me. Not in the slightest, he's been so patient, understanding, and just the best partner I could have ever asked for.

That's why I'm surprising him tonight, and I needed some socks to go with my wardrobe. I refuse to tell Penny exactly what I'm doing, but she already guesses.

"Some baseball fetish thing you all are doing?" she asks, holding up a pair of long socks.

I glare at her. "You want to talk about Lincoln?" I say, calling her out if she's going to do the same to me. The thing is, she shocks me by responding honestly.

"Yeah, I think I need to make him jealous."

"Why?"

"That's always when he acts like a caveman over me, and I like it."

"So are you two going to keep this a secret forever?"

She shrugs and sighs, handing me a pair of white long socks with two blue stripes around the top. "These are Rays' colors," she says before sighing again. "We're not just going to blow up our entire family if this is just sexual."

"Well, is it?" I ask, and she looks away from me.

"Not for me."

"Have you asked him?" I ask Penny, and she gives me a look.

"He's not one to talk about how he's feeling."

I nod my head as we continue walking through the store. I shift my weight the wrong way and can't help the little yelp that escapes me.

Penny shakes her head. "I can't decide if I want to know or not."

I'd really rather that my best friend wasn't aware of the butt plug in my ass right now, or that I'm wearing it all day to prepare myself to get fucked in the ass by her incredibly hot cousin. I just give her a little shrug and go about my business.

"The office sucks without you there, and since Aiden has been working from home, it's even more out of control."

"What's going on?" I ask as we walk through the store so I can check out.

"Tabitha and Zach broke up, so there's been plenty of drama there. I'm sure you expected him to act like a little bitch when you brought up selling your shares to Aiden, so he's just been in a continuous shitty mood."

I shrug my shoulders. Zach isn't my problem. "All he needs to do is not be an asshole."

"Oh, I agree. His spiral has at least been entertaining. It's probably best that Aiden has been working from home, in all honesty. I think he might have beaten his ass by now."

I grimace and think about Aiden's hand and how much he plays down how it hurts sometimes, and I feel guilty. "I don't want that either."

"If someone is a big enough asshole to piss Aiden off, then they deserve it," Penny says and I can't help but agree with her logic. Aiden, for the most part, is very calm and logical, but when someone gets under his skin enough and he loses it, it's honestly their own fault for getting him to that point.

"What are you guys doing for Halloween?" she asks, and when my cheeks heat, she grins at me wickedly.

"Avalon," I say quietly.

"Maybe I'll have to just show up one night and see what you two little freaks get up to."

"Gross, Penny."

"What? You want a bunch of strangers to watch you fuck, but me being one of those people is weird?"

"I don't need my best friend to see me bent over her cousin's knee, getting spanked."

She snaps her fingers. "I should have guessed you were into being spanked. It makes almost too much sense."

"Jesus Christ."

"Don't worry, I won't be at Avalon any time soon and neither should Lincoln. If you see him there, you'll let me know." She arches a brow at me.

"Scouts honor." I hold up my fingers, and she gives me an unimpressed look.

"And you haven't said anything to Aiden?"

I shake my head and she lets out a relieved breath. "Whenever you're ready for him to know, he'll know. Honestly, no offense to you or your family, but you two aren't as incognito as you think you are."

She shrugs her shoulders, and I check out. We head to lunch, and it's so nice to feel like me again. I'm not looking over my shoulder or feel like I'm being watched. I've had to train my brain to realize what happened to me was a specific person, and that person is currently locked up and should be for a very long time. I still don't like to think about going to his trial, but I do my best to not think about it. I'm not going to let Sean stop me from living. No one gets to steal this happiness from me.

I had to dig into the depths of Aiden's side of the closet, but I find what I'm looking for. With my knee high socks, Aiden's old Rays jersey, and my hair in a perky ponytail, I sit on the bed and wait for him to get home.

I'm filled with excitement and nerves, but I know without a doubt that Aiden will make this good for me. I've never felt more cared for than I do with Aiden, not even by people who were biologically programmed to love me unconditionally. He provides everything that I could want from a partner, and I want to make sure that I care for him too. I think I do a good job of letting him know he's needed and giving him the control he needs. Acts of service are his love language, and I make sure to show him I love him every day.

So, if fucking my ass is what he wants, I'll give it a try. I can't deny that I've enjoyed the butt plug, more than I imagined. However, Aiden's cock is a lot bigger than the plug, and I'm still a little nervous.

"Jessa?" I hear him say my name loudly as he walks up the stairs and through the threshold of our bedroom. When he sees me, the sexiest smirk takes over his face, and he braces himself on the door frame. "Fuck, baby," he says, taking me in. I'm feeling confident and sexy in a way I never thought a baseball jersey could make me feel. "Let me see that name on the back," he says.

I turn around and shift my ponytail so he can see his name. But that's not enough. I bend over the bed, exposing my ass so he can see the glittery end of the butt plug.

"Look at that pretty little asshole," he says, and I hear his dress shoes against the hardwood as one of his hands glides along the curve of my ass. He tugs gently on the plug, not pulling it out, just teasing the tight hole, making me moan. "Are you getting yourself ready to take me, kitten?"

"Yes, I want to make you feel good."

His hands are just on my ass, gently touching the flesh, and I have to turn around to look at his face. It's like he's hypnotized by my ass, and it makes me feel powerful and sexy.

"You always make me feel good. But this is such a good surprise. You're such a good girl for me." His hand slides down to my pussy where I can hear how wet I am when he moves his fingers back and forth from inside of me to over my clit. He kisses one of my ass cheeks before biting the flesh lightly.

I groan and he makes an echoing noise of pleasure as he continues to leisurely play with my pussy, like he has all day to toy with me.

"I think your sweet, needy pussy needs attention first," he says and I'm already eagerly nodding my head. I'm not sure what I expect him to do, but when I hear the snap of his belt and his zipper, I grip the sheets in anticipation and wonder how intense the stretch is going to be with both his cock and the plug inside of me.

There's a steadying pressure of his hand between my shoulder blades, and my cheek presses against the softness of our bed as I feel his cock against my entrance. He pushes in slowly, and I moan like the needy deviant that I am. He grips my ass with one hand as the other stays between my shoulders, and I try to remember to breathe as he stretches me.

The stretch of my pussy when my ass is filled is unreal, and the noises I'm making are unintelligible and greedy as he slowly fucks me.

"Fuck, you look so good," he says, smacking my ass, and I whimper, the feeling almost too much. I'm going to come embarrassingly fast. "You like being face down with your ass up for Daddy, don't you? I fucking love this greedy pussy."

"Yes." I whimper as he picks up the pace. I feel so fucking

full, like I might explode. But then he shifts the plug, pulling it out and back in, and then I'm keening and begging him to let me come. "Please, please, I'm so close." His hand leaves my shoulders and wraps around my waist, and his fingers strum against my clit as he fucks me.

I'm a shaking, whimpering mess as he fucks me through my orgasm. I'm still peaking when he pulls out of me. I whine from the emptiness, but there's a moment that he's gone and a clicking of a lid. Cold fluid drips down my ass, and he slowly removes the plug until I feel the push of the tip of his cock entering me.

"Breathe for me, baby," he says, and I do my best to not tense and just relax. I'm not as nervous as I'm still shivering from my orgasm.

He's so delicate as he pushes in and out, it's only a small portion of him, but it feels good. I can hear the tackiness of the lube against my ass.

"Look at you taking me like you were made for me. So goddamn good. Are you doing okay?" He checks in with me and I nod my head. He slaps my ass and I moan, knowing he wants a verbal answer.

"So good, thank you, Daddy."

"Fuck," he groans and starts pushing more of his hard, long length inside of me. I'm not sure what I expected, but it feels way better than I anticipated. There's a vibrating noise and when Aiden wraps a hand around me and puts the small vibrator on my clit, I nearly lurch forward.

"Be a good girl and hold this on your clit," he says and as much as I want to say it's too much, far more overwhelming than I can handle after coming, I take it and hold it against my clit. Both of his hands are holding on to my ass cheeks as he fucks me. The noises he's making are carnal and masculine and even on my hands and knees I feel so empowered.

Not only am I garnering pleasure from this, but the way he's so reverent and caring with me, making sure this is just as good for me, is fucking everything.

I'm on the edge as the vibrator hits my clit, and I must clench around Aiden as he groans and smacks my ass, making me jolt, and then I'm coming again.

"You feel so fucking good," he says before his pace increases. I'm nearly non-coherent as he pushes into me harder, until he pulls out and I feel ribbons of cum on my ass. The vibrator is whirling on the bed; I dropped it after I came. Aiden pants behind me.

"Can I take a picture of your ass like this?" he asks, his voice soft and almost like he's worried I'd say no. The thought of him saving the picture and looking at it when he jerks off or misses me does it for me.

"Yes," I say, and he's digging around in his pants' pocket for his phone. I stay on my hands and knees while I wait for him. When I hear the camera shutter and Aiden's groan, I look back at him and give him the best grin I can, even though I'm exhausted.

He blinks at me like his brain has checked out for a moment, and it makes me feel even better. He shakes his head, and smiles back at me. "How was that for you?"

"Good, really good," I say honestly. "But I think I could use a shower and a nap now."

He laughs and is about to help me up, but I shake my head. Sliding the jersey down my front and taking it off. "I can't get cum all over your jersey."

He scoffs and laughs, staring down at my ass, I can feel it

dripping down my legs, and I'm sure he has a certain amount of masculine pride looking at it.

"Fuck, I love you."

"I love you too. Now come wash me in the shower." He grins and does exactly that, making me feel every ounce of cherished and loved as he says.

Aiden

Marry Me

I'M NOT sure if it's stupid, reckless, or too soon, but all I know is I need Jessa Peters to know I'm all in. I've never even thought about marrying someone before Jessa, just the idea of long term dating, but now that she lives with me and I see her every day, I need this additional step. Maybe it's me being a possessive asshole, but I want my ring on her finger and for her to have my last name.

I just hope that she wants it too. I'm more than aware how fast this is, but isn't that what everyone always says. When you know, you know.

So fuck it, I need Jessa to know that this is real, that I'm going to take care of her for the rest of our lives. I thought about doing it at a baseball game, and quickly decided that was fucked up. What if she feels pressured or doesn't like the attention, though I know my girl is always down for an audience, that's too much pressure—for the both of us.

I thought about asking Penny for help, but have no idea if she can keep a secret like this. So I call my mom instead.

"Hey, sweetie." She answers the phone, and I actually feel nervous and decide to blurt it out.

"I'm going to ask Jessa to marry me."

There's a long pause over the phone until I hear light crying on the other end. "Oh, Aiden. I'm so happy for you." I take a deep breath, letting out the tension of telling her. "How are you going to ask her?"

"I think simple is the way to go."

She hums over the phone. "She loves you. It doesn't matter if it's just at home, she'll be happy. Did you buy a ring?"

"I was hoping to give her Grandma Nellie's," I say, and my mom starts crying all over again.

"Of course, you can come and get it tomorrow. You will need to get it resized for Jessa's smaller fingers. One of my sons is finally settling down, maybe there's hope for your brothers."

"Doubt it," I say in a whisper, and my mom clicks her tongue at me in disapproval.

"I'm so proud of you, Aiden," she says, and I have to hold back my own emotions. My parents have always been proud of me, even when I wasn't. Even when I hated who I was and never thought anything I did was good enough. It feels like the first time I don't need them to be proud of me. I don't know how to describe it. It's like Jessa's trust and her needing me to take control has made my confidence grow even more. Not that I was ever insecure about who I am, but seeing myself through Jessa's eyes has made me realize that I have so much to be proud of.

I'm a successful business owner, and had a great athletic career, but what matters to me most is becoming the best husband I can be.

Husband, fuck. I never thought I would think of myself in that term. Let alone be excited about it.

My mom shares more of her excitement over the phone with me. And while I don't need my family's approval of Jessa, I'm thankful I have it. Not that I ever suspected that they wouldn't like her, but it's nice to know we won't have any issues, especially since Jessa doesn't have much in the way of family herself.

It makes my heart hurt when I think about how displaced Jessa has been most of her life and how much I want to assure her that she belongs. That she'll be absorbed into my own family, no matter how annoying and chaotic they can be. My brothers might drive me fucking crazy, but I wouldn't trade them for the world.

When I hang up with mom, I make a plan, and hope to fuck that Jessa is on the same page as me.

The ring feels like it's going to burn a hole in my pocket. We ate dinner at a beach front restaurant, and now we're walking along the beach before we head home. Jessa's wearing a light blue sundress, and as the day's sun declines, it glows against her skin as we walk hand in hand.

Her hair is down and blows a little wildly around her face with the ocean breeze. I swallow thickly, waiting for the right moment.

"Oh, I spoke to the lawyer," she says as we keep walking.

"What did he say?"

"He said I should just sell you one share and keep the rest myself." She smirks, and I nod my head.

"How do you feel about that?" I ask, I would buy them all from her, but it didn't sit right with me. Collin, despite his faults, wanted her to be a part of the company. He wanted her to have a piece of this company he built, and it doesn't feel right for her to sell it to me just to put Zach in his place. One share makes me a majority shareholder and gets Jessa the payback she wants.

"I feel good. I'm never going to have a relationship with Zach, and you put so much work into making Kemper's what it is. You should be in charge of what direction the company goes. If he doesn't like it, he can sell his shares and find his own dream." She says it matter-of-factly. "Also, Colleen all but said taking the high road all the time isn't good for your inner peace." She grins at me, and I tug her closer, kissing her senseless.

"I'm proud of you," I tell her. Her cheeks heat as she leans forward and I kiss her again.

"I wouldn't have been able to do all of this without you, you know that?" I wave her off and she fists my shirt. "I'm serious, you make me feel safe to say what I'm thinking and ask for what I want. I've never had someone who cared enough to make sure I had the things I needed to be the person I wanted to be. You gave me that."

I blink at her and realize this is the moment. Fuck the light up sign at the end of the beach. I clear my throat and her eyes widen as I get down on one knee. Her hands hold one another against her heart as I pull out the ring and look up at her.

"Yes," she says before I can even speak, bouncing on her heels. I laugh and shake my head.

"Can I ask first?" I smirk at her.

"Yes," she says, and I shake my head.

"Jessa, I love everything about you. You're the most passionate, caring, and beautiful person I've ever met. You're my other half, truly. There is no better half, because only together are we perfect. You make me feel worthy and the gift of taking care of you is the best I've ever been given. I want to make sure you get everything in life, and that you always feel safe and loved when you're with me. Be my wife?"

"Yes," she shouts and nearly launches herself at me. I shut the ring box on the way down, my ass landing firmly on the sand. She grabs my face and kisses me breathless, not saying anything, just showing me her excitement through touch and affection in a way that is so her.

"Do you want to see the ring?" I ask when she parts from my lips, her hands still on my face as she nods her head.

I hold it out and open the box that shows off the pear shaped diamond with a simple white gold band.

"Holy fuck," she whispers as I take it out of the box and place it on her shaking finger. It's a perfect fit and she beams at me as she holds her hand out to the sunset. "It's gorgeous. I love it."

"It was my grandmother's. I think she would have wanted my future wife to have it."

That makes her eyes water as she wraps her arms around my neck and sits on my lap.

"I love you, I'm so happy," she says, and I can tell she's crying happy tears. I just hold her against me.

"There is a big ass marry me sign at the end of the beach with a photographer. Should we reenact it?" She laughs and pulls back. I brush off the rogue tear from her cheek.

"I don't think it gets any more perfect than this."

"I don't think so either," I say before leaning in and kissing my fiancée.

※ ※ ※

The engagement bubble is a real fucking thing. It feels like Jessa and I have been on this high since I proposed, but I'm stressing the fuck out about today.

It could set everything back. Will seeing him in court take her back to where she was after the break in? Not that it would change anything for me when it comes to our relationship, she's just worked so hard to get to where she is. I don't want this asshole to take anything else away from her. We both have to testify today, but she's first.

She wore a modest navy dress and a blazer to the court house. She's been fidgeting with her engagement ring since we got here. I'm just glad that the prosecutor said that I could be in the room while she testifies. The idea of leaving her to do this alone just wasn't an option.

We're out in the hallway when the paralegal comes to collect us.

"You're sure you're okay?" I ask Jessa with a gentle hand on her lower back.

"Yeah, I'm not letting him take anything else from me." She stands a little taller and we follow her into the court-room. I take a seat on the third row as the guard directs her to the bench. When I look over at the defense, Sean is staring at her, and I have to take a few deep breaths so that I don't make things any worse.

Jessa takes her oath and the prosecution starts. They

mostly ask her to recall the entire event, and I have to focus and mentally tell myself that she's okay now and she's with me. Hearing how afraid she was in those moments breaks my heart, and I just need this asshole to be put away for the longest time.

The prosecution asks her about her relationship with Sean, and she dissects that briefly, but the main thing they focus on are Sean's illegal actions. Jessa holds it together and makes sure to speak to the lawyer and the jury as she goes into every detail of that night.

But then everything goes to hell when the defense cross examines her. Sean's lawyer is expensive, and from what I read online, he's good at what he does. The prosecution told Jessa what to expect and how they might use tricky lines of questioning to help Sean's case.

Jessa rubs her face with her left hand, and I watch in awe as Sean's face turns red, seeing my ring on her finger. Sean glares at her, and it's the worst move he could have made as I notice the jury logging every reaction.

"Miss Peters, you were in a relationship with my client Sean McPherson for four years, is this correct?"

"That's correct," she replies, not answering any more than what he asks.

"You and my client were both members of a kink community in DC, is that correct?"

Jessa's eyes meet mine, and I give her a little nod. This slimy motherfucker. "That's correct."

"You and mister McPherson were involved in a dynamic where he was the dominant and you agreed to be submissive to him in both your public and private lives?"

"Objection, relevance," the prosecutor says.

"Sustained, Mr. Holland, I don't see the relevance of your client's sexual preferences to this case."

"I'm establishing the dynamic between my client and Miss Peters was one where Mr. McPherson was in charge of all the couple's decisions."

"Continue," the judge says.

"So in short terms, you and my client had a dynamic where he was primarily in charge?"

Jessa looks like she wants to roll her eyes. "It's not that simple, but yes, he was the authoritative figure in our relationship. Probably because he was my professor when we started dating," she says, and I have to hide my smirk behind my hand at her little dig. The lawyer was trying to make her seem like a deviant, and she just turned it around on him.

The lawyer ignores her, and Sean hasn't let his gaze drop from Jessa, or her ring that publicly marks her as mine.

"But, it's safe to say that Mr. McPherson was bringing you back home because of your relationship dynamic and there was no clear separation when you left Virginia."

Jessa raises an eyebrow at the lawyer and looks over at Sean. She looks so strong sitting up there, not letting this piece of shit man take anything else from her.

"No, there was no confusion. I had a conversation on the phone that was overheard by my old coworker where I explicitly told Sean that we were no longer together and to stop calling me and reaching out to me."

"But with your dynamic—"

With balls of steel Jessa interrupts the lawyer. "No, because I have the same dynamic with my fiancée and he would never disrespect my boundaries like Sean did. Not only did he break into my home with a deadly weapon, hit me, and ruined my peace, he left me with emotional scars that others can't see. His actions have nothing to do with the dynamic we had in or out of the bedroom. He is a small man who threw a tantrum because he was told no, and he should be locked away so he can never do this to anyone else again."

"No further questions," the defense lawyer says, and Jessa is dismissed. Sean tracts her movements until she's in my arms. I lean forward and kiss her cheek, placing my hand behind her head and giving him the middle finger in a way that no one can see.

"So proud of you," I tell her and she exhales thickly.

"Can we leave now?"

"Penny is out in the hallway. Why don't you sit with her while I finish up?" She nods against my chest and I squeeze her close to me. Sean is shaking in anger in his seat, his arm is limply hanging against his chest, and it's a dark thought, but I wish the cop would have aimed just a little higher and toward the middle.

Jessa hugs me one more time before leaving the court-room. My testimony is short and to the point. I think the defense knows he doesn't have a case, especially when the officer on scene talks about him threatening all of us with his weapon.

I give Sean a look that says I won. Being petty feels better than I imagined. Jessa had a point. I leave the courtroom feeling proud and lighter. This only proves how strong Jessa is and something like this isn't going to break her. We're stronger together and we always will be.

Jessa

Kitten

I SHOW my engagement ring off like it's a championship ring. Anyone who even looks at it, I go into how Aiden proposed and how much I love him. We're a bunch of lovesick idiots, and I truly don't care who notices or feels like we're too in their face. It's taken me a while to realize we both deserve this happiness, and I'm not going to hide it.

I certainly didn't when we went to Sean's trial, and I'm not ashamed of how I acted at all. I've just been so tired of being this person who accepts everyone stepping all over them. Aiden entering my life really helped me realize how often I let people take advantage of me. Having him there, knowing I'm protected and safe, makes me feel like I have the spine to stand up for myself. And if I'm at a point where I can't fend for myself, I know he will carry the weight. It's something I've always wanted, to be someone's person. For someone to love me so much, they would do everything and anything to take care of me, and it's sad, but being with Aiden is the first time I've ever felt like that.

Despite the fact that there are so many other people who had the opportunity to fill this position in my life, I'm glad it

was Aiden. I finally know what truly loving someone unconditionally looks like, and I plan on reciprocating as often as
I can.

I squeeze into the small black dress and put on my cat
ears before I head downstairs. I can tell that Aiden didn't
want to dress up, but he did for me. He's wearing a white and
black striped shirt and black trousers, so I'm a cat, and he's
the cat burglar. I give him a wide smile as I step between his
legs at the kitchen island. He pushes my hair behind my back
and kisses my collarbone.

"You ready to go, kitten?" he asks with a devious smirk.

I fiddle with the end of my dress, excited to go back to
Avalon, but there's also a nervous tension from what
happened last time. "Will Leo be there?"

"I don't know, but if he is, I'll make sure he comes
nowhere near you." The thing is, that promise out of another
man's mouth I wouldn't believe it. Aiden saying it, however,
puts me completely at ease. I nod and lean my body more
against his. "You look very pretty, baby."

"And you look like the Hamburglar, let's go," I say, gripping his shirt. He gives me a dark look that just says he wants
to spank my ass for that comment—perfect.

He swats at my ass as he grabs our bag of spare clothes as
we head out to the car. I felt bad about not leaving candy out
for the kids in the neighborhood, so I put a bucket on the
front porch even though Aiden said the first little fucker to
the house would probably take the whole bucket. Sure
enough, as we pull out of the driveway, there's a little boy
dressed like the Hulk dumping the whole bucket into his
pillow case bag. I just shrug my shoulders while Aiden gives
me a look that screams I told you so.

"We had to leave out candy, we don't want to be that house," I say, and he shakes his head.

"What house?"

"The house that everyone knows is the dickhead couple. I might not want kids, but I do like them. Plus, don't you want them coming to the door to sell Girl Scout cookies?"

He shrugs his shoulders and acts like I don't know about all the Thin Mints in the freezer that I steal on occasion.

"Fine, it's not like you didn't get your way, anyway. Now that Bruce Banner took all the candy, can we go to Avalon so I can get my treat?"

"So greedy," I joke. He just slips his hand on my bare thigh, dragging his fingertips against the smooth skin, never sliding up my skirt, but just promising me that he's going to turn me into an absolute mess tonight—I welcome it.

※ ※ ※

Leo is not at Avalon tonight, thank God. Carmen is, however, sitting on a man's lap I don't recognize. She doesn't even look over in our direction and I wonder how long she's been unhappy in her marriage and if he knows she's here tonight.

"How do you want to play tonight, kitten?" Aiden asks, an arm wrapped around my waist in a possessive hold, letting everyone know that they can look but not touch.

"I think I want strict daddy tonight," I say, looking up at him and gauging his response. I love how sweet and loving Aiden can be, but I also love seeing these little snippets of his dark side. I know that he will never hurt me, and if I tell him anything is off limits, he will immediately stop. I just want to be told what to do tonight and see how happy he is with my obedience.

His hand slides down to my ass as his other wraps around my throat, a tight squeeze on each side, but not enough to cut off my airway or hinder me from speaking.

"Are you going to be so good for me tonight, kitten? You want to be Daddy's little fuck toy and do what he tells you?"

I swallow and nod my head, my lips parting as he slides his thumb in between my lips. Without being told, I suck on his finger as he sighs.

His wet thumb drags down my chin as he directs us over to our usual couch. Maybe one day I'll graduate to being on a stage or doing an amateur show, but for now, I like that this room provides me the ability to not have to perform. I can just be me and get off on the fact that people are watching without the pressure of being on a stage, but I can't deny that the idea is definitely growing on me.

Aiden sits, his legs wide, and I guess that he wants me on his lap. He clicks his tongue and shakes his head. "On your knees," he says.

Immediately wet.

I use his thighs as leverage as I get on my knees for him, the back of my thighs resting on my calves as I tilt my head at him for more direction. He laughs, and I realize I still have my cat ears on. He takes them off and rests them next to his hips before cradling my jaw with his larger hand. "Pull that skirt up, show them how pretty that ass is," he says.

I follow his direction instantly, sliding my dress up so that my cheeks are on display for the room. Part of why I like people watching me is because I love how zoned out I get with Aiden. I like knowing that people are getting off on seeing us together almost as much as I like Aiden's ability to make me forget we aren't the only people in the room.

My hands are on his thighs, and he grabs them by the wrist. "Hands behind your back." I tangle my fingers together at the base of my spine and wish I had something to hold them together. While I might be an excellent listener, not touching Aiden is hard for me.

Aiden looks larger than life when I'm on the floor like this for him. He looks like a fucking king, and all I want to do is please him and make him lose control over how much he wants me. It's heady having a man with this much presence only wanting you. I feel loved, even with my knees pressed against the hardwood. I'm in a position of submissiveness, yet, I hold all the power.

I know I'm going to make Aiden feel good, just like I know he will reward me ten-fold for gifting him with my total submission.

"Feel how hard my cock is," he says. His pants are still on, and I have no other recourse except to use my face. I rub my cheek along the inside of his thigh until I reach the bulge against his pants. Rubbing my cheeks along the length and licking him, the taste of his pants isn't strong. But the way his eyes are blazing down at me as I follow his commands and put myself in what could be considered a demeaning position for him is worth it. I think about the people around us watching and how it must look. How men want to be in Aiden's position and how many others wish they were on their knees for him, like I am.

"You want my cock in that greedy little mouth, don't you?" I nod with my cheek against his cock, and he groans. Unbuckling his pants and pushing them down just enough to fist his cock. He gives it three slow strokes, and my mouth waters looking at him. I like that we never get fully naked at the club. I like even more how Aiden usually only takes out his cock, like it's the only piece of himself he's willing for everyone in the club to see. The rest of the man is reserved for his time alone with me.

"Please, Daddy," I say, giving him needy eyes as I look up at him.

"I want you to take all of it," he says, and I nod. Keeping my hands behind my back as I open my mouth and slightly rise on my knees. No doubt anyone watching can see the wet patch on my thong as I lean forward and swipe my tongue around the head of his length. His fist still holds the base of him as he lets me get him wet.

"Head up," he says, and I stop what I'm doing to watch him. He gives me a smile as a trail of spit leaves his lips and drips on his cock.

Holy fucking shit. I swear my clit throbs as he smirks at me.

"Now take all of it," he demands. One of his hands tangles in my hair at the top of my head and the other grips my chin. He controls the pace as he fucks my throat. The noises my body makes as he uses me are obscene and only have me feeling more turned on. I shift my weight as he takes what he wants, trying to get some friction between my thighs. "Come on, baby, I know you can take more," he says.

It spurs me on, this never ending need to please him, as I open up my throat as he pushes further. My nose hits his pelvis as his cock hits the back of my throat. His hand slides down my neck, squeezing gently where he can feel his cock, before groaning and letting me go.

A line of spit trails from my lips to the head of his dick. I take a gasping breath as Aiden uses his thumb to clean up my chin and rub it on his pants.

"Always so good for Daddy, aren't you?" I nod my head and open my mouth again, ready to please him, but he has other plans in mind. "Give me your hand." I give it to him, and he helps me up, his large hands brushing off my knees before he places a soft kiss on my thigh.

I expect him to toss me over his lap and spank me in that position, but he stands up, pushing back my hair before placing a soft kiss on my lips. "All fours, on the couch," he says. I nod, and Aiden has an outreached hand if I need it as I use my forearms to balance the upper part of my body as my knees and shins rest on the leather.

Aiden doesn't waste any time as he tugs on my thong, the material stretching between my thighs as the first slap of his palm hits my ass. I can feel more eyes on us in that moment— there's nothing better than an audible smack to get people's attention. I press my face against the leather and watch him as he winds up again, hitting the same spot in a delicious way that stings so fucking good.

"Look at your pretty little cunt dripping for me. All that from sucking your daddy's cock?"

"Yes." I groan as he spanks me again.

I'm expecting another swat to my ass when his hand smacks my pussy, nowhere near as hard as he would my ass, but the feeling has me on edge and whimpering like the needy, wanton whore I feel like at this moment.

One of his hands grips my pink ass cheek as his other plays with my pussy. His fingers toying with my wetness before entering me. Aiden's fingers are magical, and he's relentless with the way he fucks me. His two fingers curl at the right pace and right amount of friction. When he spanks my ass at the same time, I shatter. My thighs start to give out, but Aiden simply removes his fingers and replaces them with his hard length. My orgasm feels like it's riding a wave, and the added stretch of him only helps me come again.

He's relentless as he pushes against me. The front half of my body can't handle it. As I collapse, the only thing in the air is my ass as Aiden uses my pussy as he wants. His grip is tight on my ass as I clench around him, needing him to come inside of me.

He's breathing heavily behind me, as he smacks my ass and pushes so deeply inside of me that I nearly shout. His hips stutter and my cheek is plastered and sweaty against the couch. His moan is low and deep as he fills me. His grip on my body loosens slightly as he takes a moment before pulling out.

I blink a few times and find two couples watching us. They clap lightly, and I can't help the blush that spreads over my face as Aiden starts fussing with me. Picking me up and having me straddle his lap as he rubs my back.

"How are you feeling?"

I pull back and run my fingers through his hair.

"Perfect... I feel perfect." I lean forward and give him a gentle kiss, which he returns. There's so much love here that I feel like I might explode. I don't think either of us ever imagined that we could have the best of both worlds. But here we are, dressed like a cat and a burglar having sex in front of a crowd. But I know that tomorrow he's taking me to my first hockey game and will treat me like an absolute princess the whole time.

I lean against his chest, wondering how we got here, and I can't help but feel proud of us.

"I love you," I whisper against his chest.

He squeezes me tightly, putting my cat ears back on. "I love you too, kitten," he says with a laugh and a final kiss before wrapping me back up in his arms.

I thank the road that got me here, even if it was a difficult one, because being with Aiden is worth every single trial of my past. I hold on to him like a lifeline and know that I'm never going to spend a day away from this man for the rest of my life.

Aiden

Epilogues Are For Lovers

MAYBE I WENT over the top for our honeymoon, but when I convinced Jessa that it was also my fortieth birthday, she agreed that nothing would be over the top. So here we are in the South of France on a chartered yacht for the next five days, just the two of us.

I let her sleep in as I sit on the aft deck and drink a coffee. The sun is beaming brightly, and I soak up the summer Mediterranean sun. When I raise my mug to my lips, I smile at the shining gold ring on my finger.

Truthfully, I didn't think this was in the cards for me. Fuck, I didn't even think I wanted it, but I want everything with Jessa. I'm selfish with her, and she seems more than eager to soak up all my affections and my desperation for her time.

The sliding door takes me away from my thoughts as she walks over to me. She has on a tiny white bathing suit and a white cover up as she steps toward me.

"Morning, wife," I say, grinning at her. She blushes, but eagerly comes to sit on my lap.

"Good morning, birthday boy," she says, kissing my chest

and stealing my coffee. "What do you want to do on your birthday?"

"To fuck you so many times that I'm drawing blanks." She throws her head back and laughs, and she looks so beautiful. She's no longer that woman I met at a funeral who was scared of her own place in life. Jessa's confidence grows every day, and I'm more than happy to be the one to help foster that glow.

"I need to give you your present first," she says.

"I thought that was my present?"

She shakes her head and ignores me, going back to the interior of the boat before coming back with a manila folder. She hands it to me as she sits at the end of the lounge chair. I open the top of the document and pull it out. I skim over the first few pages and look back at her.

"You're giving me two of your shares?"

"Fifty-one percent just didn't have the same ring to it, but fifty-two, that sounds like a majority shareholder to me."

"I told you I would buy them from you."

She shakes her head and crawls up my lap. "You're my husband now, and I wanted you to have more say in the company. It's yours. Honestly, the more I thought about it, the more I realized that Collin might have given me that ten-percent to protect you almost as much as he did out of guilt."

I shake my head, and I'm going to speak when she cuts me off.

"I might never have closure about Collin, or that part of my family, and as fucked up as it might be, I'm glad I was at that funeral. That despite everything, I got you, which is priceless. I never thought this kind of happiness existed. Even though my parents let me down, I just know that they would both be happy with how things turned out."

I swallow and nod at her. I feel guilty for not thinking about Collin in a long time, but I think she's right. He wanted Kemper's to stay under my control, and if he were alive, it might have been an adjustment seeing me with his daughter. But I know he would be happy that I'm taking care of her in a way no one else can.

"Thank you, baby," I say instead of arguing with her over the shares. I'm sure I'll have enough shit to deal with when I'm back at work, but Zach can kiss my ass.

"You're welcome, Daddy," she says cheekily, and I pinch her ass, making her squeak and jump off me slightly.

"I think I'm ready for the rest of my gift though," I say, grinding up against her. She grabs a towel, wrapping it around her waist as she tugs my shorts down and pushes her bikini bottoms to the side. I slide inside of my wife, knowing that life doesn't get any better than this.

ACKNOWLEDGMENTS

Stephanie – Thank you for being my designated Omega reader and finding any last-minute errors. I appreciate all your hard work and for always being able to jump on and read my stories.

Sandra – Thank you for my beautiful covers and design work. You're always my voice of reason when I'm feeling low. I love you so much!

Nikki - Thank you for your notes and for pushing me to add the poker chapter!

Leisha – Thank you for being such a good daddy's girl.

Lindsay & Kassie - Thank you both for checking the final file and helping me find last minute slip ups.

Jeffrey Dean Morgan and Pedro Pascal – You know what you did.

Content Creators – To anyone who posts an image, a comment, or a video about any of my books just know I absolutely adore you. The work that goes into creating content is one of passion and it really warms my heart that you liked my book enough to post about it. Thank you for your hard work and effort.

ABOUT THE AUTHOR

Sarah Blue writes contemporary sweet omegaverse, erotic, why choose romances. She loves romance in nearly any genre. When she isn't writing you can find her nose buried in a book or lit up from her kindle. She loves the sweeter side of romance and creating interesting characters while adding adventure and spice. Writing strong female characters and male characters willing to show weakness is something that makes her gooey on the inside.

Sarah lives in Maryland with her husband, two sons, and two annoying cats. If she isn't reading or writing she is probably working on a craft project or scrolling on Tik Tok.

- instagram.com/sarahblueauthor
- amazon.com/stores/Sarah-Blue/author/B09DHZ1YW6?ref=ap_rdr&store_ref=ap_rdr&isDramIntegrated=true&shoppingPortalEnabled=true
- tiktok.com/@sarahblueauthor

Printed in Great Britain
by Amazon

24352774R00187